30 DAYS OF NIGHT™

STEVE NILES
STORY

BEN TEMPLESMITH
ART

ROBBIE ROBBINS
LETTERS & DESIGN

PUBLISHED BY
IDEA AND DESIGN WORKS, LLC
4411 MORENA BLVD., SUITE 106
SAN DIEGO, CA 92117

www.IDWPUBLISHING.com

ISBN: 0-9719775-5-0
08 07 06 05   9 8 7 6
PRINTED IN KOREA

 IDW PUBLISHING IS:
ROBBIE ROBBINS, PRESIDENT
CHRIS RYALL, PUBLISHER/EDITOR-IN-CHIEF
TED ADAMS, VICE PRESIDENT
KRIS OPRISKO, VICE PRESIDENT
NEIL UYETAKE, ART DIRECTOR
DAN TAYLOR, EDITOR
AARON MYERS, DISTRIBUTION MANAGER
TOM B. LONG, DESIGNER
CHANCE BOREN, EDITORIAL ASSISTANT
MATTHEW RUZICKA, CPA, CONTROLLER
ALEX GARNER, CREATIVE DIRECTOR
YUMIKO MIYANO, BUSINESS DEVELOPMENT
RICK PRIVMAN, BUSINESS DEVELOPMENT

COLD BLOOD

IN THE INTERESTS OF FULL DISCLOSURE LET ME TELL YOU
THAT I'VE KNOWN STEVE NILES MORE YEARS THAN EITHER
OF US PROBABLY CARE TO REMEMBER. WE'VE WORKED
TOGETHER, DRUNK TOGETHER, AND DEBATED THE MERITS
OF A LOT OF HORROR MOVIES TOGETHER.

THE COMIC IN YOUR HANDS HAS MUCH OF THE RAW, EVEN
BRUTAL ENERGY OF A HORROR MOVIE FROM THE GOOD OLD
DAYS. SHORT, SHARP AND UNFORGIVING. IT'S GOT A CATCHY
TITLE, A WONDERFULLY CLEVER, BUT SIMPLE IDEA AT ITS
CHILLY HEART, AND A NARRATIVE THAT STARTS AT A RUN
AND NEVER SLOWS DOWN.

HIS COLLABORATOR BEN TEMPLESMITH HAS PROVIDED
30 DAYS OF NIGHT WITH A GRAPHIC STYLE THAT IS
STRIPPED TO THE ESSENTIALS. ALL REDUNDANCIES ARE
REMOVED. THE IMAGES THROW THE BLEAK WORLD OF
BARROW INTO SOFT FOCUS IN ORDER TO CONCENTRATE
OUR ATTENTION ON THE EYES OF THE VICTIMS, ON THEIR
BLOOD, OR ON THE DELICATE SYMMETRY OF A SET OF
FANGS. IT'S NOT PRETTY. BUT WHEN WAS A GREAT
HORROR STORY EVER PRETTY? I SUPPOSE THERE ARE A
FEW DECADENT PREDATORS OUT THERE WHO DO LOOK
FANCY IN VELVET, BUT STEVE'S VAMPIRES ARE NOT OF THAT
CLAN. HE'S TAPPED A NEW VEIN IN THESE PAGES, EVOKING A
COLD, JOYLESS WORLD IN WHICH APPETITE CAN NEVER BE
SATED, AND LOVE GIVES NO COMFORT, EVEN IN
THE BRIGHT LIGHT OF DAY. IN FACT, ESPECIALLY THEN.

I WON'T SPOIL THE TALE BY SAYING ANY MORE. LET ME
ONLY COMMEND *30 DAYS OF NIGHT* TO YOU, WITH THE
CERTAINTY THAT IF YOU HAVE A TASTE FOR THE REAL
STUFF OF HORROR FICTION, YOU'LL FIND IT IN THE PAGES
THAT FOLLOW. UNLIKE THOSE OF US WHO GOT CAUGHT
BY STEVE AND BEN'S SKILLS IN THE FIRST ISSUE, AND
HAD TO WAIT FOR THE NEXT, AND THE NEXT, YOU HAVE
THE TALE COMPLETE BETWEEN THESE COVERS.

ALL THE WAY TO ITS BITTER, BITTER END.

CLIVE BARKER
LOS ANGELES 2002

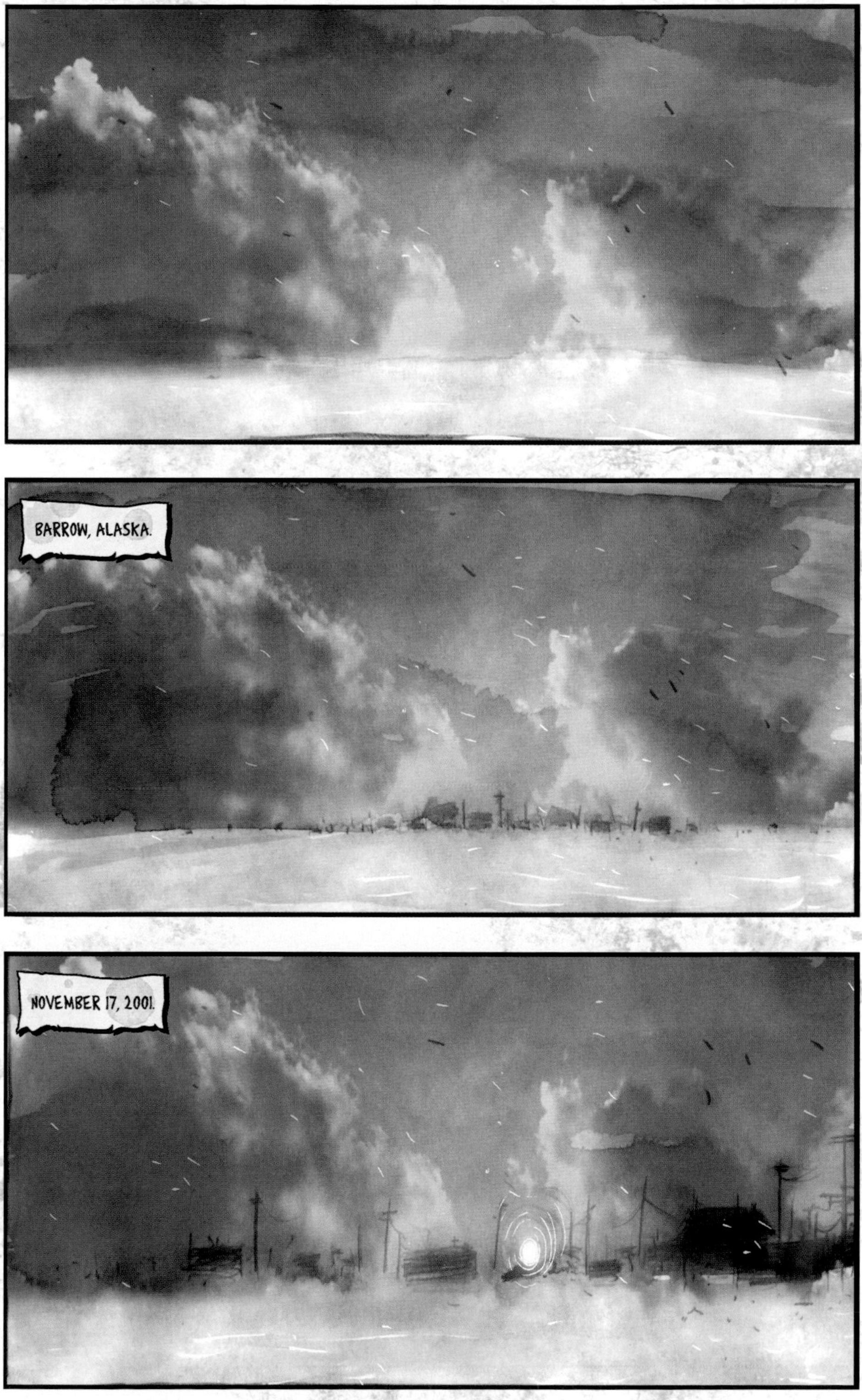
BARROW, ALASKA.
NOVEMBER 17, 2001.

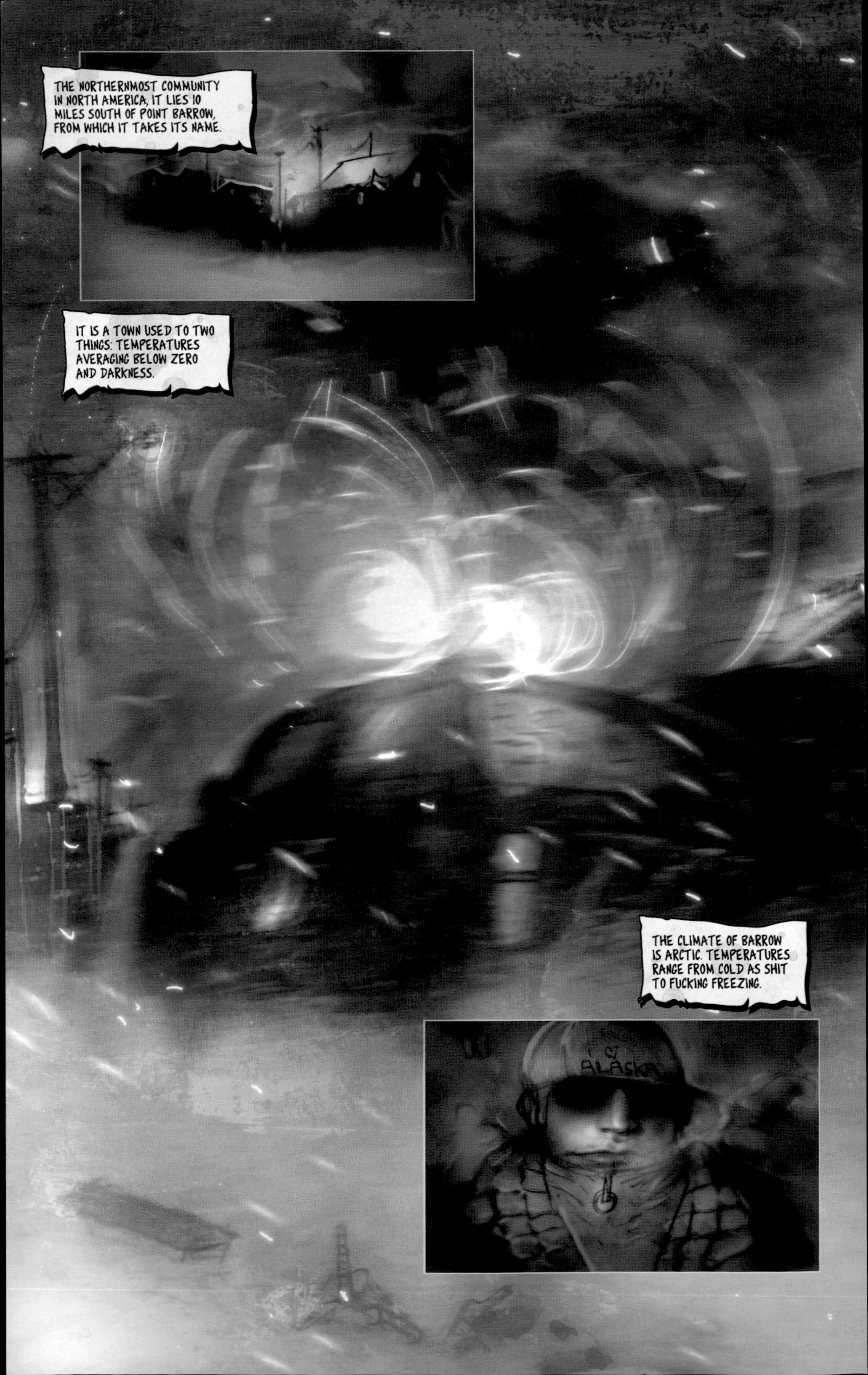

THE NORTHERNMOST COMMUNITY IN NORTH AMERICA, IT LIES 10 MILES SOUTH OF POINT BARROW, FROM WHICH IT TAKES ITS NAME.
IT IS A TOWN USED TO TWO THINGS: TEMPERATURES AVERAGING BELOW ZERO AND DARKNESS.
THE CLIMATE OF BARROW IS ARCTIC. TEMPERATURES RANGE FROM COLD AS SHIT TO FUCKING FREEZING.
I ♡ ALASKA

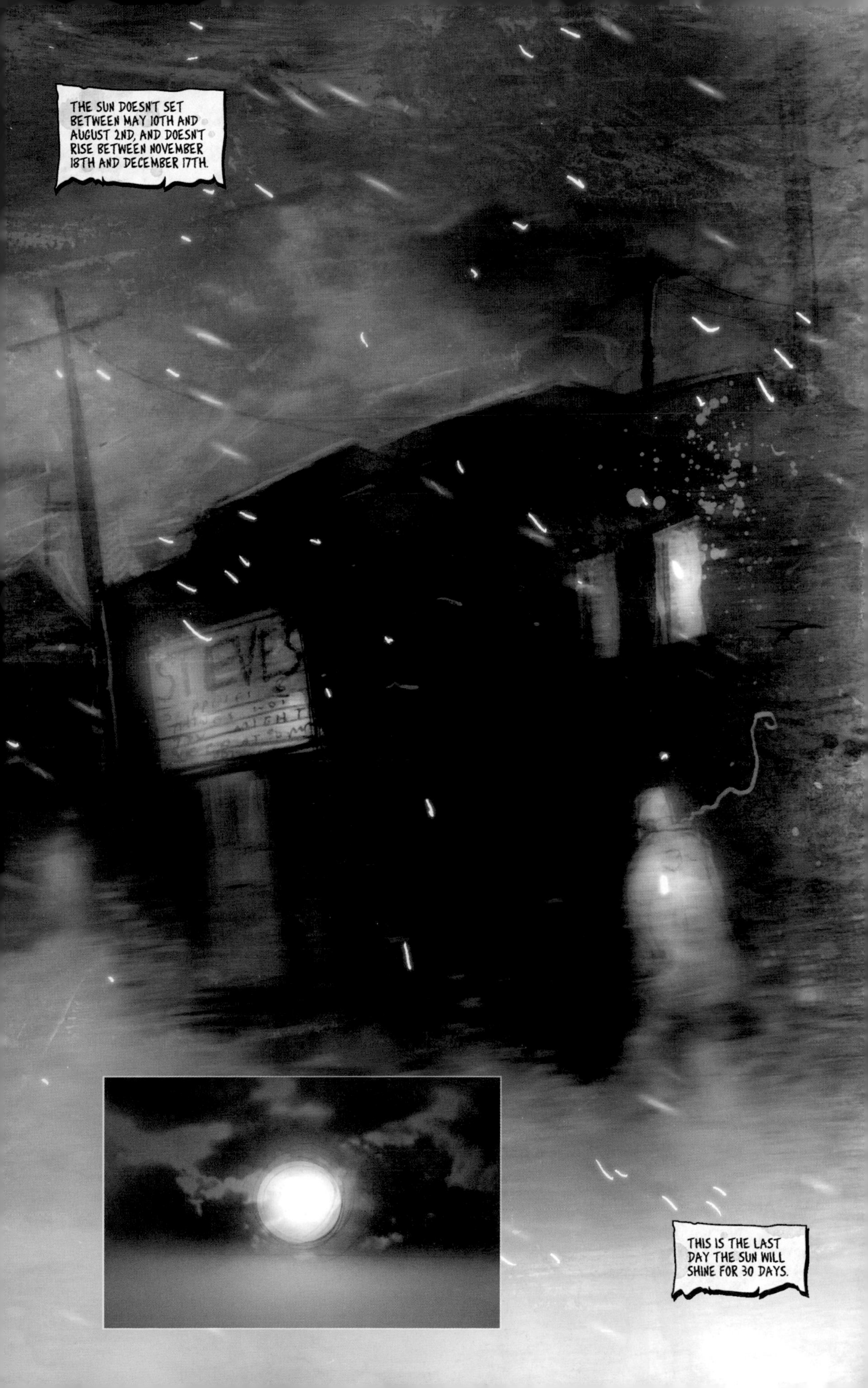
THE SUN DOESN'T SET BETWEEN MAY 10TH AND AUGUST 2ND, AND DOESN'T RISE BETWEEN NOVEMBER 18TH AND DECEMBER 17TH.
THIS IS THE LAST DAY THE SUN WILL SHINE FOR 30 DAYS.

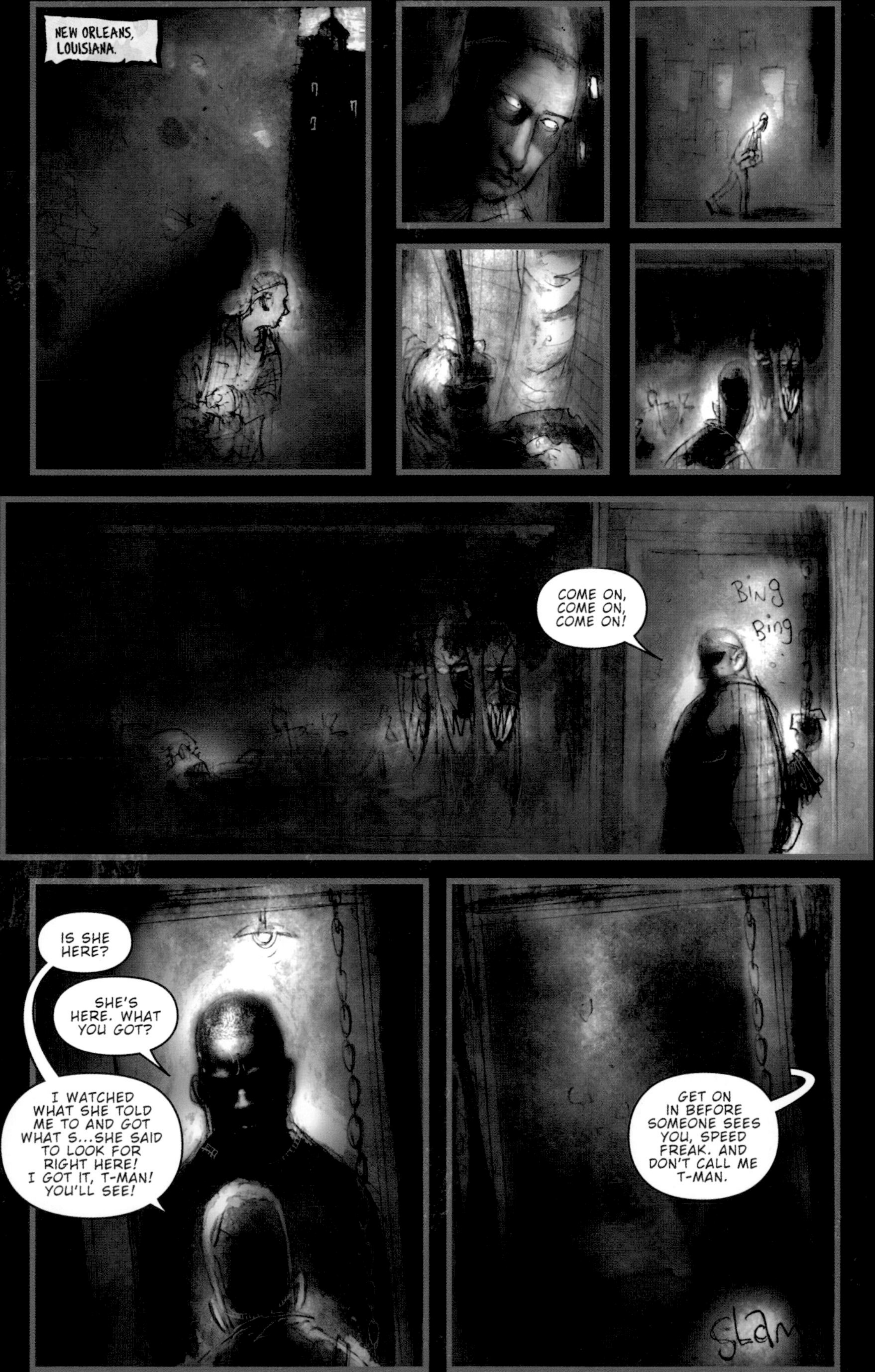
NEW ORLEANS, LOUISIANA.
COME ON, COME ON, COME ON!
BING
BING
IS SHE HERE?
SHE'S HERE. WHAT YOU GOT?
I WATCHED WHAT SHE TOLD ME TO AND GOT WHAT S...SHE SAID TO LOOK FOR RIGHT HERE! I GOT IT, T-MAN! YOU'LL SEE!
GET ON IN BEFORE SOMEONE SEES YOU, SPEED FREAK. AND DON'T CALL ME T-MAN.
SLAM

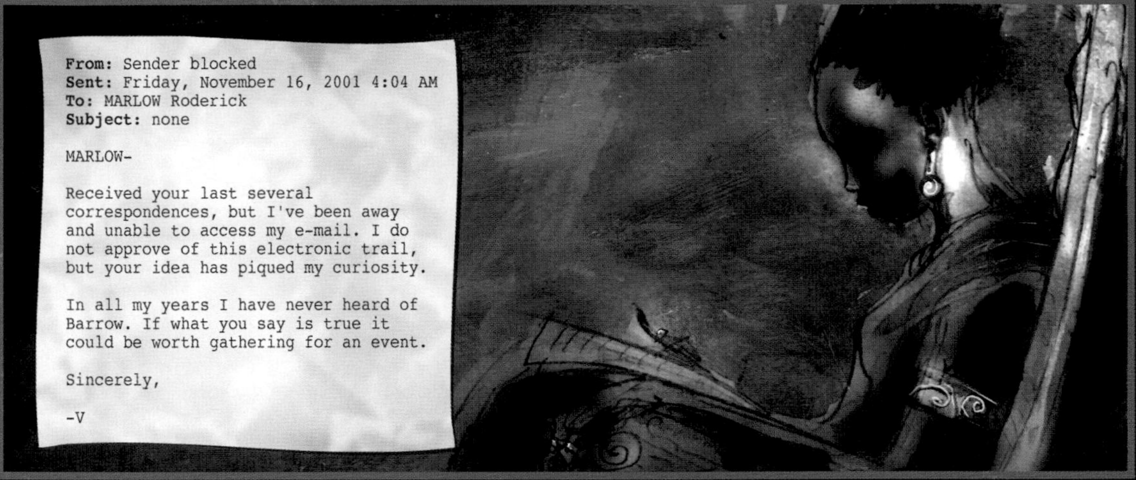
From: Sender blocked
Sent: Friday, November 16, 2001 4:04 AM
To: MARLOW Roderick
Subject: none
MARLOW-
Received your last several correspondences, but I've been away and unable to access my e-mail. I do not approve of this electronic trail, but your idea has piqued my curiosity.
In all my years I have never heard of Barrow. If what you say is true it could be worth gathering for an event.
Sincerely,
-V

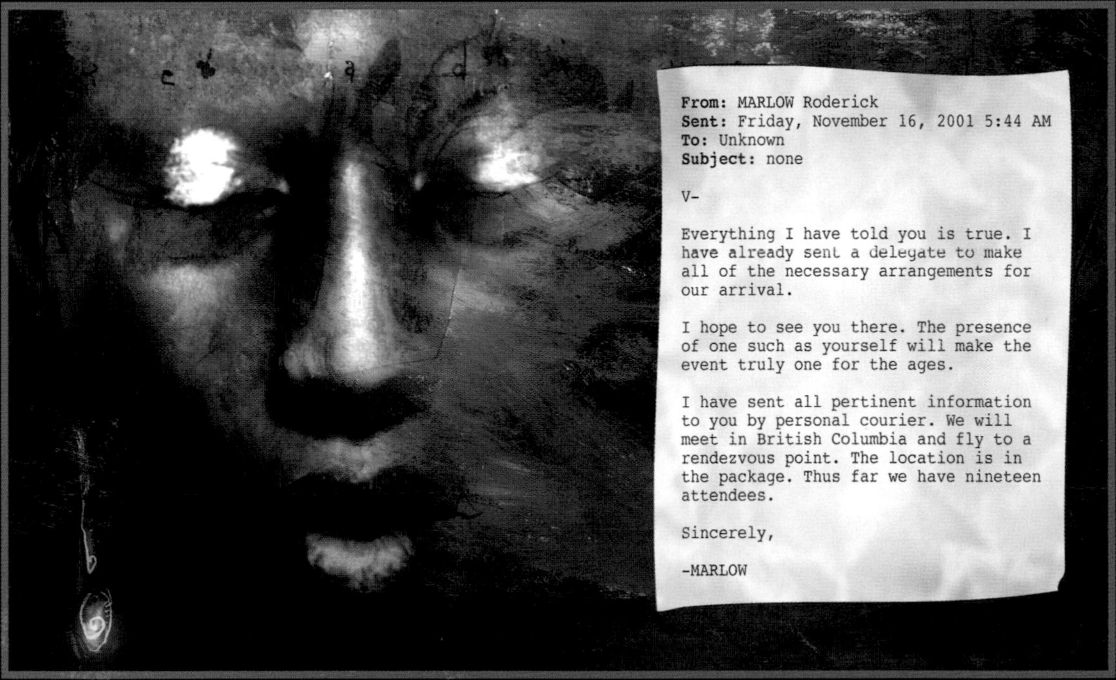
From: MARLOW Roderick
Sent: Friday, November 16, 2001 5:44 AM
To: Unknown
Subject: none
V-
Everything I have told you is true. I have already sent a delegate to make all of the necessary arrangements for our arrival.
I hope to see you there. The presence of one such as yourself will make the event truly one for the ages.
I have sent all pertinent information to you by personal courier. We will meet in British Columbia and fly to a rendezvous point. The location is in the package. Thus far we have nineteen attendees.
Sincerely,
-MARLOW

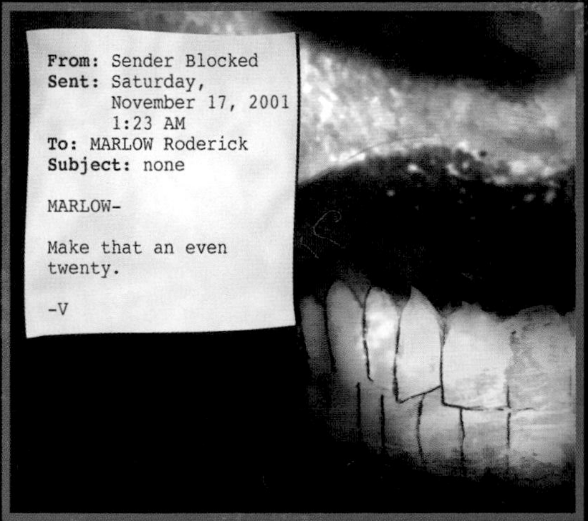
From: Sender Blocked
Sent: Saturday, November 17, 2001 1:23 AM
To: MARLOW Roderick
Subject: none
MARLOW-
Make that an even twenty.
-V

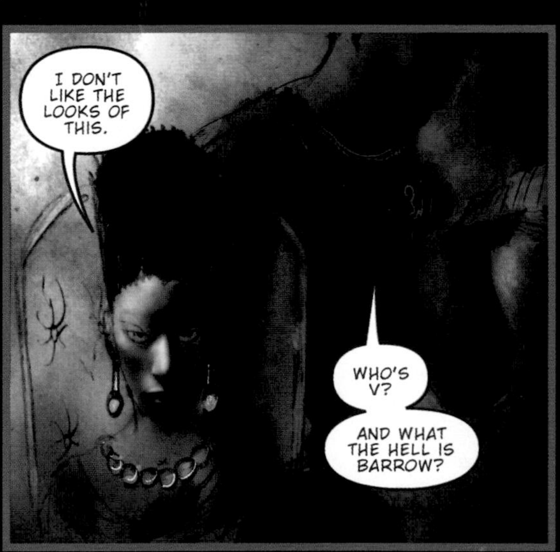
I DON'T LIKE THE LOOKS OF THIS.
WHO'S V?
AND WHAT THE HELL IS BARROW?

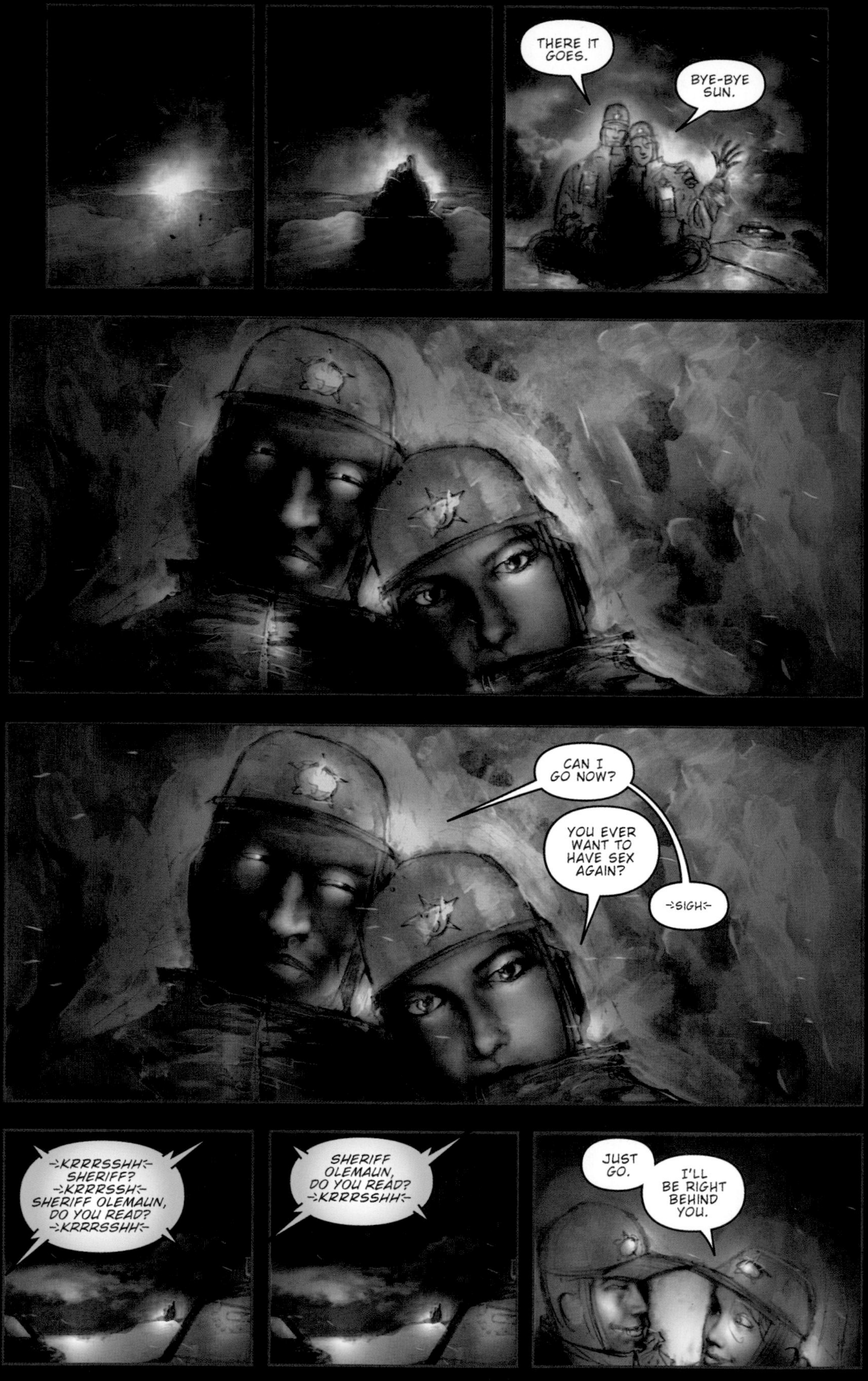
THERE IT GOES.
BYE-BYE SUN.
CAN I GO NOW?
YOU EVER WANT TO HAVE SEX AGAIN?
-SIGH-
-KRRRSSHH- SHERIFF? -KRRRSSH- SHERIFF OLEMAUN, DO YOU READ? -KRRRSSHH-
SHERIFF OLEMAUN, DO YOU READ? -KRRRSSHH-
JUST GO.
I'LL BE RIGHT BEHIND YOU.

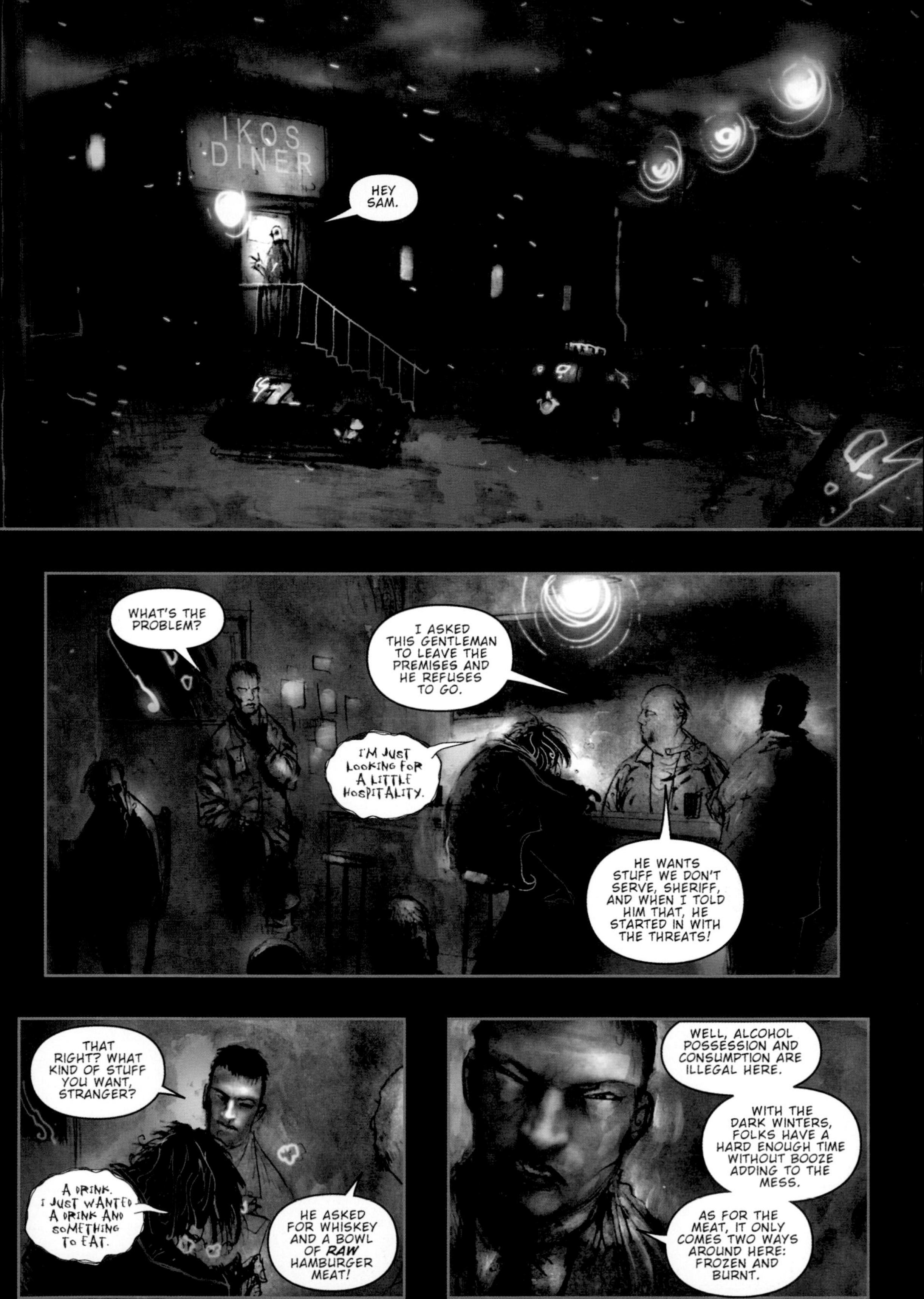
IKOS DINER
HEY SAM.
WHAT'S THE PROBLEM?
I ASKED THIS GENTLEMAN TO LEAVE THE PREMISES AND HE REFUSES TO GO.
I'M JUST LOOKING FOR A LITTLE HOSPITALITY.
HE WANTS STUFF WE DON'T SERVE, SHERIFF, AND WHEN I TOLD HIM THAT, HE STARTED IN WITH THE THREATS!
THAT RIGHT? WHAT KIND OF STUFF YOU WANT, STRANGER?
A DRINK. I JUST WANTED A DRINK AND SOMETHING TO EAT.
HE ASKED FOR WHISKEY AND A BOWL OF RAW HAMBURGER MEAT!
WELL, ALCOHOL POSSESSION AND CONSUMPTION ARE ILLEGAL HERE.
WITH THE DARK WINTERS, FOLKS HAVE A HARD ENOUGH TIME WITHOUT BOOZE ADDING TO THE MESS.
AS FOR THE MEAT, IT ONLY COMES TWO WAYS AROUND HERE: FROZEN AND BURNT.

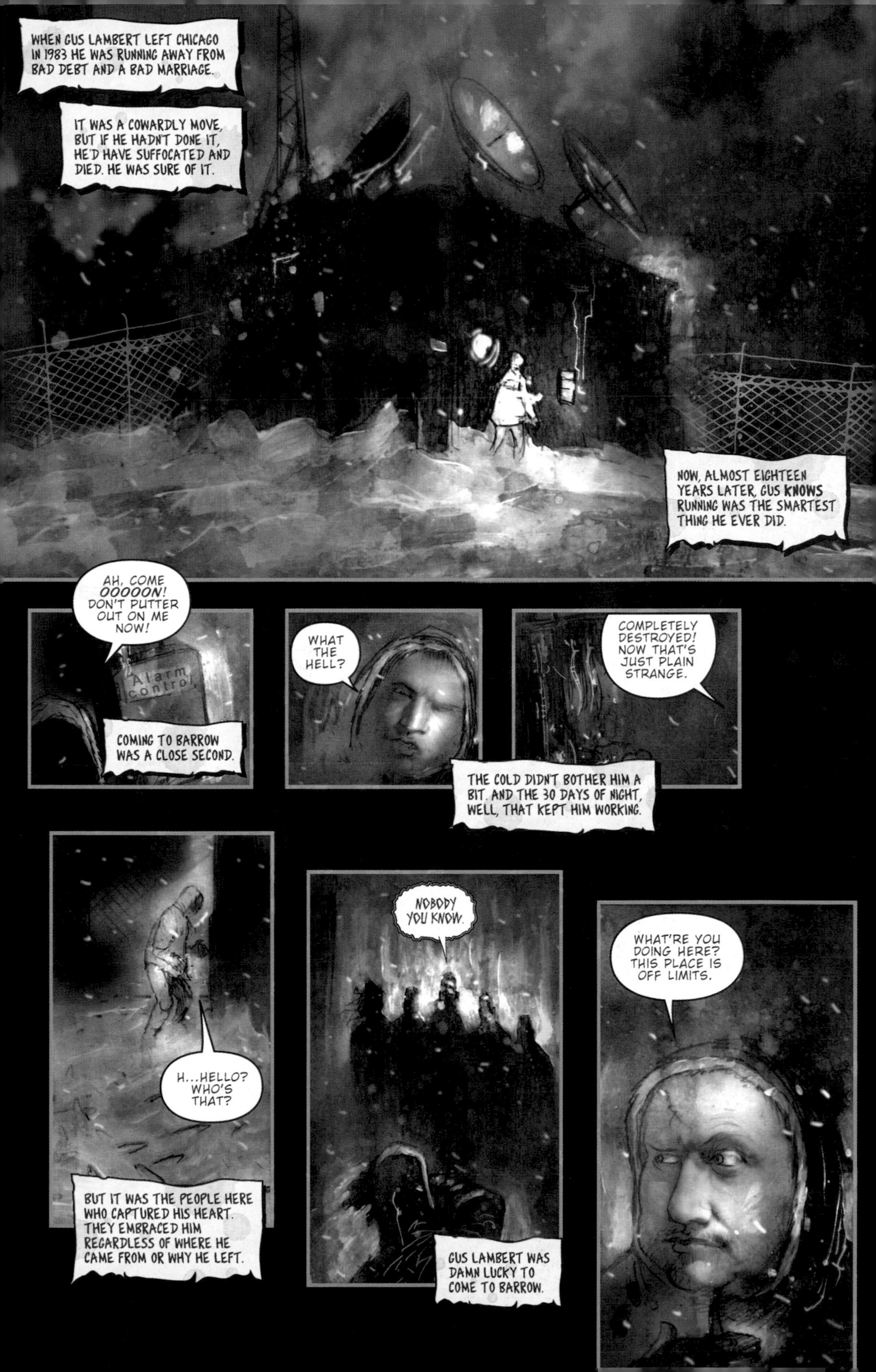
WHEN GUS LAMBERT LEFT CHICAGO IN 1983 HE WAS RUNNING AWAY FROM BAD DEBT AND A BAD MARRIAGE.
IT WAS A COWARDLY MOVE, BUT IF HE HADN'T DONE IT, HE'D HAVE SUFFOCATED AND DIED. HE WAS SURE OF IT.
NOW, ALMOST EIGHTEEN YEARS LATER, GUS KNOWS RUNNING WAS THE SMARTEST THING HE EVER DID.
AH, COME OOOOON! DON'T PUTTER OUT ON ME NOW!
Alarm control
COMING TO BARROW WAS A CLOSE SECOND.
WHAT THE HELL?
COMPLETELY DESTROYED! NOW THAT'S JUST PLAIN STRANGE.
THE COLD DIDN'T BOTHER HIM A BIT. AND THE 30 DAYS OF NIGHT, WELL, THAT KEPT HIM WORKING.
H...HELLO? WHO'S THAT?
BUT IT WAS THE PEOPLE HERE WHO CAPTURED HIS HEART. THEY EMBRACED HIM REGARDLESS OF WHERE HE CAME FROM OR WHY HE LEFT.
NOBODY YOU KNOW.
GUS LAMBERT WAS DAMN LUCKY TO COME TO BARROW.
WHAT'RE YOU DOING HERE? THIS PLACE IS OFF LIMITS.

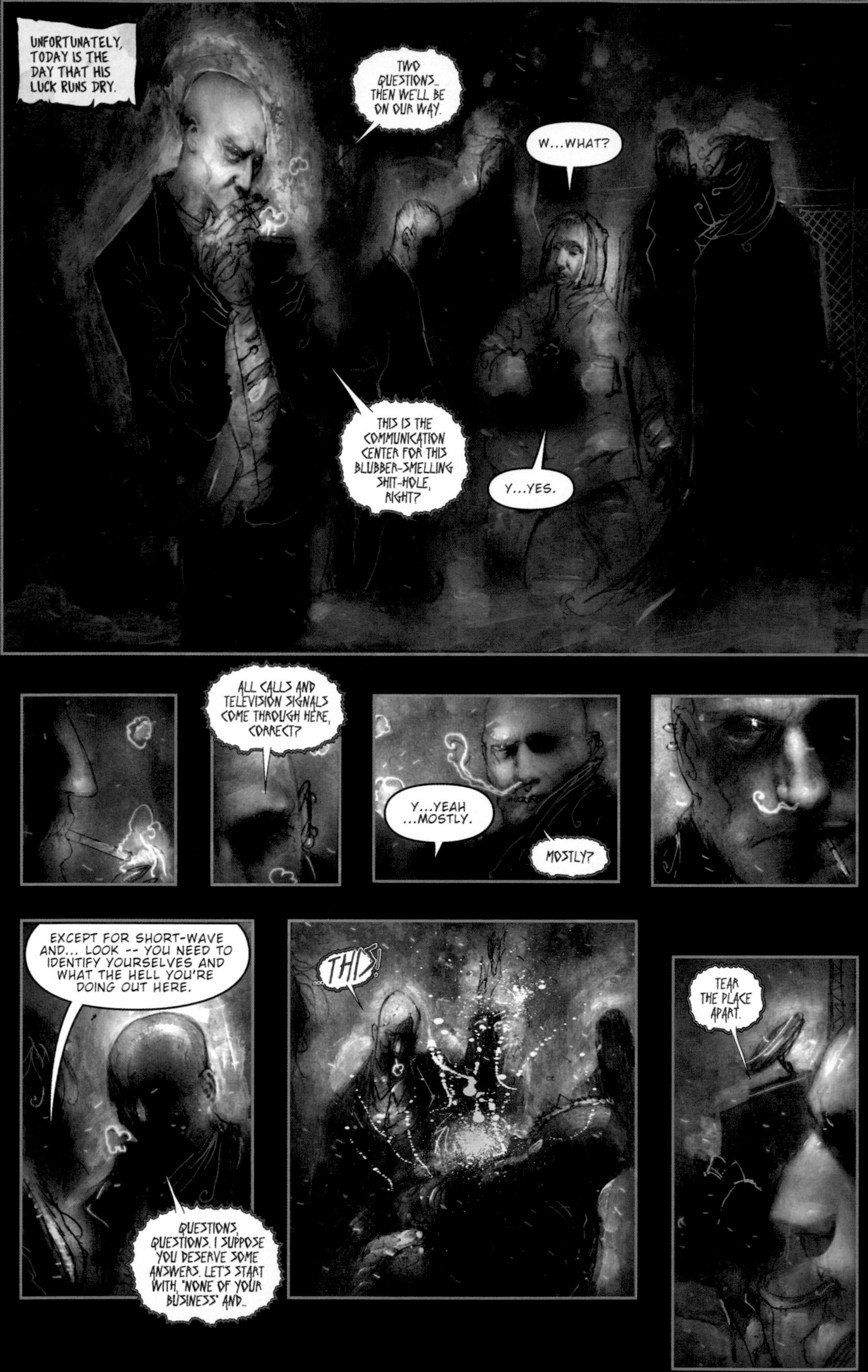
UNFORTUNATELY, TODAY IS THE DAY THAT HIS LUCK RUNS DRY.
TWO QUESTIONS... THEN WE'LL BE ON OUR WAY.
W...WHAT?
THIS IS THE COMMUNICATION CENTER FOR THIS BLUBBER-SMELLING SHIT-HOLE, RIGHT?
Y...YES.
ALL CALLS AND TELEVISION SIGNALS COME THROUGH HERE, CORRECT?
Y...YEAH ...MOSTLY.
MOSTLY?
EXCEPT FOR SHORT-WAVE AND... LOOK -- YOU NEED TO IDENTIFY YOURSELVES AND WHAT THE HELL YOU'RE DOING OUT HERE.
QUESTIONS, QUESTIONS. I SUPPOSE YOU DESERVE SOME ANSWERS. LET'S START WITH, "NONE OF YOUR BUSINESS" AND...
THIS!
TEAR THE PLACE APART.

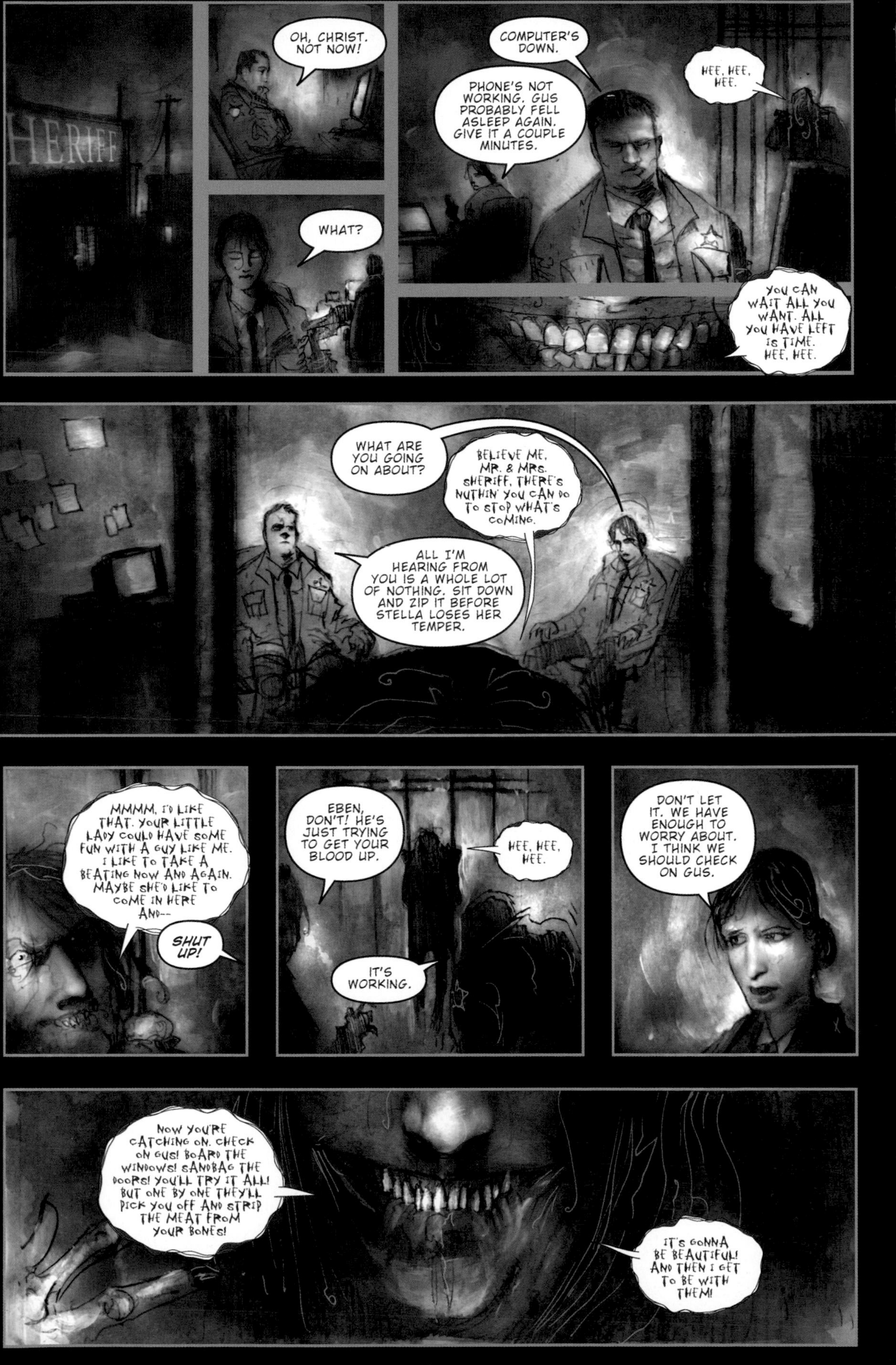
HERIFF
OH, CHRIST. NOT NOW!
WHAT?
COMPUTER'S DOWN.
PHONE'S NOT WORKING. GUS PROBABLY FELL ASLEEP AGAIN. GIVE IT A COUPLE MINUTES.
HEE, HEE, HEE.
YOU CAN WAIT ALL YOU WANT. ALL YOU HAVE LEFT IS TIME. HEE, HEE.
WHAT ARE YOU GOING ON ABOUT?
BELIEVE ME, MR. & MRS. SHERIFF, THERE'S NUTHIN' YOU CAN DO TO STOP WHAT'S COMING.
ALL I'M HEARING FROM YOU IS A WHOLE LOT OF NOTHING. SIT DOWN AND ZIP IT BEFORE STELLA LOSES HER TEMPER.
MMMM, I'D LIKE THAT. YOUR LITTLE LADY COULD HAVE SOME FUN WITH A GUY LIKE ME. I LIKE TO TAKE A BEATING NOW AND AGAIN. MAYBE SHE'D LIKE TO COME IN HERE AND--
SHUT UP!
EBEN, DON'T! HE'S JUST TRYING TO GET YOUR BLOOD UP.
HEE, HEE, HEE.
IT'S WORKING.
DON'T LET IT. WE HAVE ENOUGH TO WORRY ABOUT. I THINK WE SHOULD CHECK ON GUS.
NOW YOU'RE CATCHING ON. CHECK ON GUS! BOARD THE WINDOWS! SANDBAG THE DOORS! YOU'LL TRY IT ALL! BUT ONE BY ONE THEY'LL PICK YOU OFF AND STRIP THE MEAT FROM YOUR BONES!
IT'S GONNA BE BEAUTIFUL! AND THEN I GET TO BE WITH THEM!

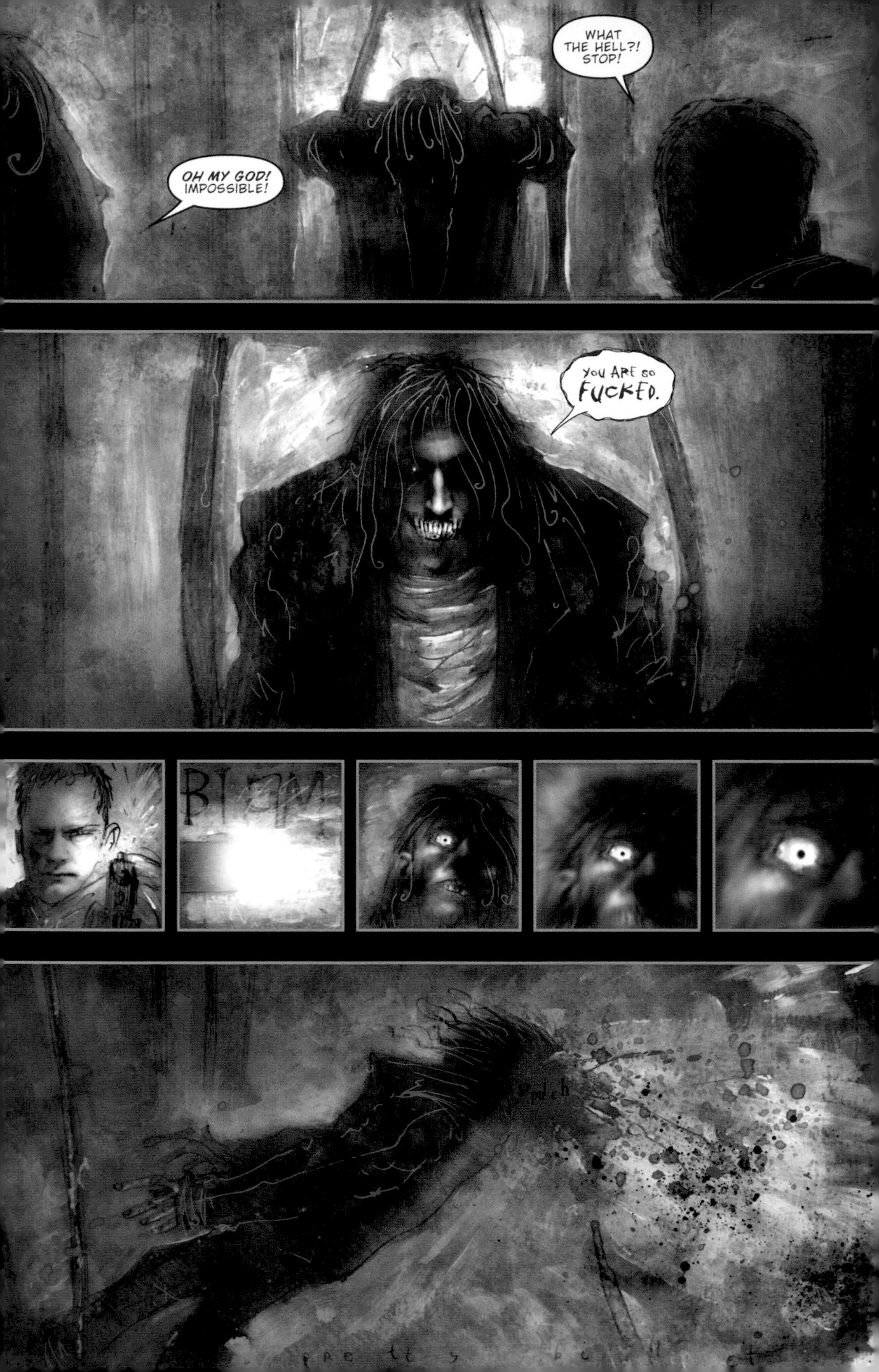
WHAT THE HELL?! STOP!
OH MY GOD! IMPOSSIBLE!
YOU ARE SO FUCKED.
BLAM

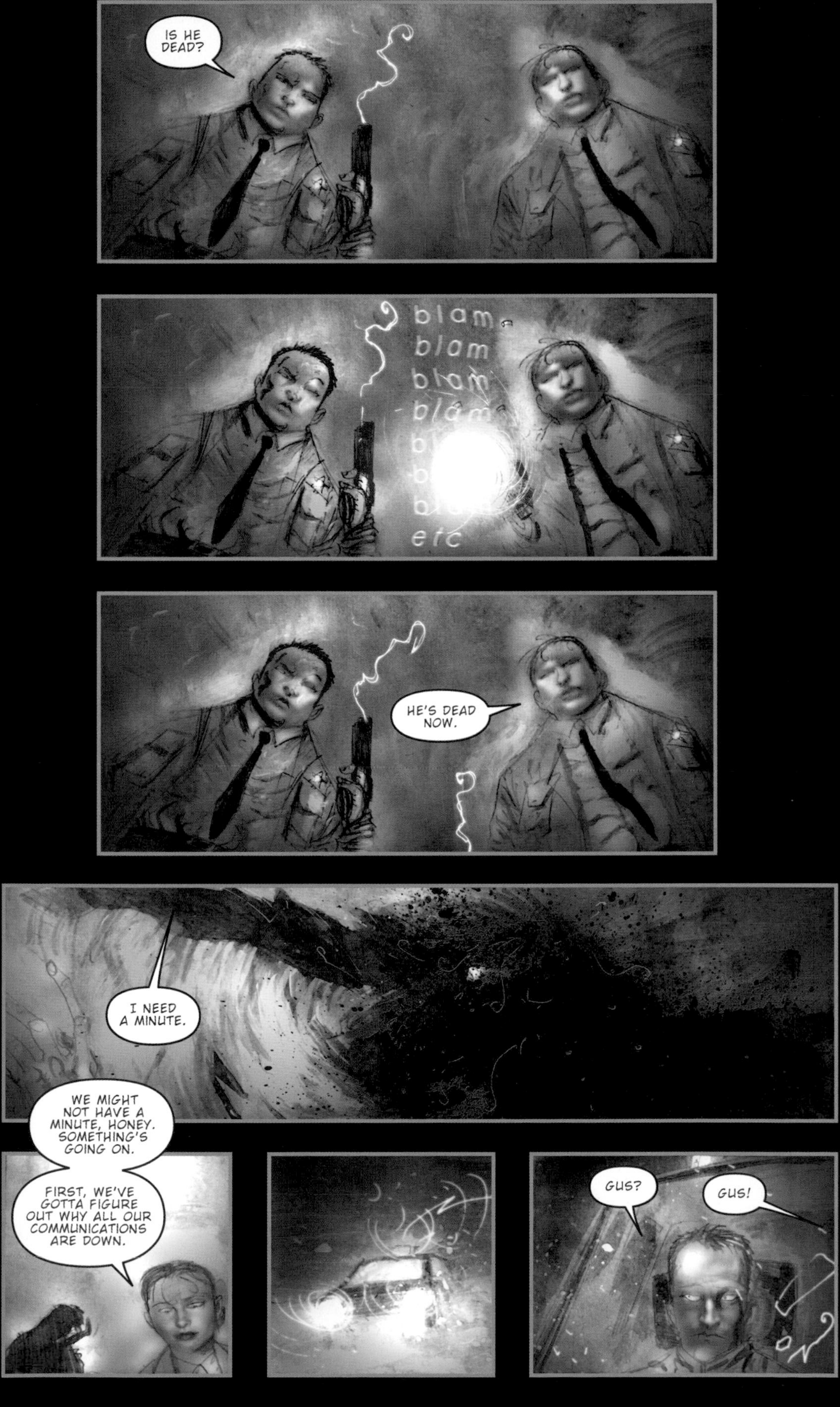
IS HE DEAD?
blam
blam
blam
blam
etc
HE'S DEAD NOW.
I NEED A MINUTE.
WE MIGHT NOT HAVE A MINUTE, HONEY. SOMETHING'S GOING ON.
FIRST, WE'VE GOTTA FIGURE OUT WHY ALL OUR COMMUNICATIONS ARE DOWN.
GUS?
GUS!

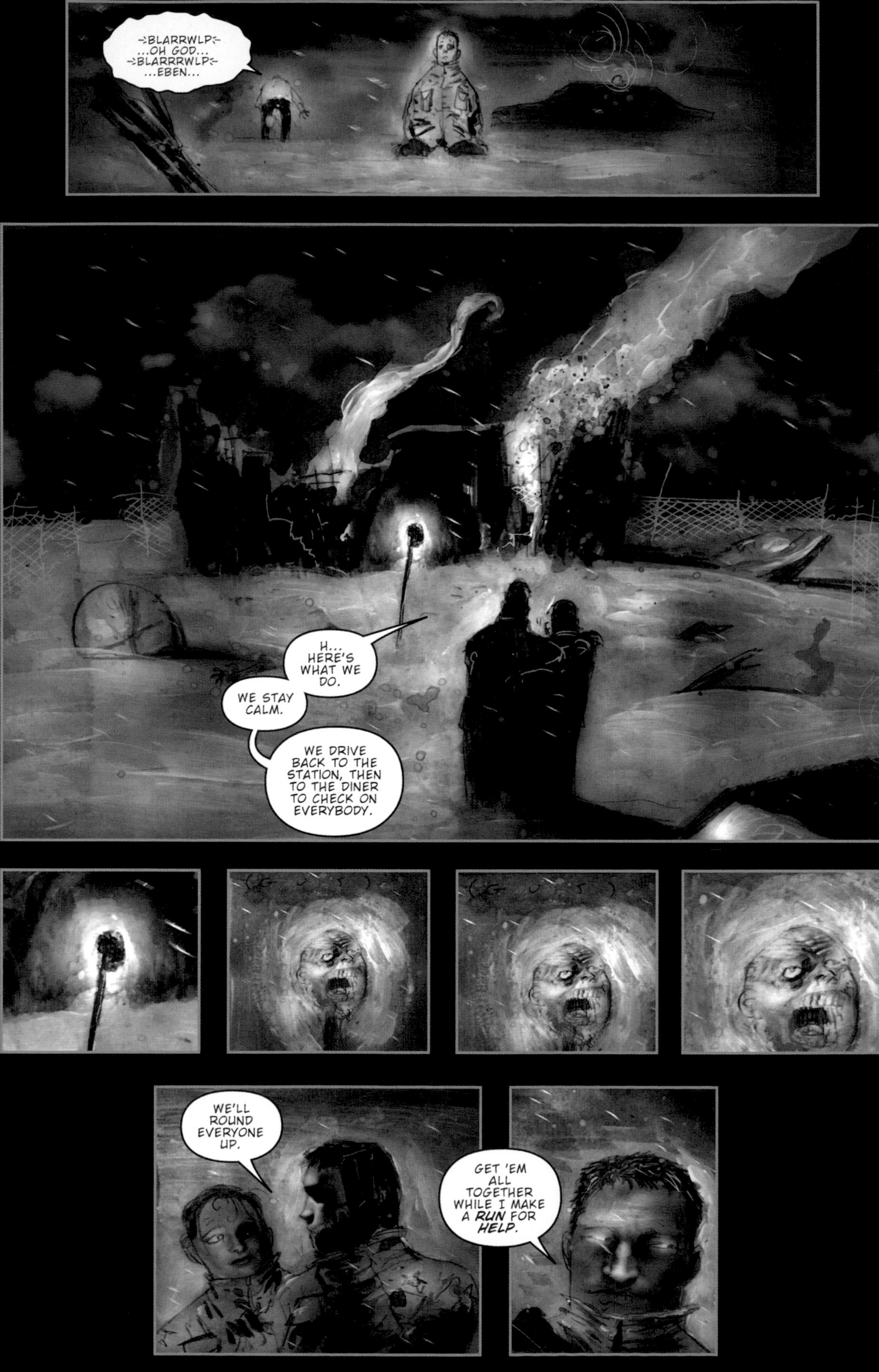
-BLARRWLP-
...OH GOD...
-BLARRRWLP-
...EBEN...
H... HERE'S WHAT WE DO.
WE STAY CALM.
WE DRIVE BACK TO THE STATION, THEN TO THE DINER TO CHECK ON EVERYBODY.
WE'LL ROUND EVERYONE UP.
GET 'EM ALL TOGETHER WHILE I MAKE A ***RUN*** FOR ***HELP***.

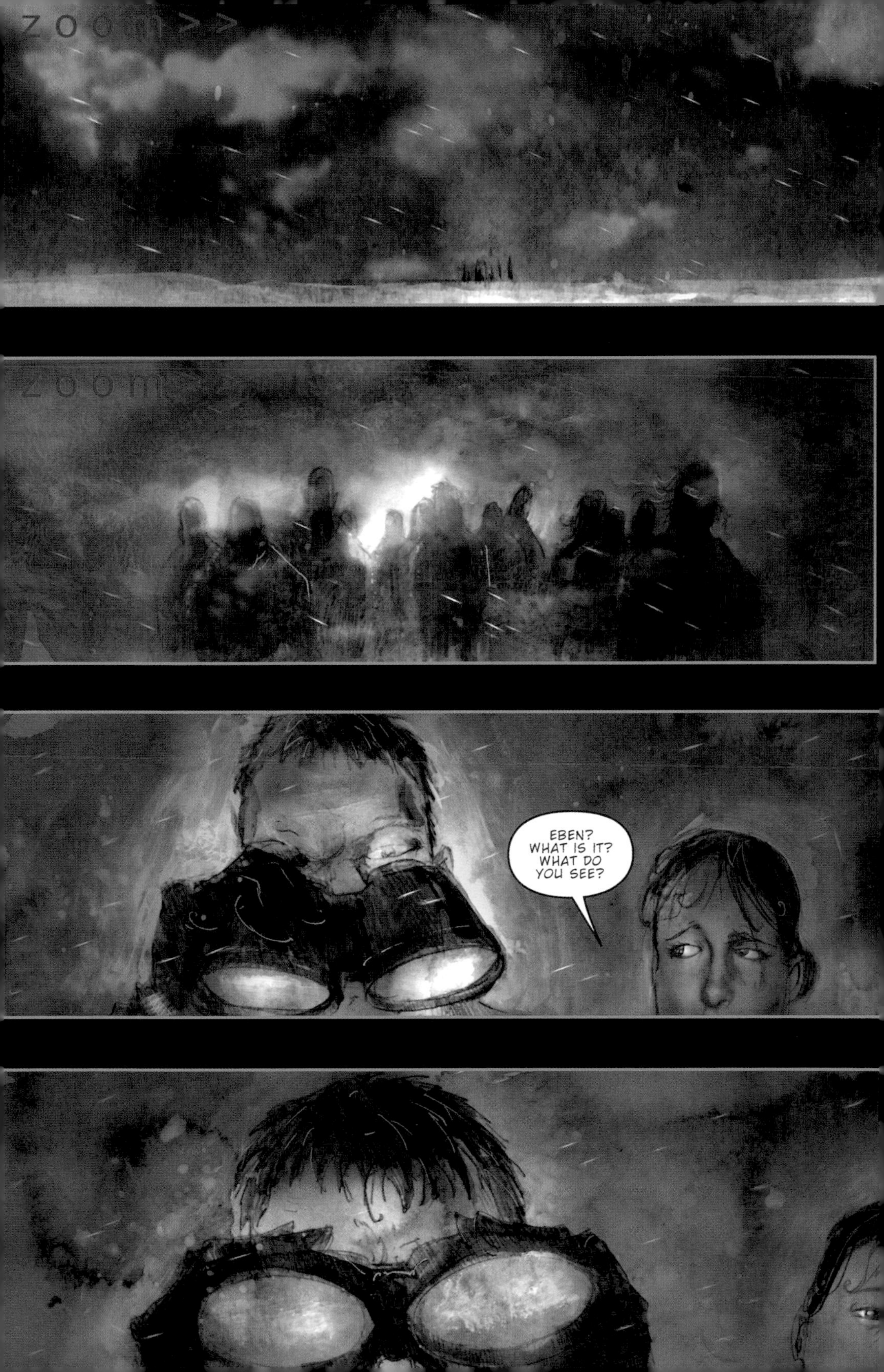
zoom>>
zoom
EBEN? WHAT IS IT? WHAT DO YOU SEE?

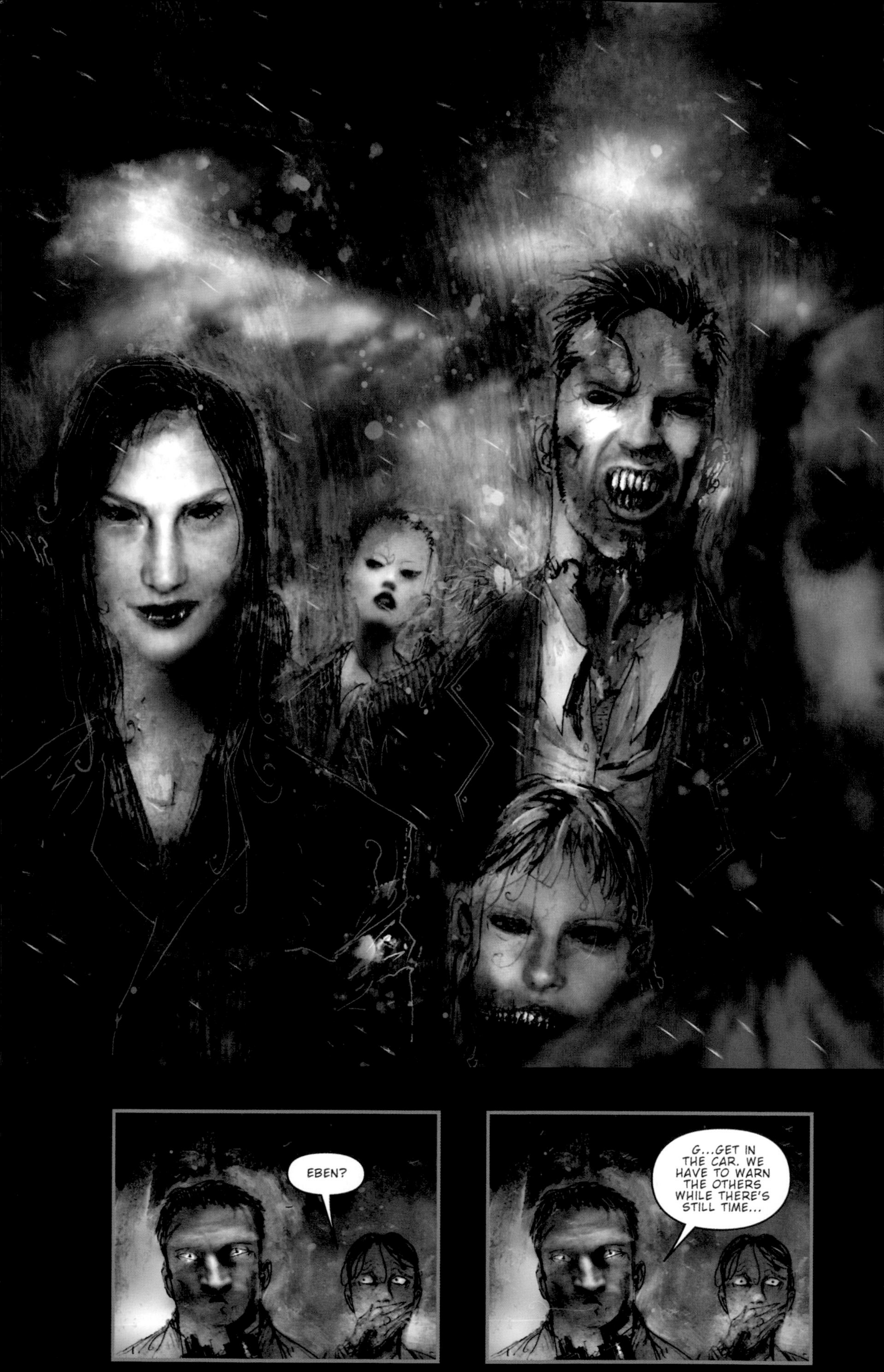
EBEN?
G...GET IN THE CAR. WE HAVE TO WARN THE OTHERS WHILE THERE'S STILL TIME...

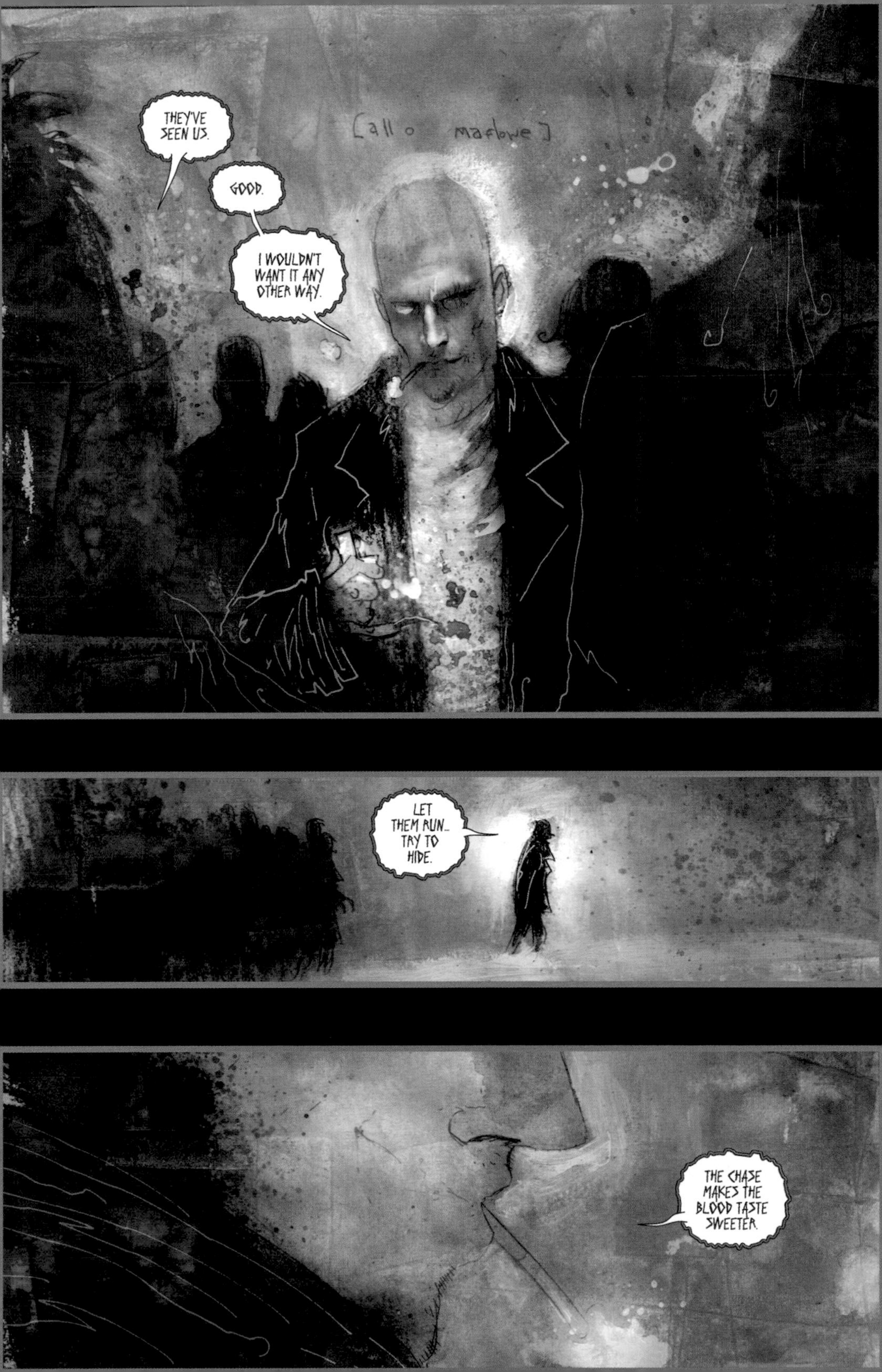
THEY'VE SEEN US.
GOOD.
I WOULDN'T WANT IT ANY OTHER WAY.
LET THEM RUN... TRY TO HIDE.
THE CHASE MAKES THE BLOOD TASTE SWEETER.

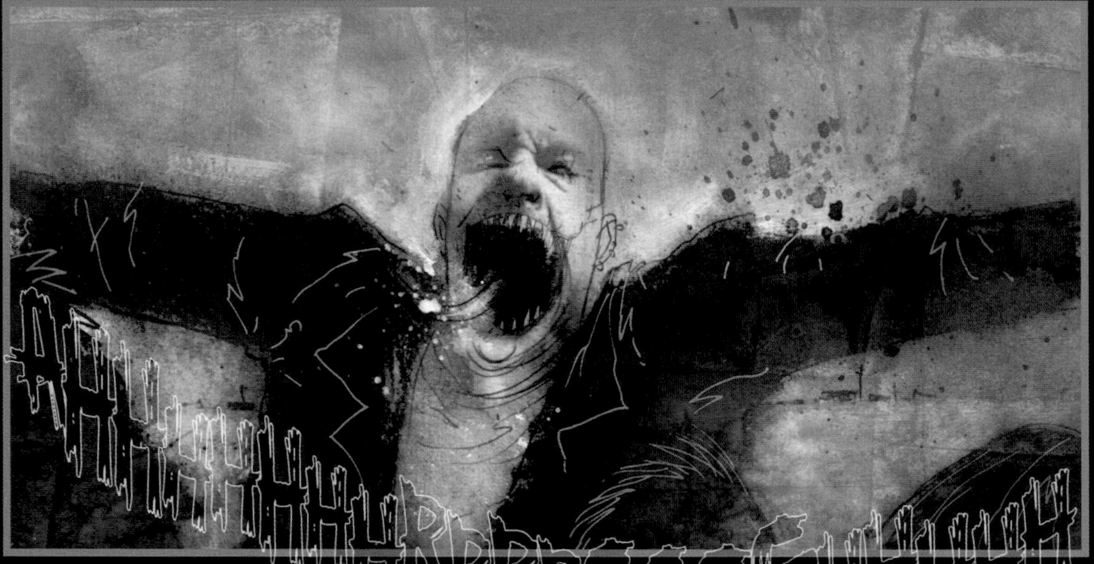

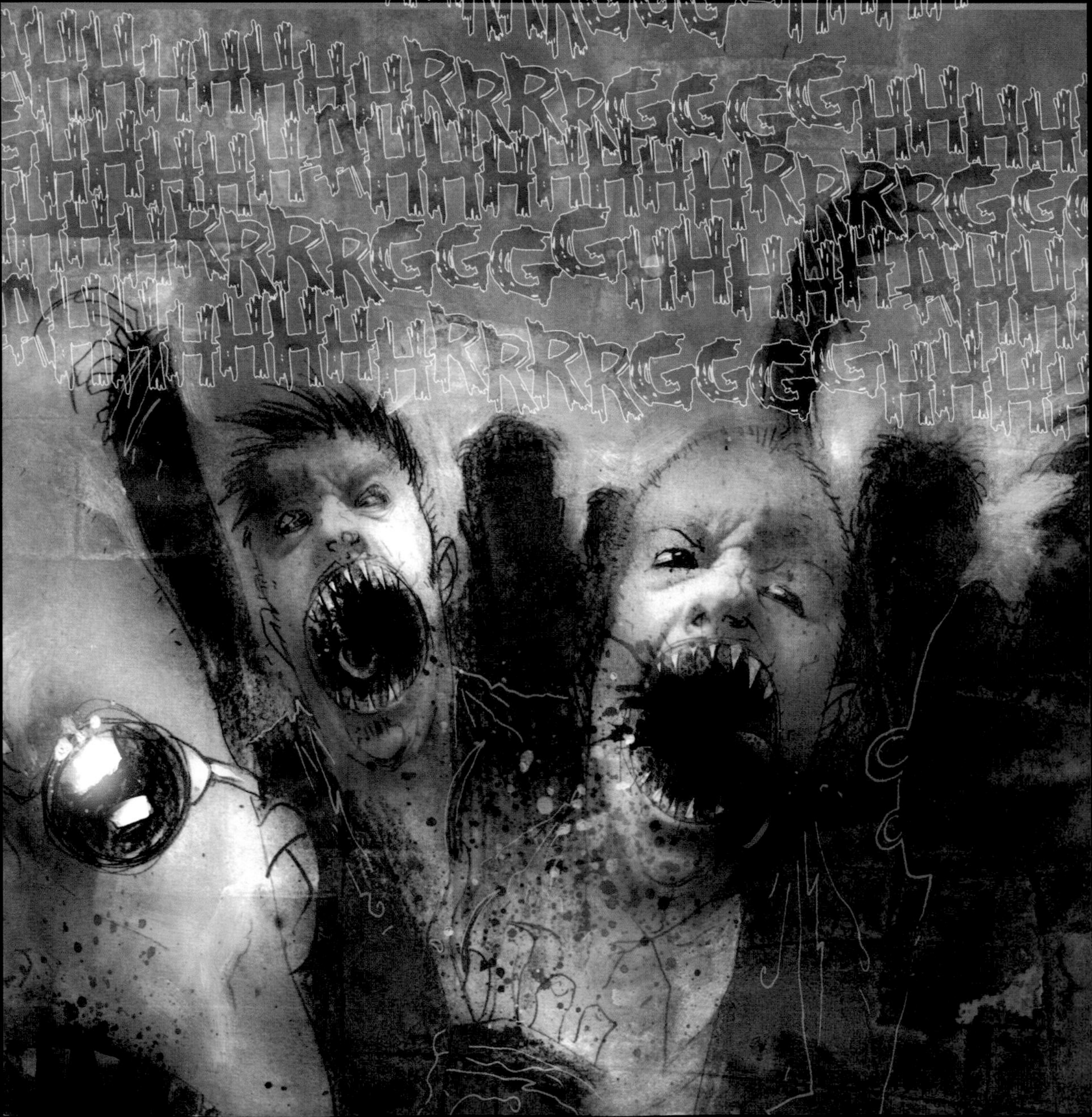

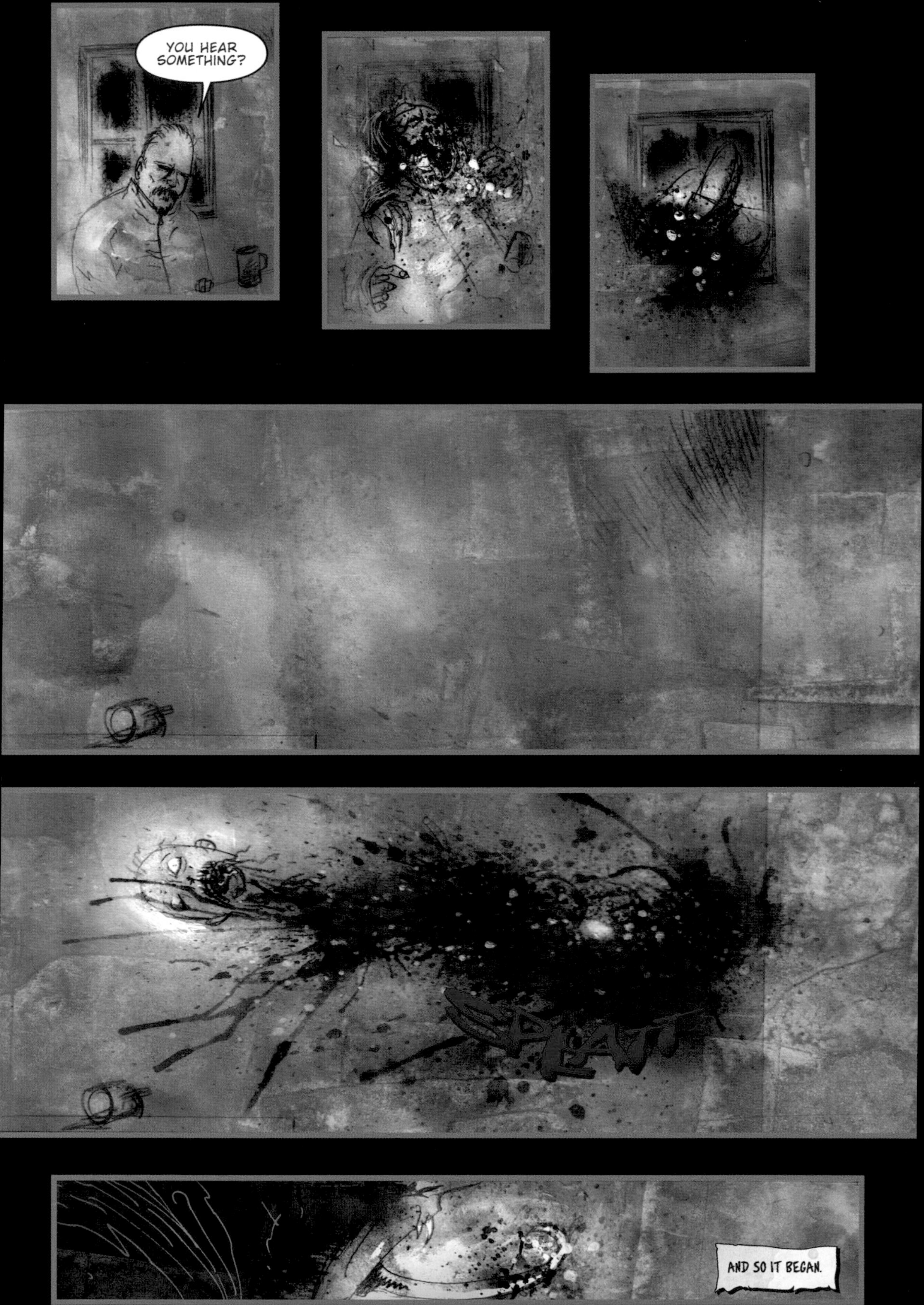
YOU HEAR SOMETHING?
AND SO IT BEGAN.

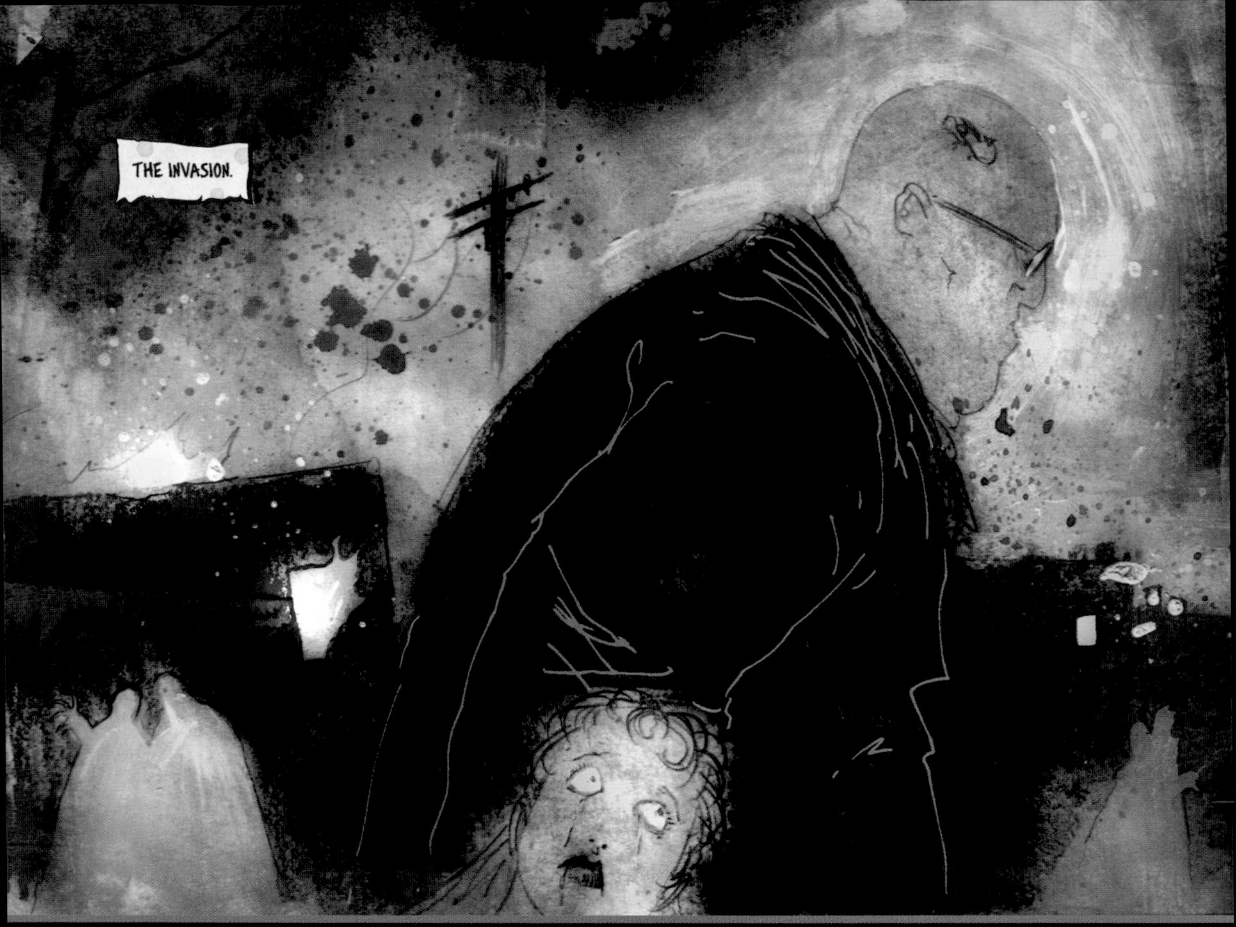
THE INVASION.

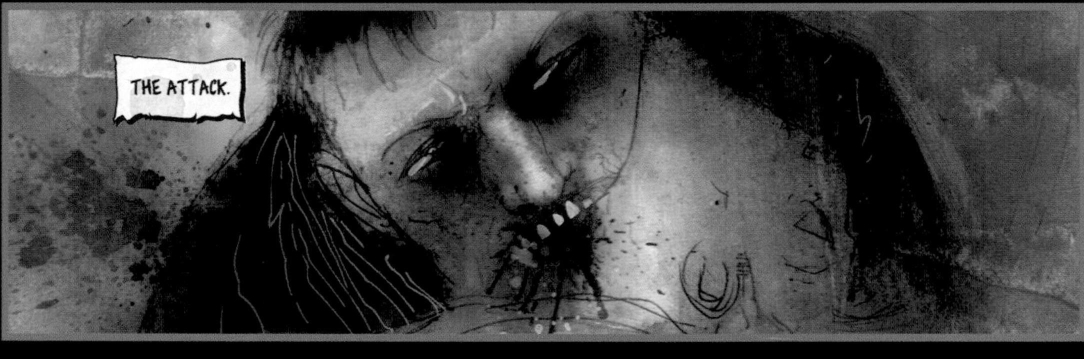
THE ATTACK.

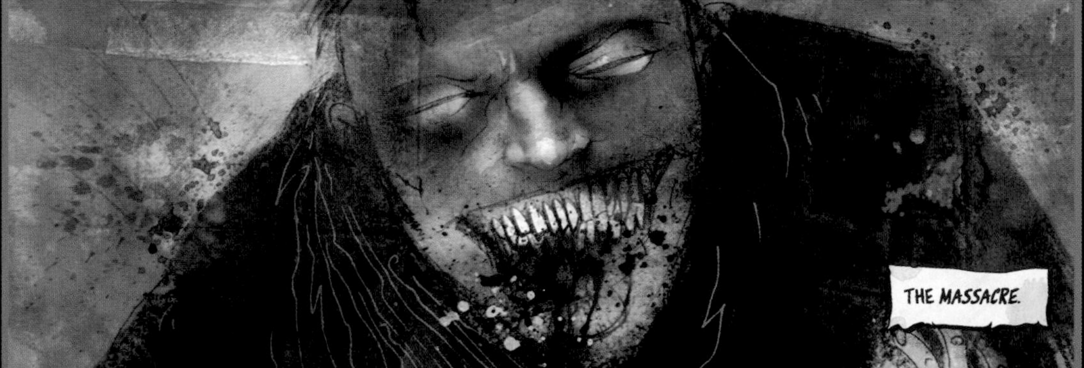
THE MASSACRE.

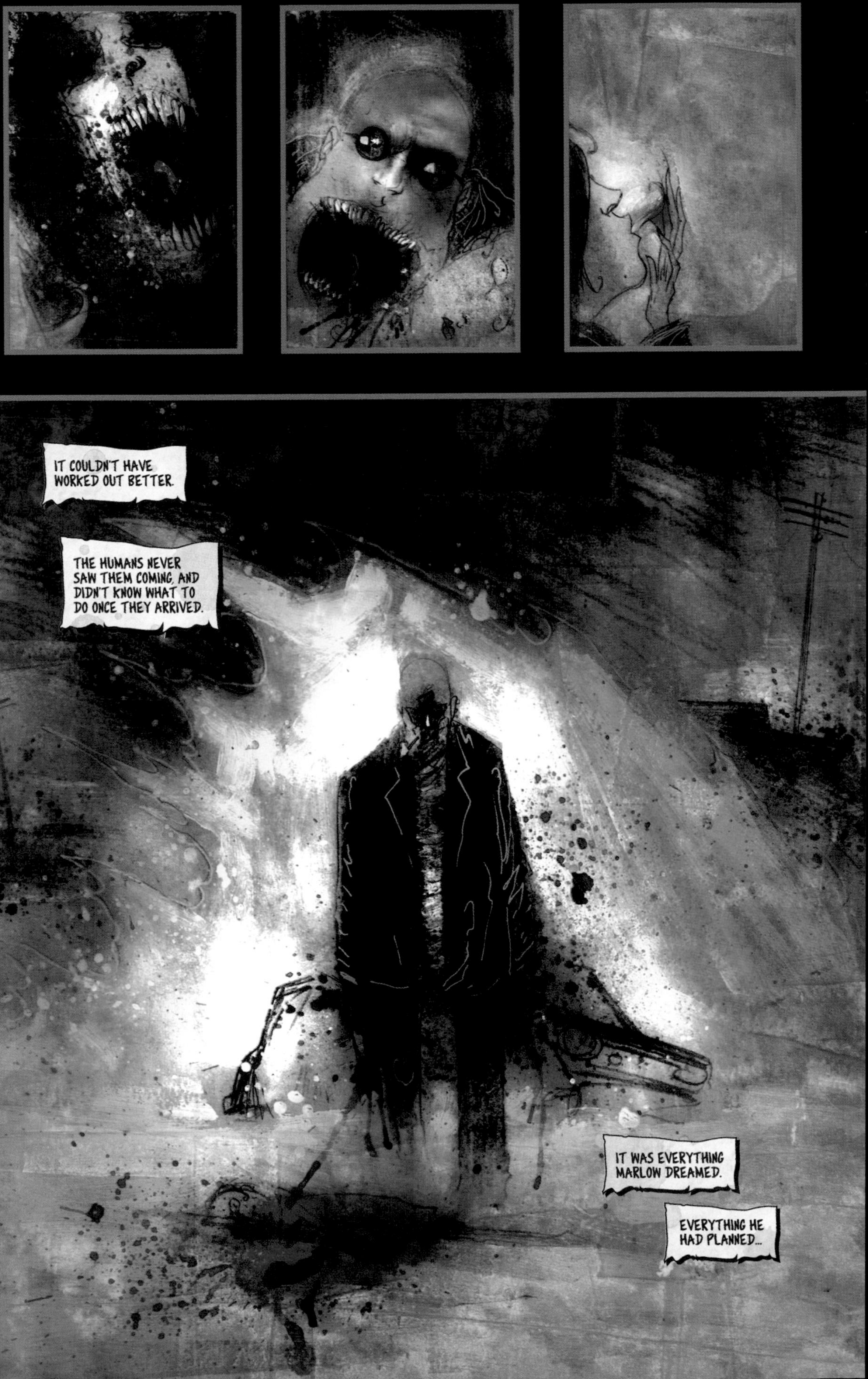
IT COULDN'T HAVE WORKED OUT BETTER.
THE HUMANS NEVER SAW THEM COMING, AND DIDN'T KNOW WHAT TO DO ONCE THEY ARRIVED.
IT WAS EVERYTHING MARLOW DREAMED.
EVERYTHING HE HAD PLANNED...

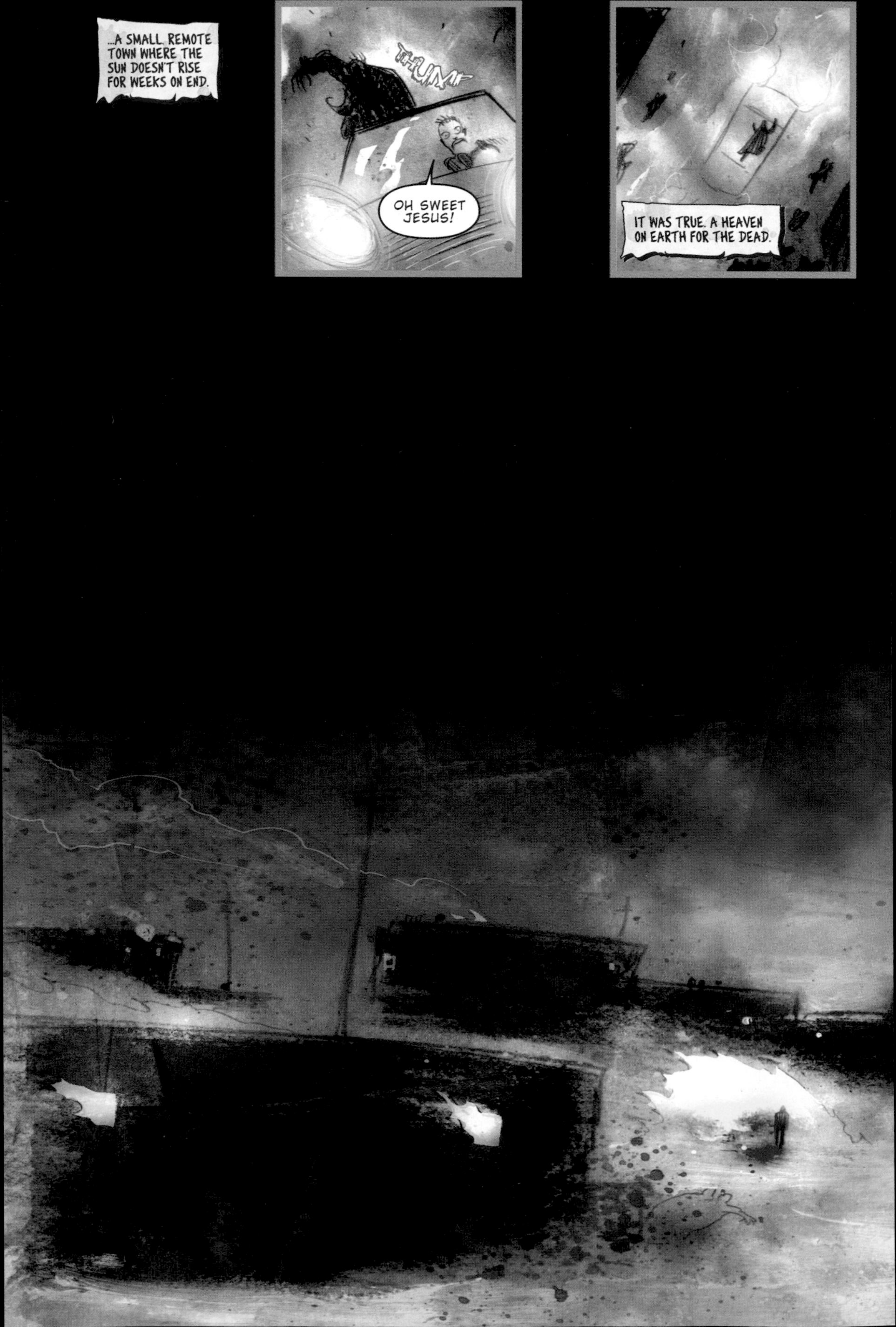
...A SMALL, REMOTE TOWN WHERE THE SUN DOESN'T RISE FOR WEEKS ON END.
THUMP
OH SWEET JESUS!
IT WAS TRUE. A HEAVEN ON EARTH FOR THE DEAD.

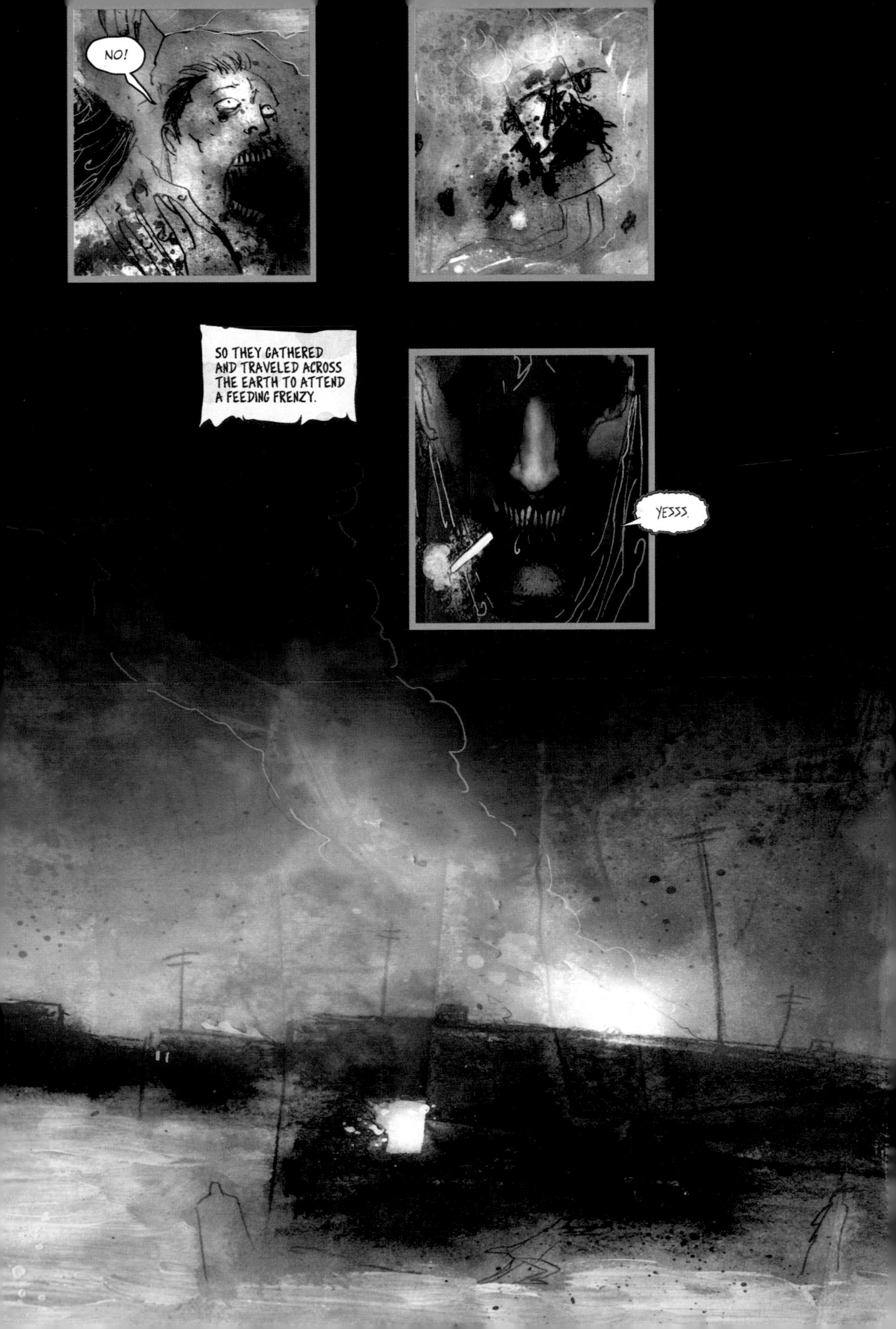
NO!
SO THEY GATHERED AND TRAVELED ACROSS THE EARTH TO ATTEND A FEEDING FRENZY.
YESSS.

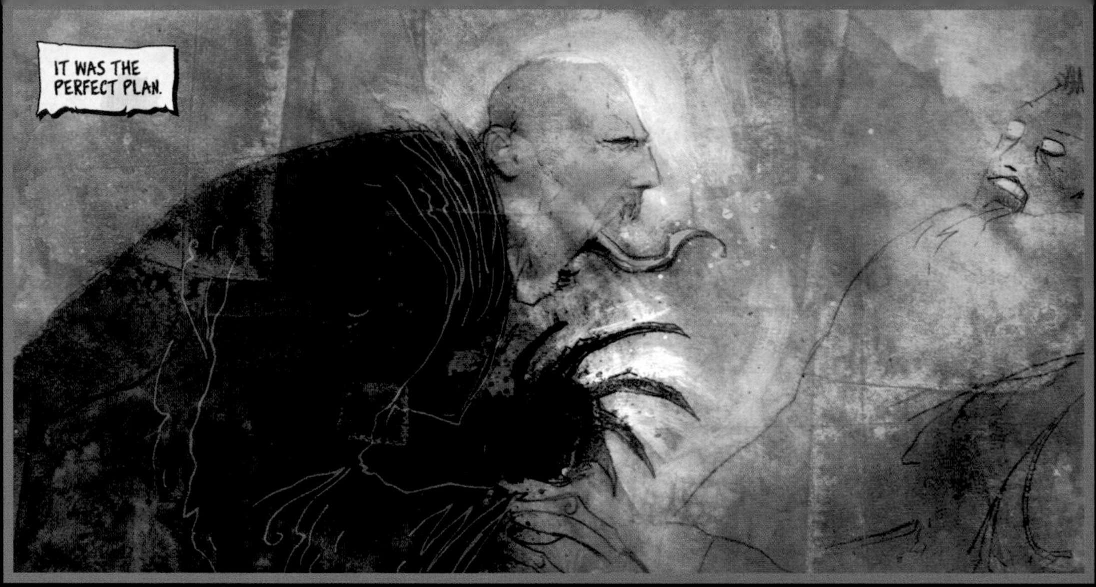
IT WAS THE PERFECT PLAN.

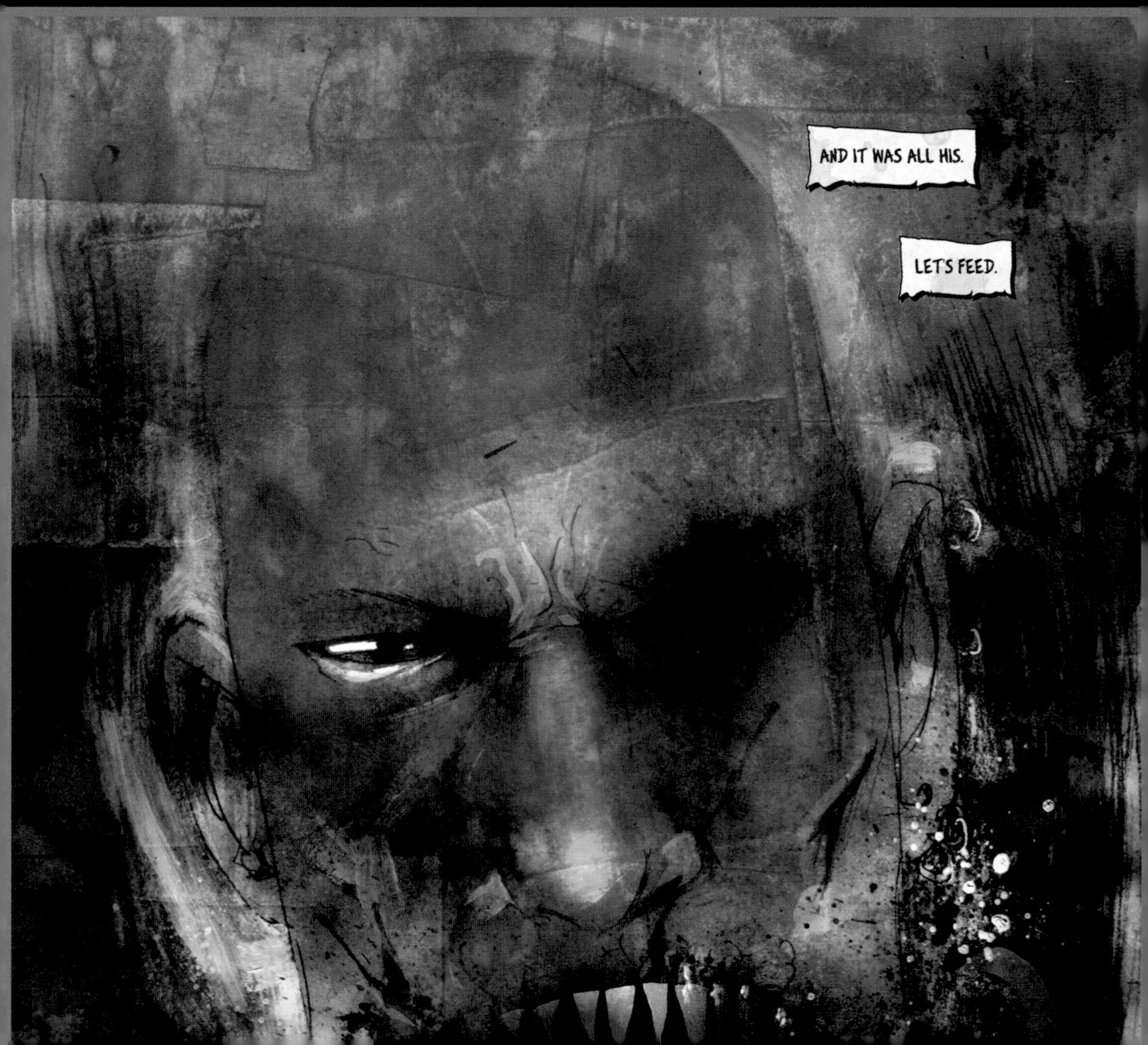
AND IT WAS ALL HIS.
LET'S FEED.

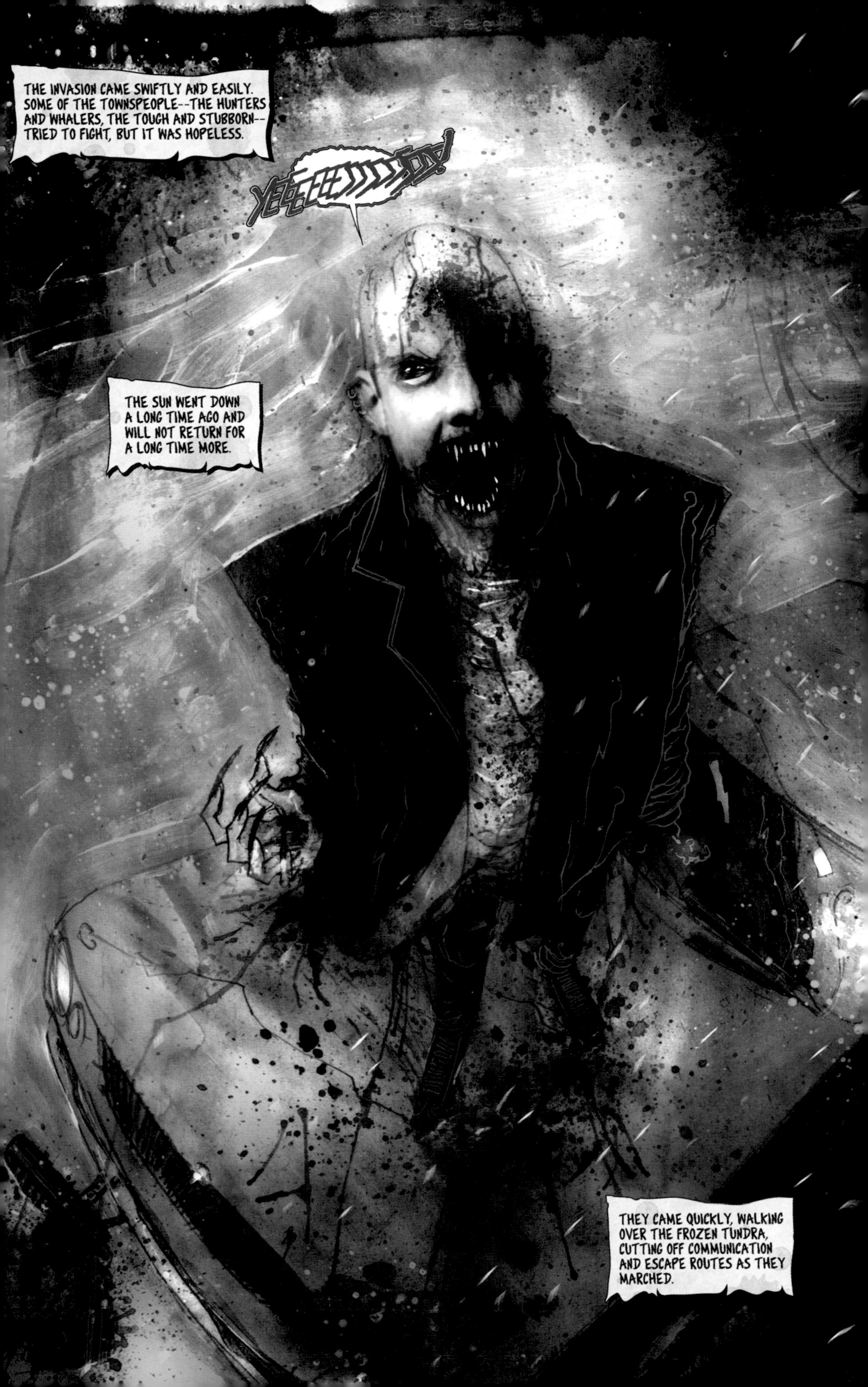
THE INVASION CAME SWIFTLY AND EASILY. SOME OF THE TOWNSPEOPLE--THE HUNTERS AND WHALERS, THE TOUGH AND STUBBORN--TRIED TO FIGHT, BUT IT WAS HOPELESS.
THE SUN WENT DOWN A LONG TIME AGO AND WILL NOT RETURN FOR A LONG TIME MORE.
THEY CAME QUICKLY, WALKING OVER THE FROZEN TUNDRA, CUTTING OFF COMMUNICATION AND ESCAPE ROUTES AS THEY MARCHED.

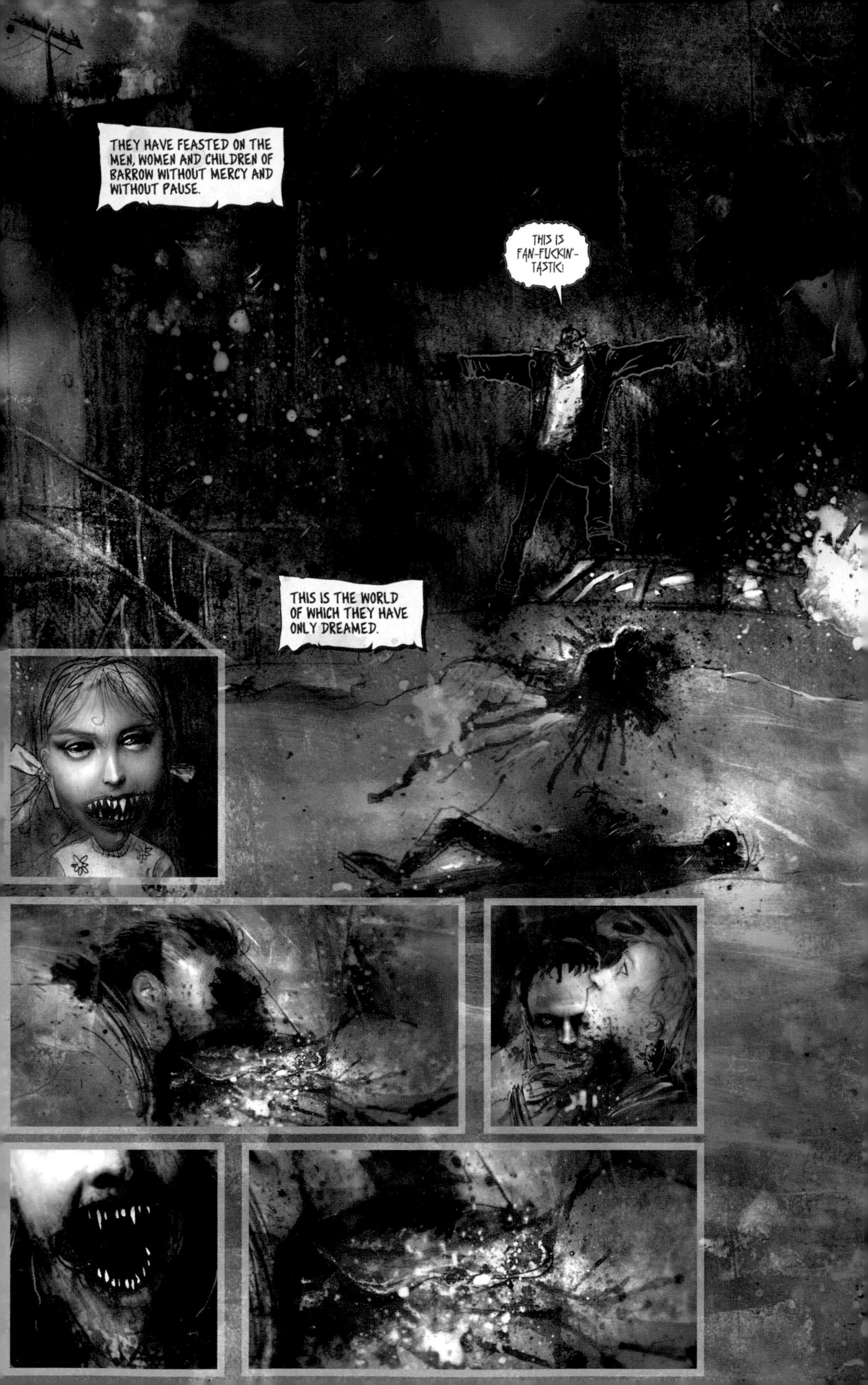
THEY HAVE FEASTED ON THE MEN, WOMEN AND CHILDREN OF BARROW WITHOUT MERCY AND WITHOUT PAUSE.
THIS IS FAN-FUCKIN'-TASTIC!
THIS IS THE WORLD OF WHICH THEY HAVE ONLY DREAMED.

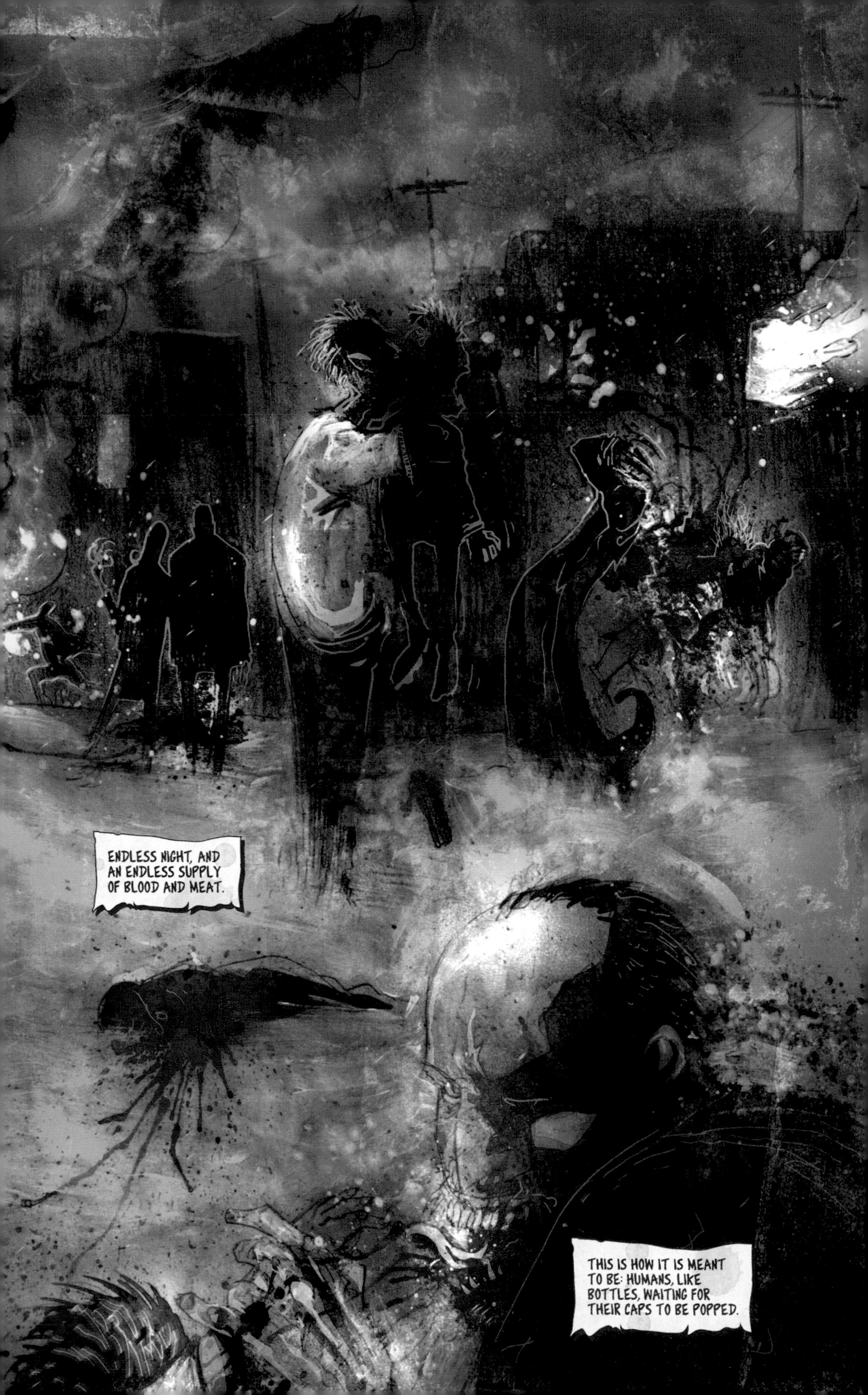
ENDLESS NIGHT, AND AN ENDLESS SUPPLY OF BLOOD AND MEAT.
THIS IS HOW IT IS MEANT TO BE: HUMANS, LIKE BOTTLES, WAITING FOR THEIR CAPS TO BE POPPED.

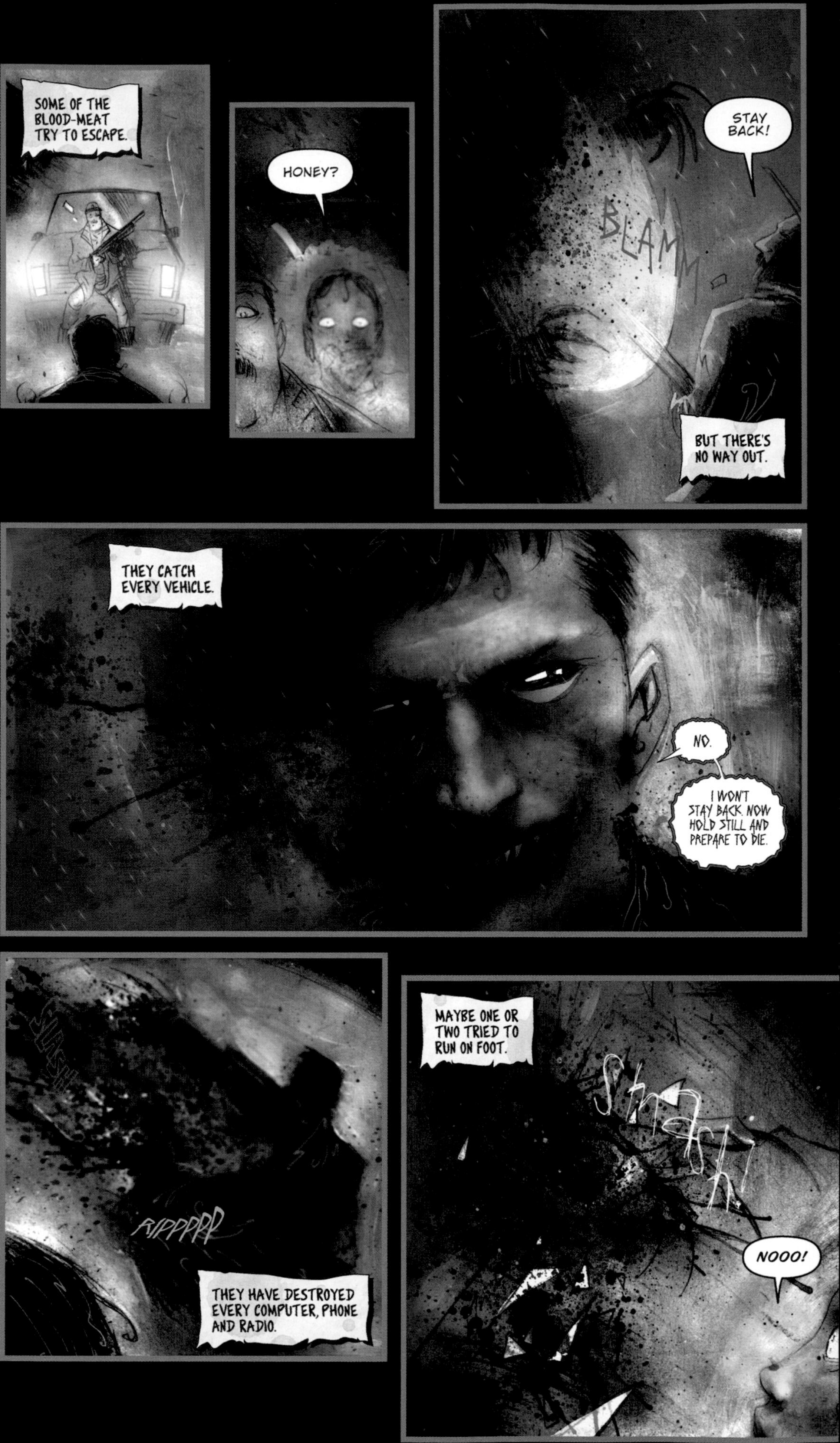

SOME OF THE BLOOD-MEAT TRY TO ESCAPE.
HONEY?
STAY BACK!
BLAMM
BUT THERE'S NO WAY OUT.
THEY CATCH EVERY VEHICLE.
NO.
I WON'T STAY BACK. NOW HOLD STILL AND PREPARE TO DIE.
RIPPPPP
THEY HAVE DESTROYED EVERY COMPUTER, PHONE AND RADIO.
MAYBE ONE OR TWO TRIED TO RUN ON FOOT.
Smash!
NOOO!

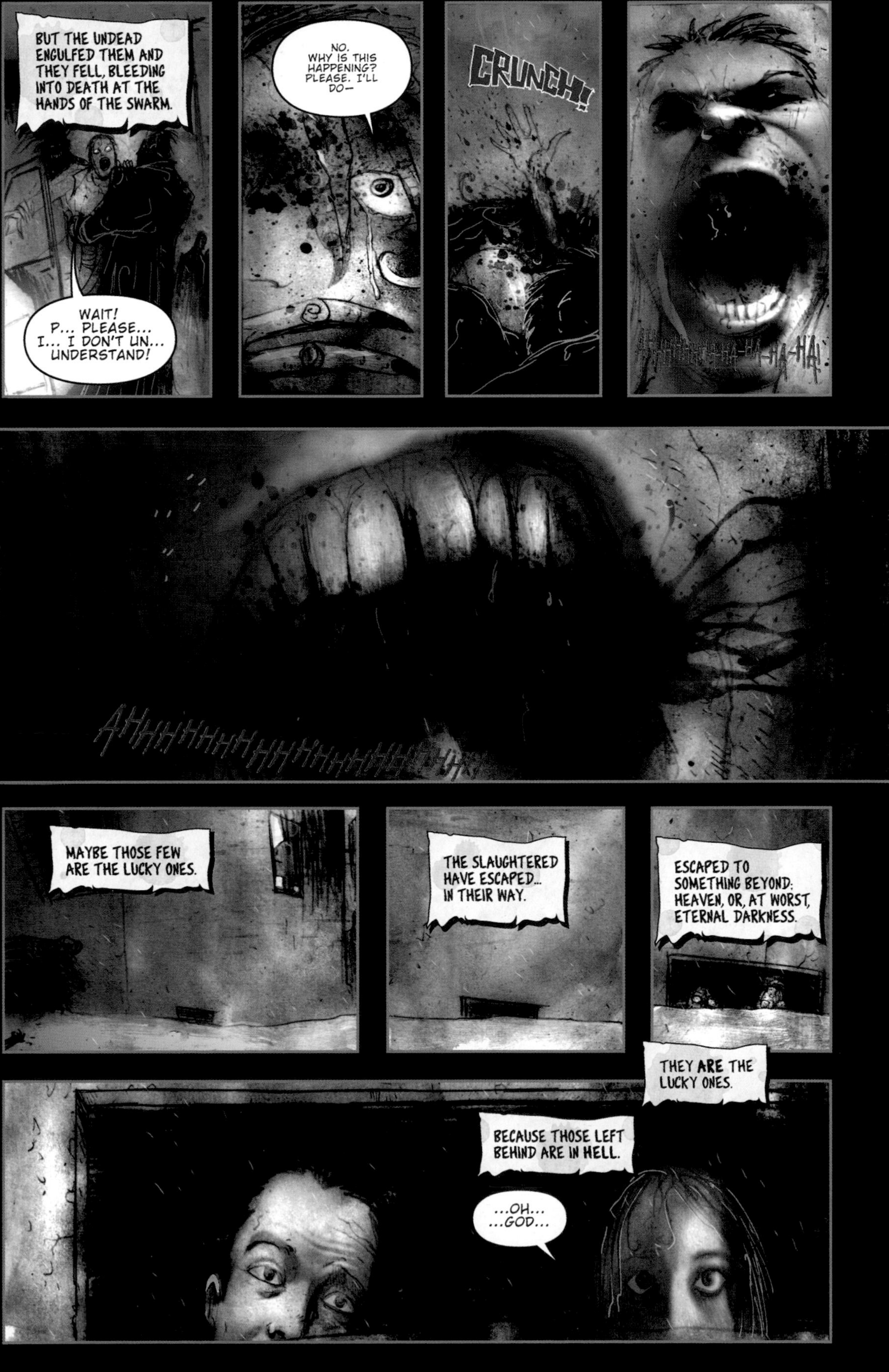
BUT THE UNDEAD ENGULFED THEM AND THEY FELL, BLEEDING INTO DEATH AT THE HANDS OF THE SWARM.
WAIT! P... PLEASE... I... I DON'T UN... UNDERSTAND!
NO. WHY IS THIS HAPPENING? PLEASE. I'LL DO—
CRUNCH!
MAYBE THOSE FEW ARE THE LUCKY ONES.
THE SLAUGHTERED HAVE ESCAPED... IN THEIR WAY.
ESCAPED TO SOMETHING BEYOND: HEAVEN, OR, AT WORST, ETERNAL DARKNESS.
THEY ARE THE LUCKY ONES.
BECAUSE THOSE LEFT BEHIND ARE IN HELL.
...OH... ...GOD...

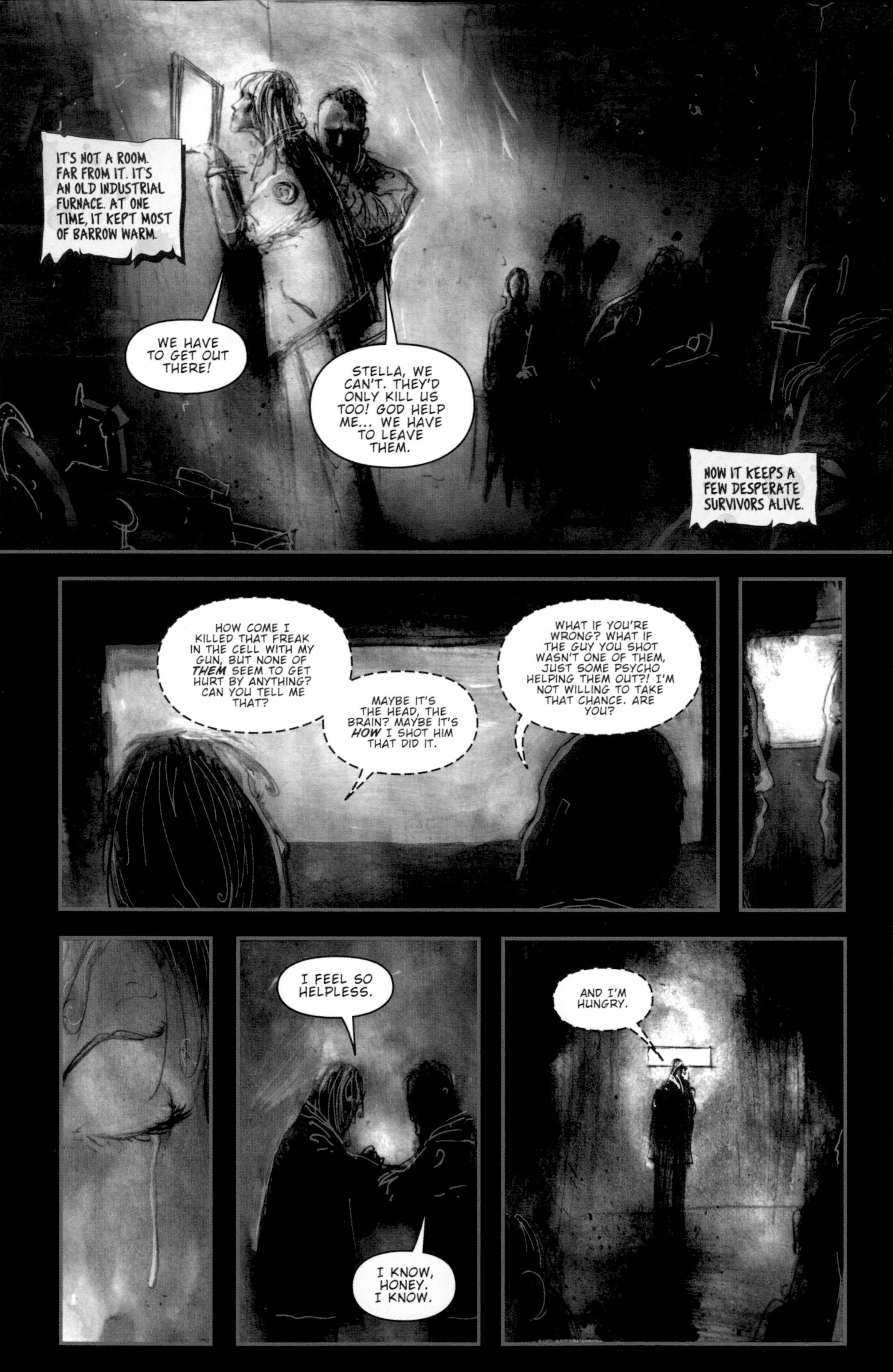
IT'S NOT A ROOM. FAR FROM IT. IT'S AN OLD INDUSTRIAL FURNACE. AT ONE TIME, IT KEPT MOST OF BARROW WARM.
WE HAVE TO GET OUT THERE!
STELLA, WE CAN'T. THEY'D ONLY KILL US TOO! GOD HELP ME... WE HAVE TO LEAVE THEM.
NOW IT KEEPS A FEW DESPERATE SURVIVORS ALIVE.
HOW COME I KILLED THAT FREAK IN THE CELL WITH MY GUN, BUT NONE OF THEM SEEM TO GET HURT BY ANYTHING? CAN YOU TELL ME THAT?
MAYBE IT'S THE HEAD, THE BRAIN? MAYBE IT'S HOW I SHOT HIM THAT DID IT.
WHAT IF YOU'RE WRONG? WHAT IF THE GUY YOU SHOT WASN'T ONE OF THEM, JUST SOME PSYCHO HELPING THEM OUT?! I'M NOT WILLING TO TAKE THAT CHANCE. ARE YOU?
I FEEL SO HELPLESS.
I KNOW, HONEY. I KNOW.
AND I'M HUNGRY.

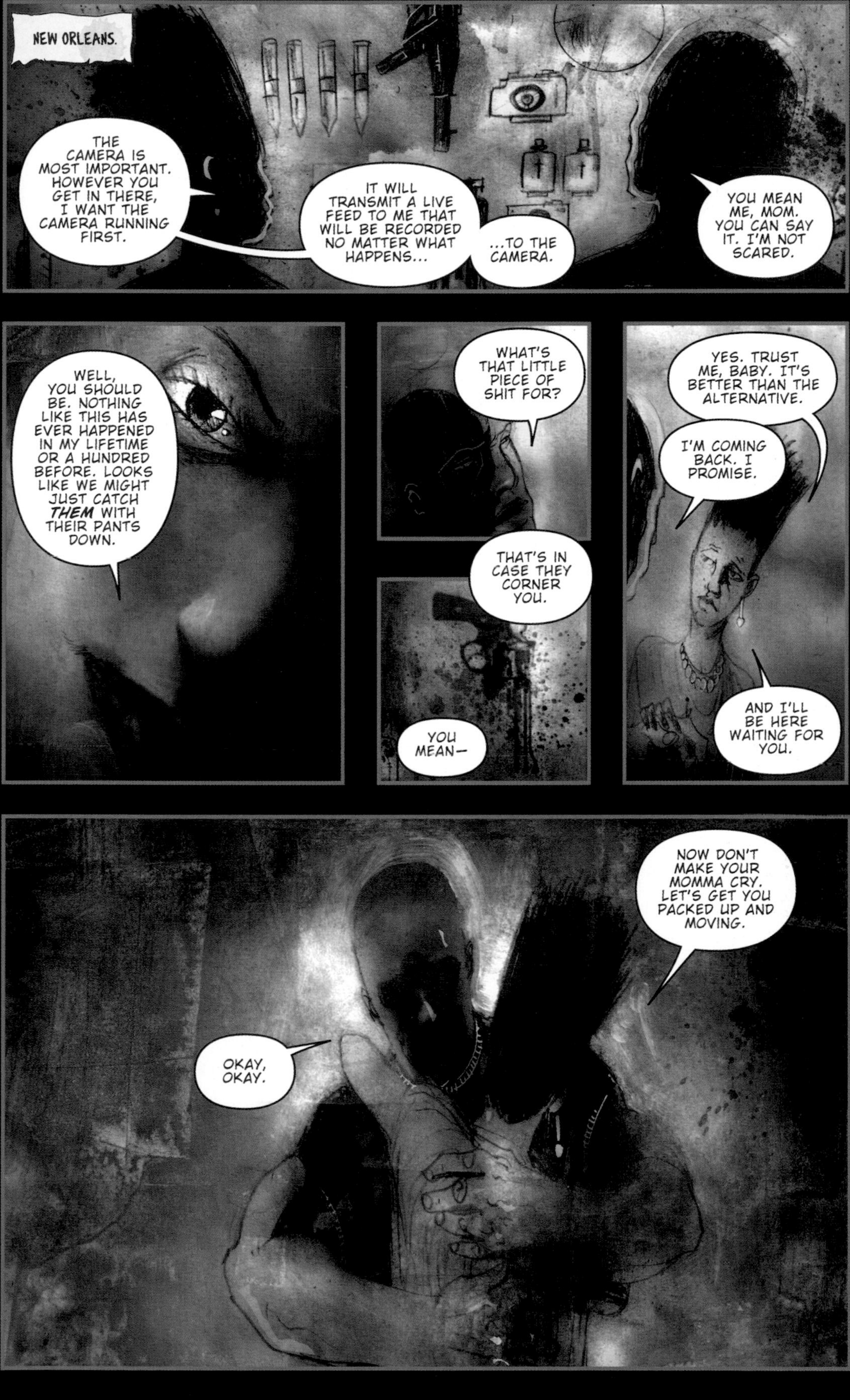
NEW ORLEANS.
THE CAMERA IS MOST IMPORTANT. HOWEVER YOU GET IN THERE, I WANT THE CAMERA RUNNING FIRST.
IT WILL TRANSMIT A LIVE FEED TO ME THAT WILL BE RECORDED NO MATTER WHAT HAPPENS...
...TO THE CAMERA.
YOU MEAN ME, MOM. YOU CAN SAY IT. I'M NOT SCARED.
WELL, YOU SHOULD BE. NOTHING LIKE THIS HAS EVER HAPPENED IN MY LIFETIME OR A HUNDRED BEFORE. LOOKS LIKE WE MIGHT JUST CATCH *THEM* WITH THEIR PANTS DOWN.
WHAT'S THAT LITTLE PIECE OF SHIT FOR?
THAT'S IN CASE THEY CORNER YOU.
YOU MEAN—
YES. TRUST ME, BABY. IT'S BETTER THAN THE ALTERNATIVE.
I'M COMING BACK. I PROMISE.
AND I'LL BE HERE WAITING FOR YOU.
NOW DON'T MAKE YOUR MOMMA CRY. LET'S GET YOU PACKED UP AND MOVING.
OKAY, OKAY.

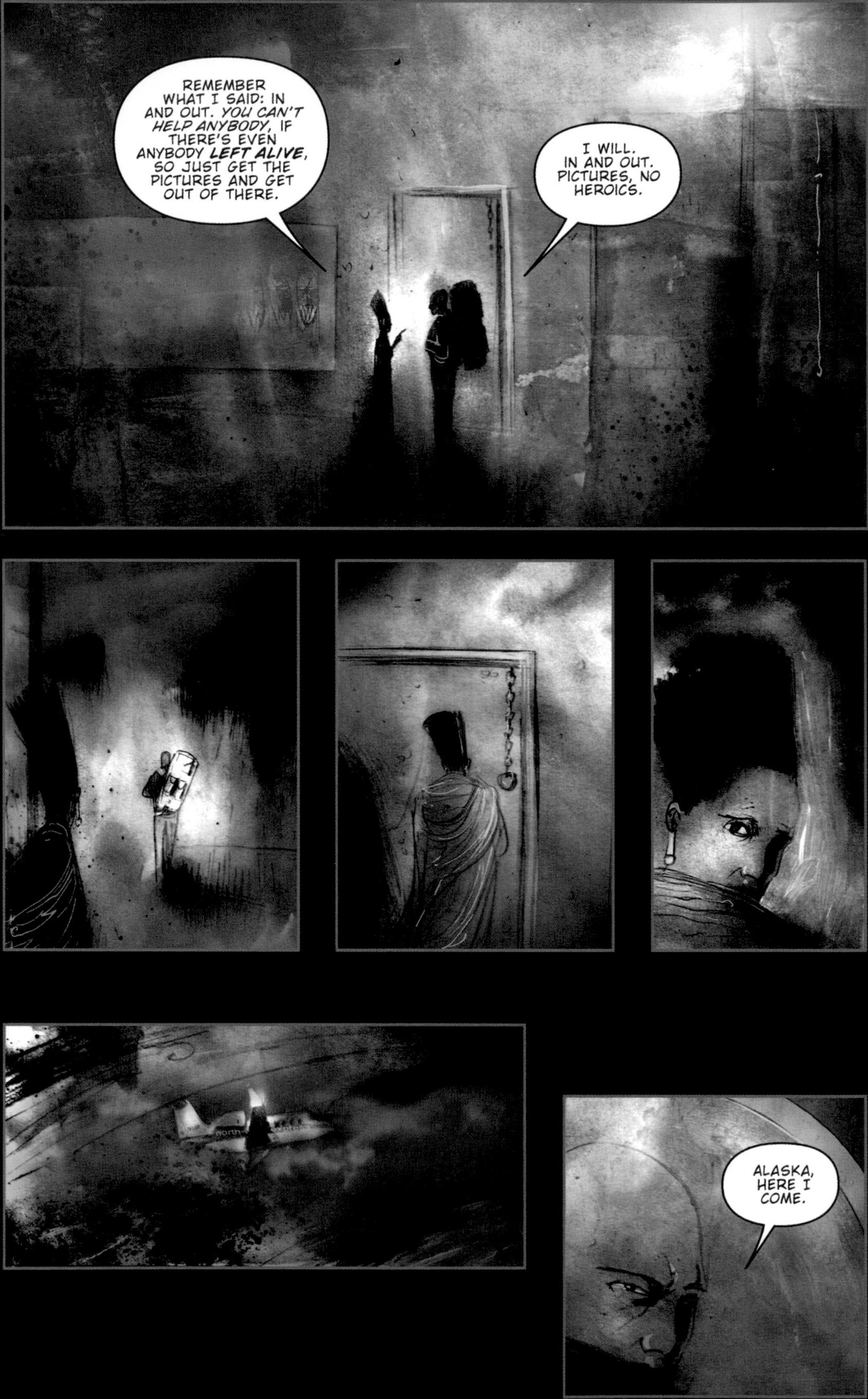
REMEMBER WHAT I SAID: IN AND OUT. *YOU CAN'T HELP ANYBODY*, IF THERE'S EVEN ANYBODY ***LEFT ALIVE***, SO JUST GET THE PICTURES AND GET OUT OF THERE.
I WILL. IN AND OUT. PICTURES, NO HEROICS.
ALASKA, HERE I COME.

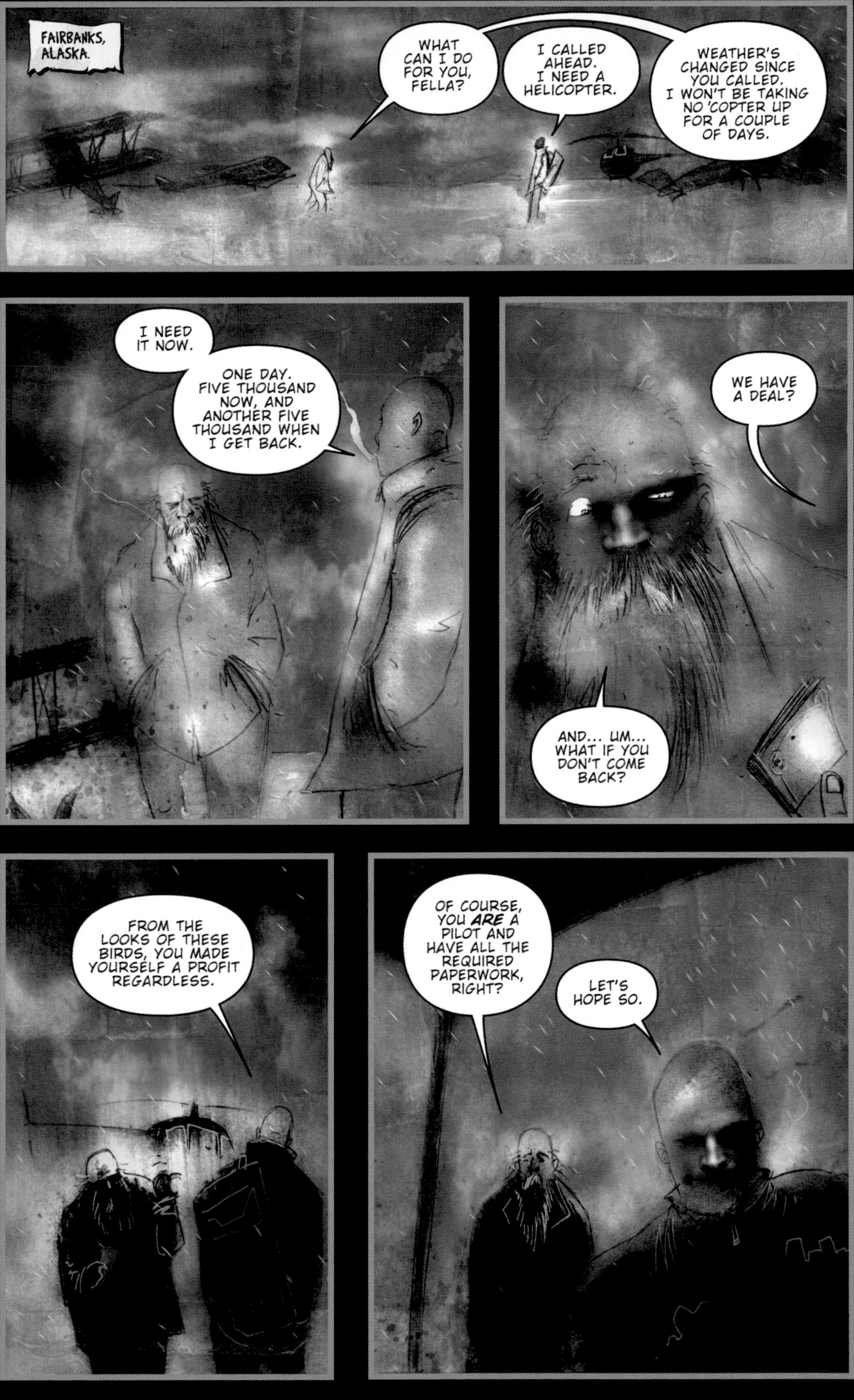
FAIRBANKS, ALASKA.
WHAT CAN I DO FOR YOU, FELLA?
I CALLED AHEAD. I NEED A HELICOPTER.
WEATHER'S CHANGED SINCE YOU CALLED. I WON'T BE TAKING NO 'COPTER UP FOR A COUPLE OF DAYS.
I NEED IT NOW.
ONE DAY. FIVE THOUSAND NOW, AND ANOTHER FIVE THOUSAND WHEN I GET BACK.
WE HAVE A DEAL?
AND... UM... WHAT IF YOU DON'T COME BACK?
FROM THE LOOKS OF THESE BIRDS, YOU MADE YOURSELF A PROFIT REGARDLESS.
OF COURSE, YOU **ARE** A PILOT AND HAVE ALL THE REQUIRED PAPERWORK, RIGHT?
LET'S HOPE SO.

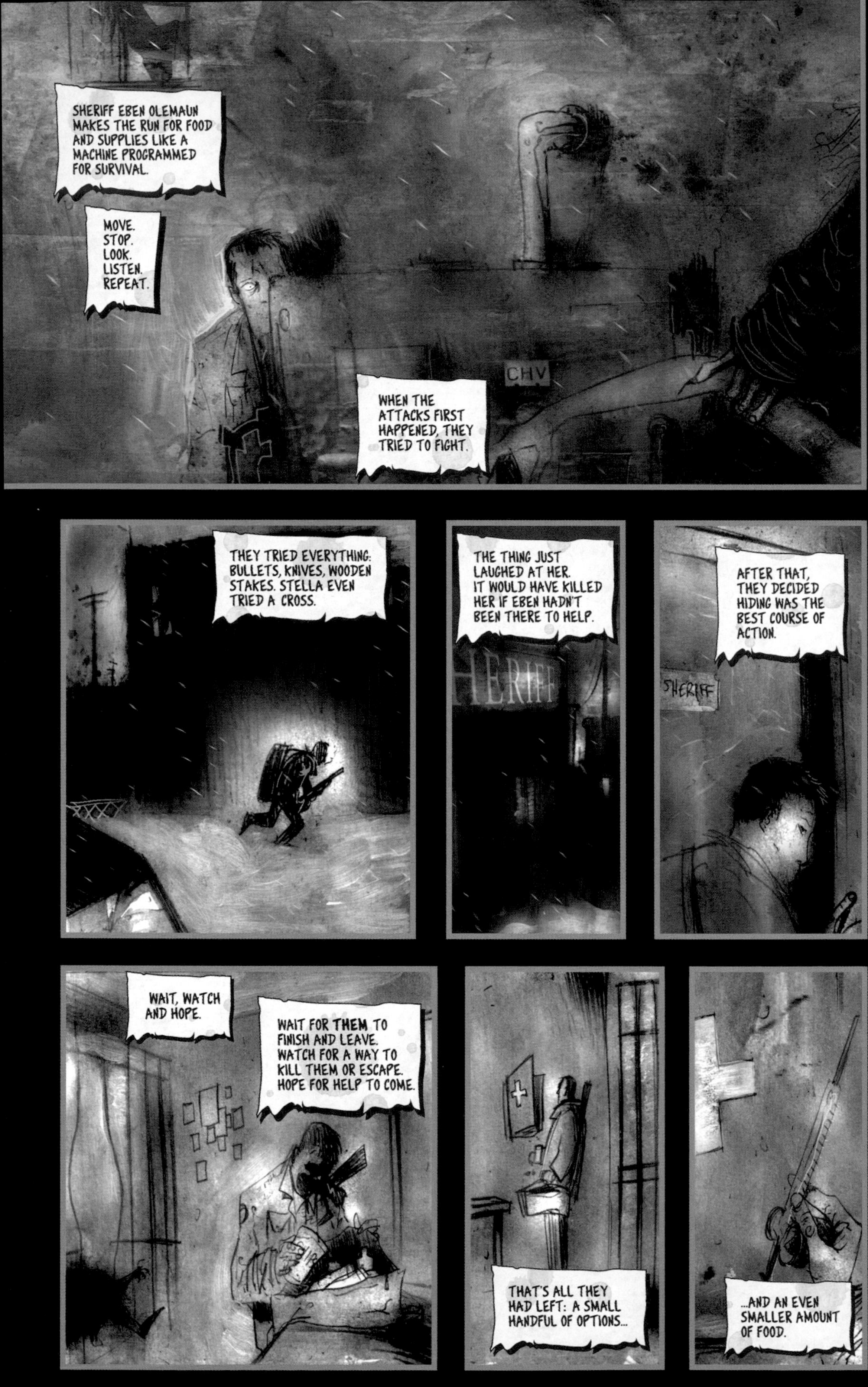
SHERIFF EBEN OLEMAUN MAKES THE RUN FOR FOOD AND SUPPLIES LIKE A MACHINE PROGRAMMED FOR SURVIVAL.
MOVE. STOP. LOOK. LISTEN. REPEAT.
CHV
WHEN THE ATTACKS FIRST HAPPENED, THEY TRIED TO FIGHT.
THEY TRIED EVERYTHING: BULLETS, KNIVES, WOODEN STAKES. STELLA EVEN TRIED A CROSS.
THE THING JUST LAUGHED AT HER. IT WOULD HAVE KILLED HER IF EBEN HADN'T BEEN THERE TO HELP.
AFTER THAT, THEY DECIDED HIDING WAS THE BEST COURSE OF ACTION.
SHERIFF
WAIT, WATCH AND HOPE.
WAIT FOR THEM TO FINISH AND LEAVE. WATCH FOR A WAY TO KILL THEM OR ESCAPE. HOPE FOR HELP TO COME.
THAT'S ALL THEY HAD LEFT: A SMALL HANDFUL OF OPTIONS...
...AND AN EVEN SMALLER AMOUNT OF FOOD.

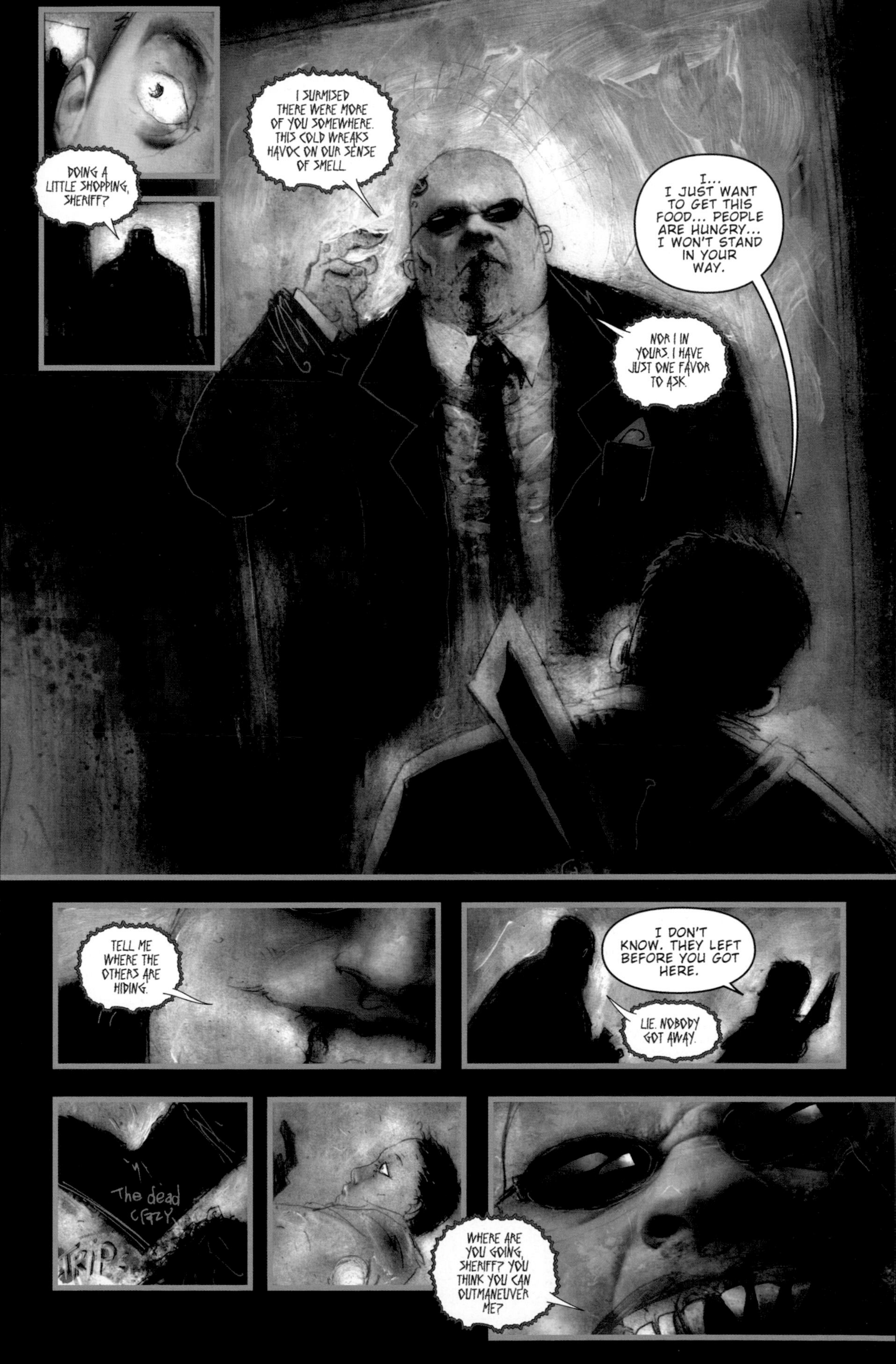
DOING A LITTLE SHOPPING, SHERIFF?
I SURMISED THERE WERE MORE OF YOU SOMEWHERE. THIS COLD WREAKS HAVOC ON OUR SENSE OF SMELL.
I... I JUST WANT TO GET THIS FOOD... PEOPLE ARE HUNGRY... I WON'T STAND IN YOUR WAY.
NOR I IN YOURS. I HAVE JUST ONE FAVOR TO ASK.
TELL ME WHERE THE OTHERS ARE HIDING.
I DON'T KNOW. THEY LEFT BEFORE YOU GOT HERE.
LIE. NOBODY GOT AWAY.
The dead crazy
WHERE ARE YOU GOING, SHERIFF? YOU THINK YOU CAN OUTMANEUVER ME?

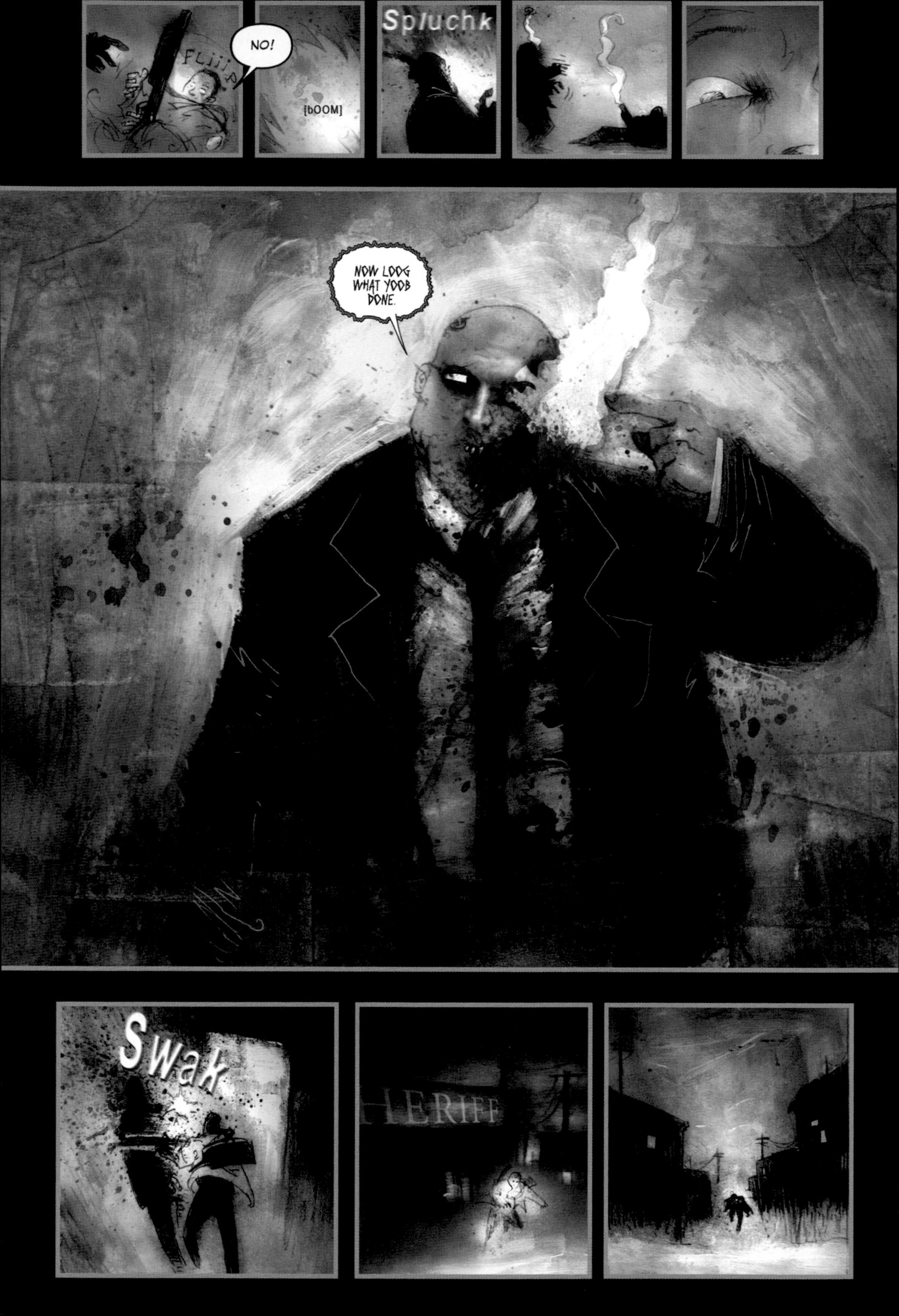
FLiiiP
NO!
[bOOM]
Spluchk
NOW LOOG WHAT YOOB DONE.
Swak
HERIFF

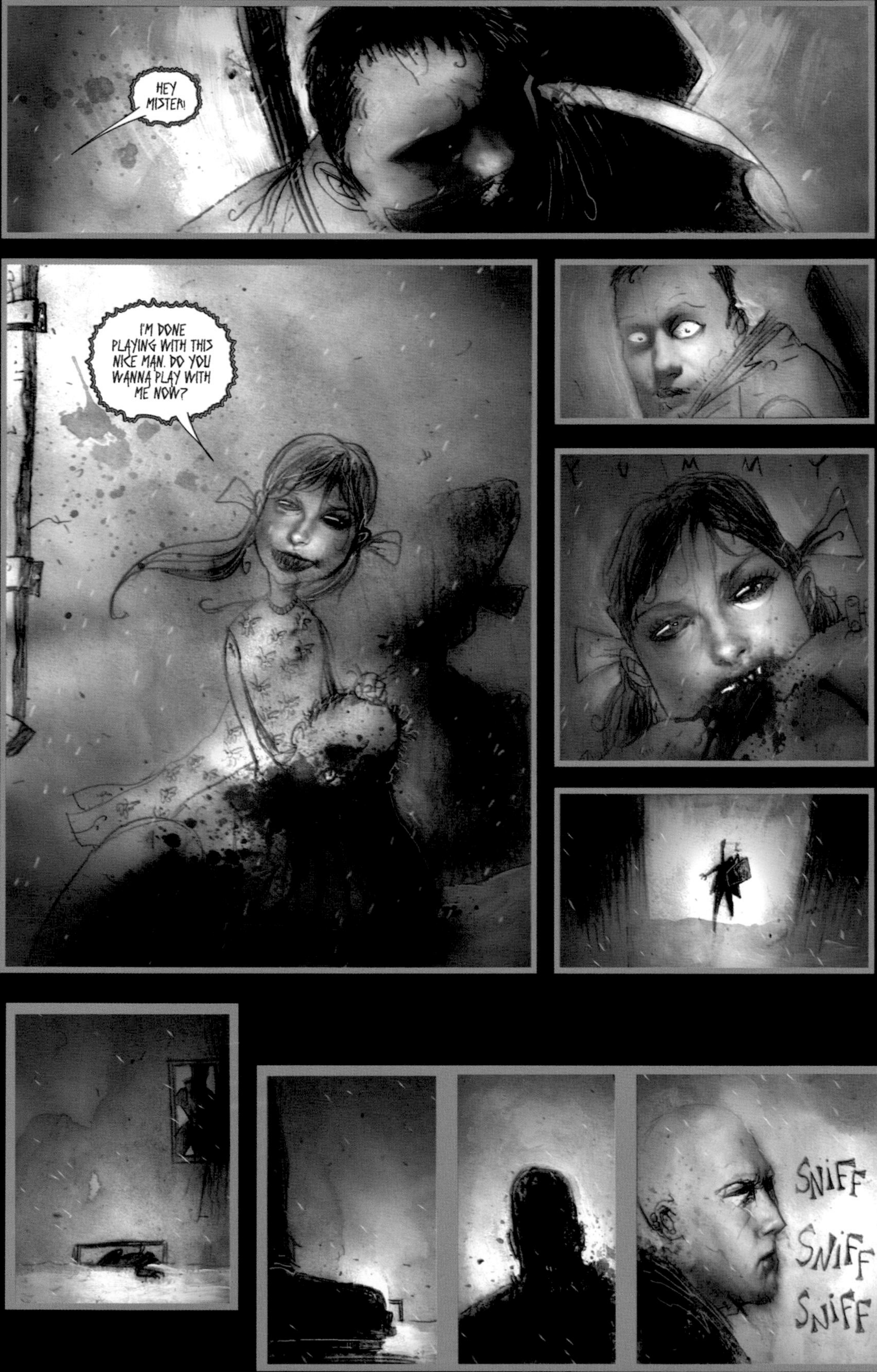
HEY MISTER!
I'M DONE PLAYING WITH THIS NICE MAN. DO YOU WANNA PLAY WITH ME NOW?
Y U M M Y
SNIFF
SNIFF
SNIFF

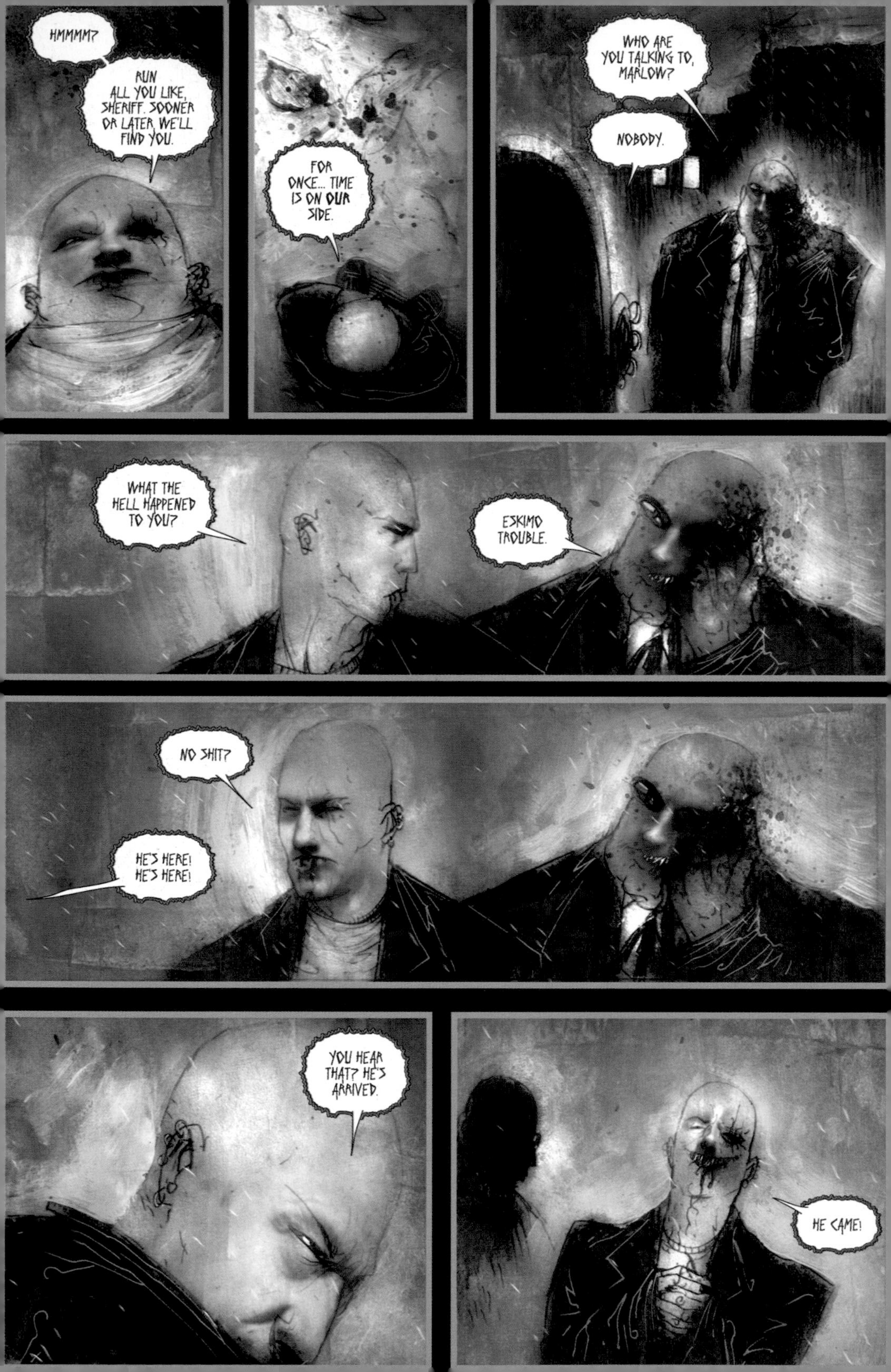
HMMMM?
RUN ALL YOU LIKE, SHERIFF. SOONER OR LATER WE'LL FIND YOU.
FOR ONCE... TIME IS ON **OUR** SIDE.
WHO ARE YOU TALKING TO, MARLOW?
NOBODY.
WHAT THE HELL HAPPENED TO YOU?
ESKIMO TROUBLE.
NO SHIT?
HE'S HERE! HE'S HERE!
YOU HEAR THAT? HE'S ARRIVED.
HE CAME!

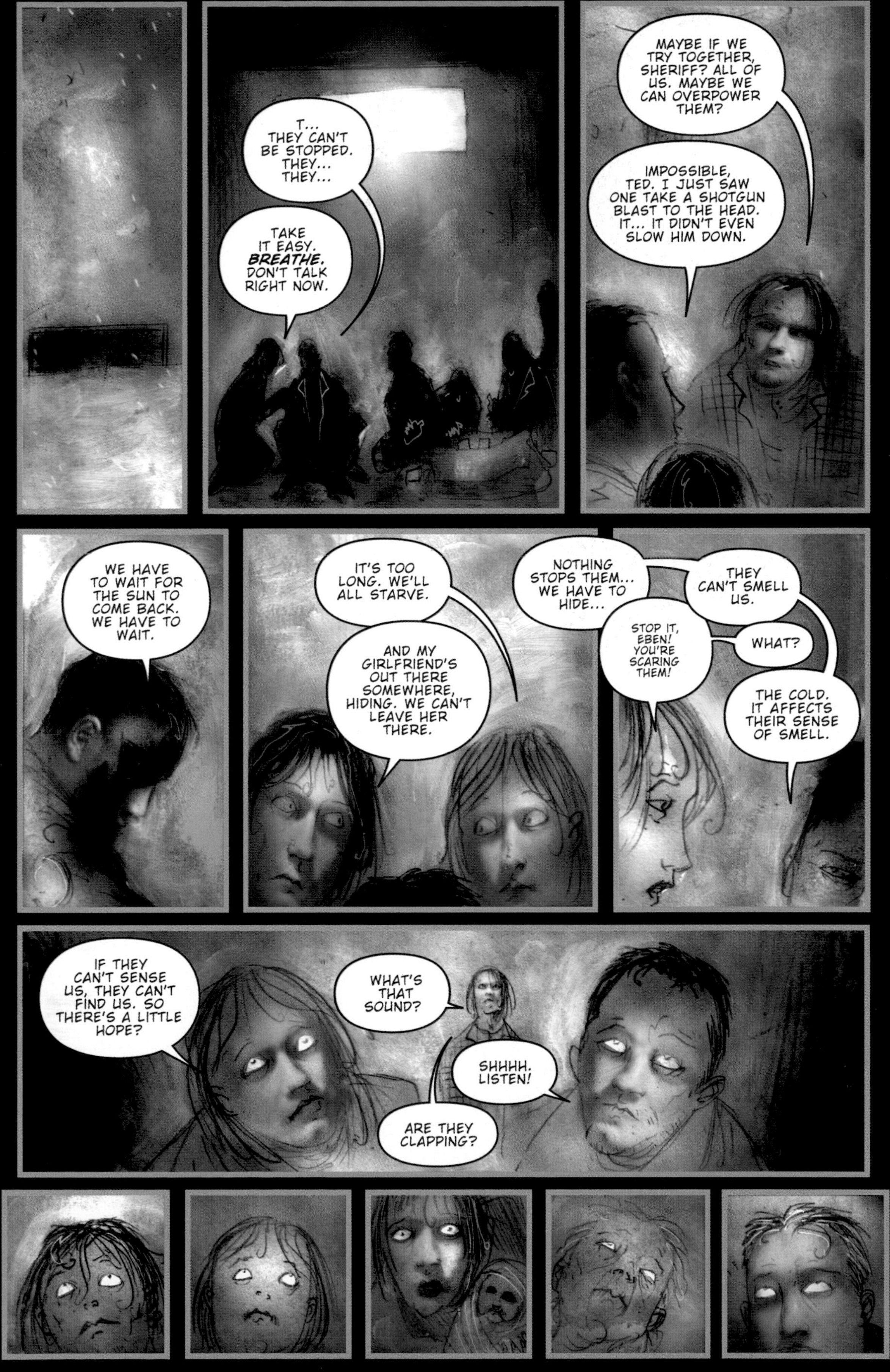
T... THEY CAN'T BE STOPPED. THEY... THEY...
TAKE IT EASY. **BREATHE.** DON'T TALK RIGHT NOW.
MAYBE IF WE TRY TOGETHER, SHERIFF? ALL OF US. MAYBE WE CAN OVERPOWER THEM?
IMPOSSIBLE, TED. I JUST SAW ONE TAKE A SHOTGUN BLAST TO THE HEAD. IT... IT DIDN'T EVEN SLOW HIM DOWN.
WE HAVE TO WAIT FOR THE SUN TO COME BACK. WE HAVE TO WAIT.
IT'S TOO LONG. WE'LL ALL STARVE.
AND MY GIRLFRIEND'S OUT THERE SOMEWHERE, HIDING. WE CAN'T LEAVE HER THERE.
NOTHING STOPS THEM... WE HAVE TO HIDE...
THEY CAN'T SMELL US.
STOP IT, EBEN! YOU'RE SCARING THEM!
WHAT?
THE COLD. IT AFFECTS THEIR SENSE OF SMELL.
IF THEY CAN'T SENSE US, THEY CAN'T FIND US. SO THERE'S A LITTLE HOPE?
WHAT'S THAT SOUND?
SHHHH. LISTEN!
ARE THEY CLAPPING?

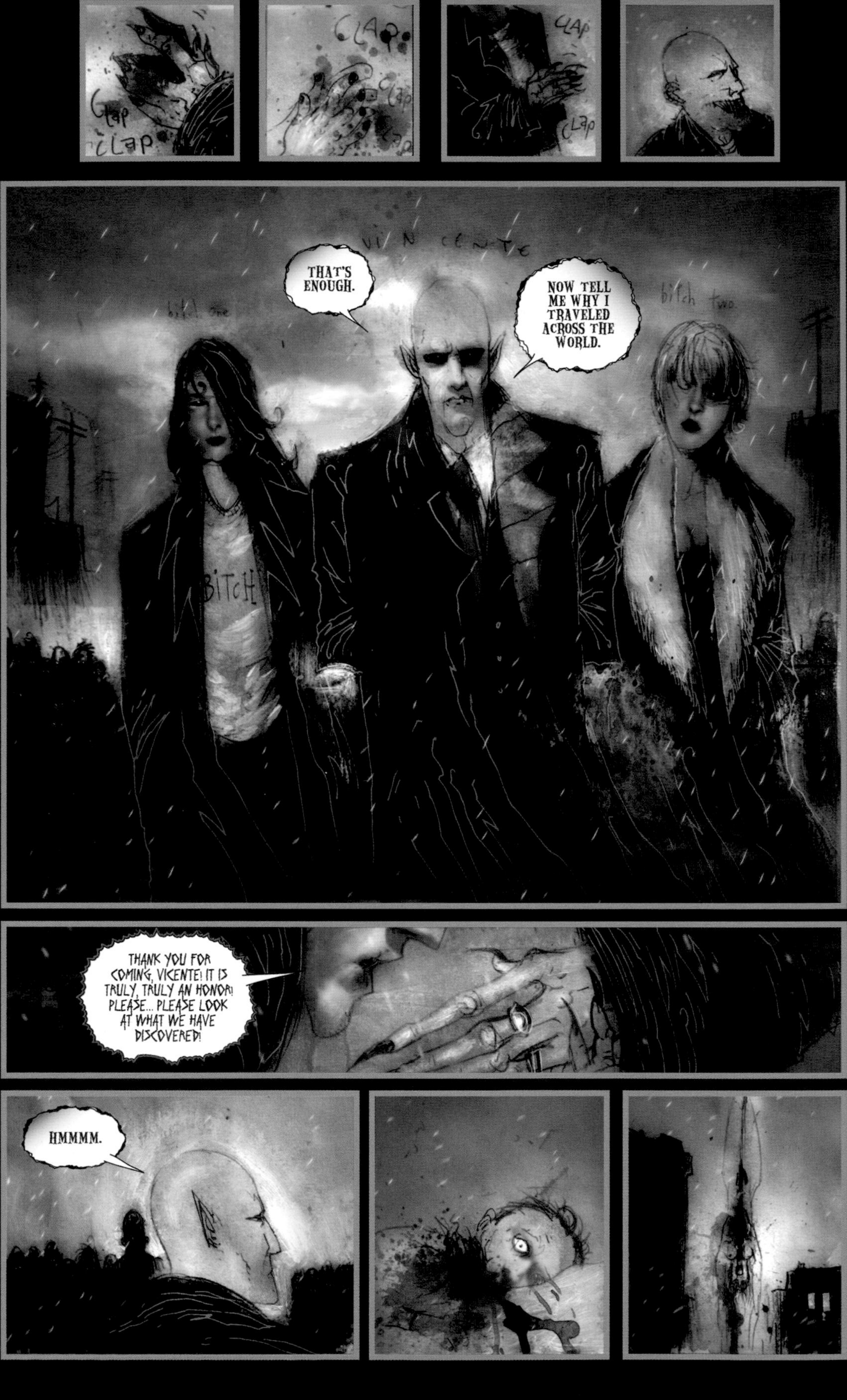
CLAP CLAP
CLAP CLAP CLAP
CLAP CLAP
THAT'S ENOUGH.
NOW TELL ME WHY I TRAVELED ACROSS THE WORLD.
bitch two
BITCH
THANK YOU FOR COMING, VICENTE! IT IS TRULY, TRULY AN HONOR! PLEASE... PLEASE LOOK AT WHAT WE HAVE DISCOVERED!
HMMMM.

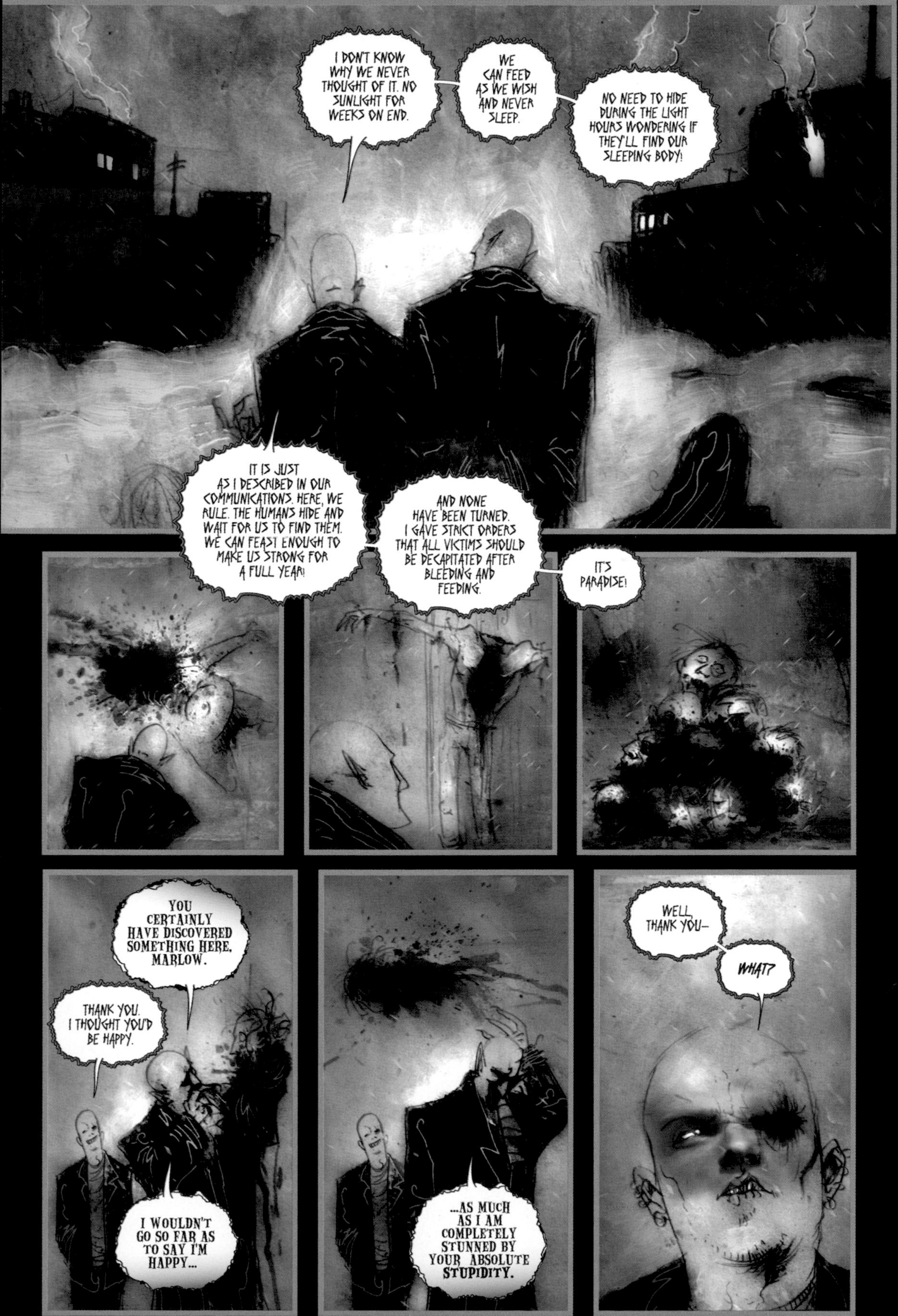
I DON'T KNOW WHY WE NEVER THOUGHT OF IT. NO SUNLIGHT FOR WEEKS ON END.
WE CAN FEED AS WE WISH AND NEVER SLEEP.
NO NEED TO HIDE DURING THE LIGHT HOURS WONDERING IF THEY'LL FIND OUR SLEEPING BODY!
IT IS JUST AS I DESCRIBED IN OUR COMMUNICATIONS. HERE, WE RULE. THE HUMANS HIDE AND WAIT FOR US TO FIND THEM. WE CAN FEAST ENOUGH TO MAKE US STRONG FOR A FULL YEAR!
AND NONE HAVE BEEN TURNED. I GAVE STRICT ORDERS THAT ALL VICTIMS SHOULD BE DECAPITATED AFTER BLEEDING AND FEEDING.
IT'S PARADISE!
YOU CERTAINLY HAVE DISCOVERED SOMETHING HERE, MARLOW.
THANK YOU. I THOUGHT YOU'D BE HAPPY.
I WOULDN'T GO SO FAR AS TO SAY I'M HAPPY...
...AS MUCH AS I AM COMPLETELY STUNNED BY YOUR ABSOLUTE STUPIDITY.
WELL, THANK YOU—
WHAT?

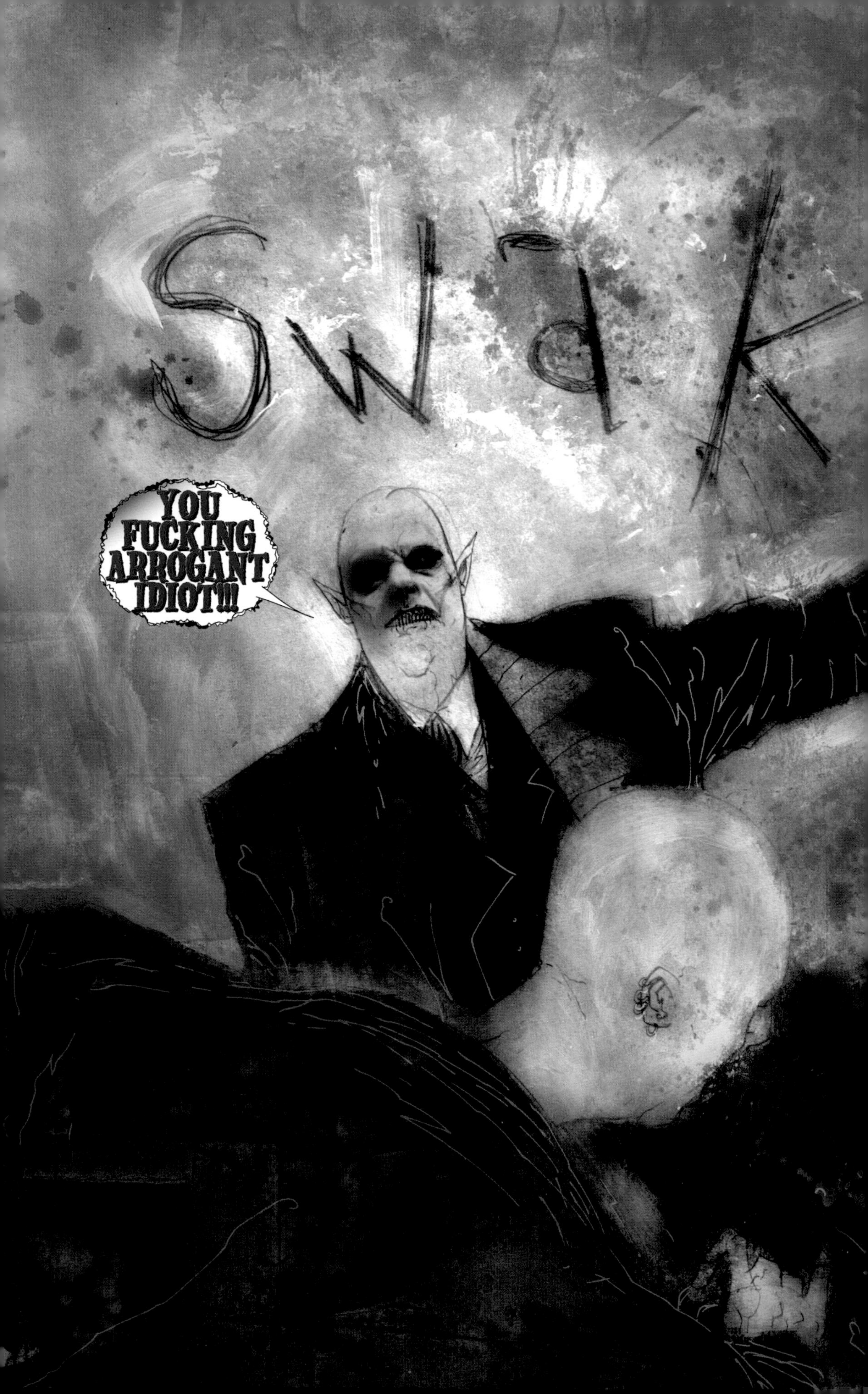
SWACK
YOU FUCKING ARROGANT IDIOT!!!

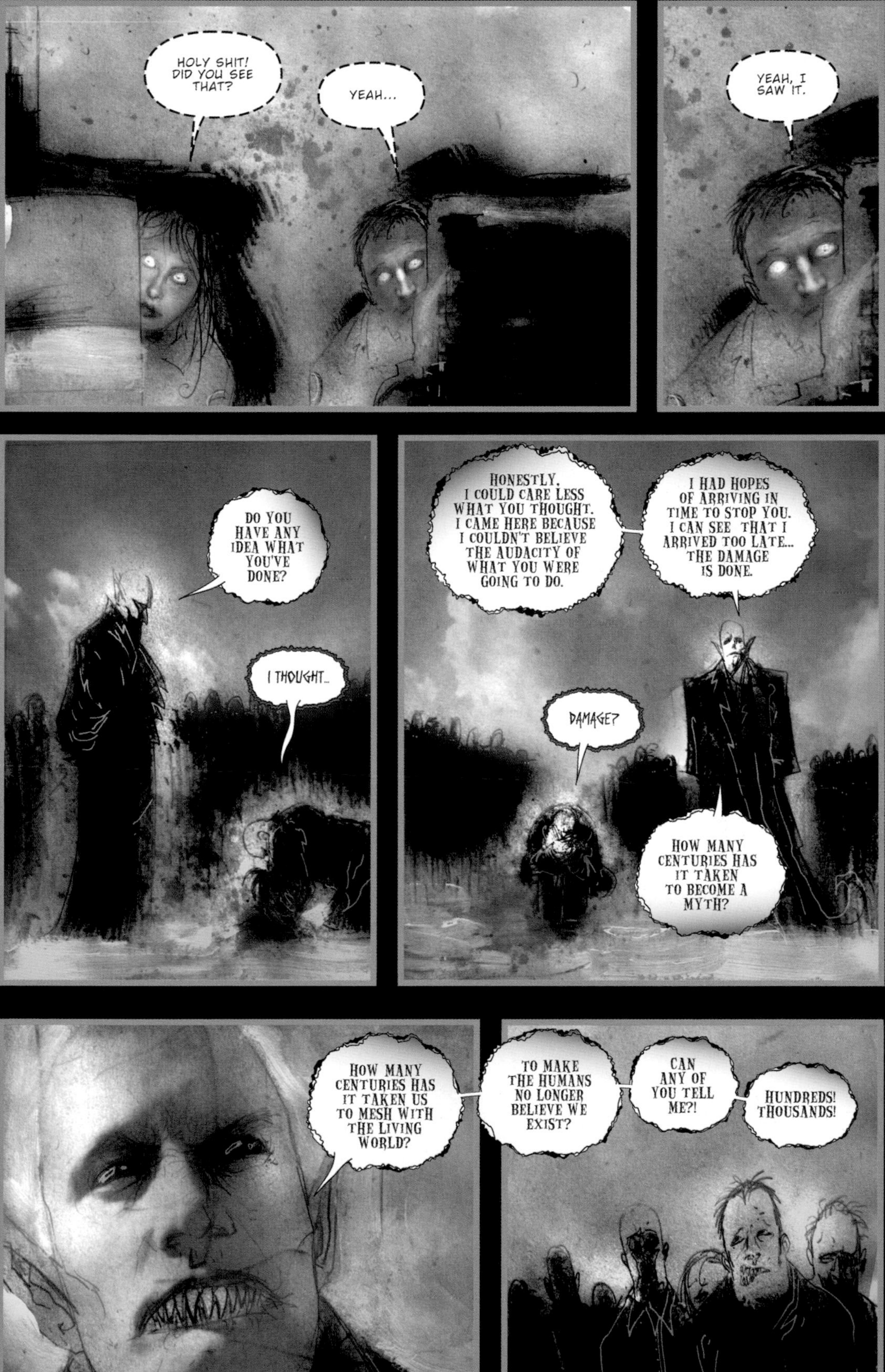

HOLY SHIT! DID YOU SEE THAT?
YEAH...
YEAH, I SAW IT.
DO YOU HAVE ANY IDEA WHAT YOU'VE DONE?
I THOUGHT...
HONESTLY, I COULD CARE LESS WHAT YOU THOUGHT. I CAME HERE BECAUSE I COULDN'T BELIEVE THE AUDACITY OF WHAT YOU WERE GOING TO DO.
I HAD HOPES OF ARRIVING IN TIME TO STOP YOU. I CAN SEE THAT I ARRIVED TOO LATE... THE DAMAGE IS DONE.
DAMAGE?
HOW MANY CENTURIES HAS IT TAKEN TO BECOME A MYTH?
HOW MANY CENTURIES HAS IT TAKEN US TO MESH WITH THE LIVING WORLD?
TO MAKE THE HUMANS NO LONGER BELIEVE WE EXIST?
CAN ANY OF YOU TELL ME?!
HUNDREDS! THOUSANDS!

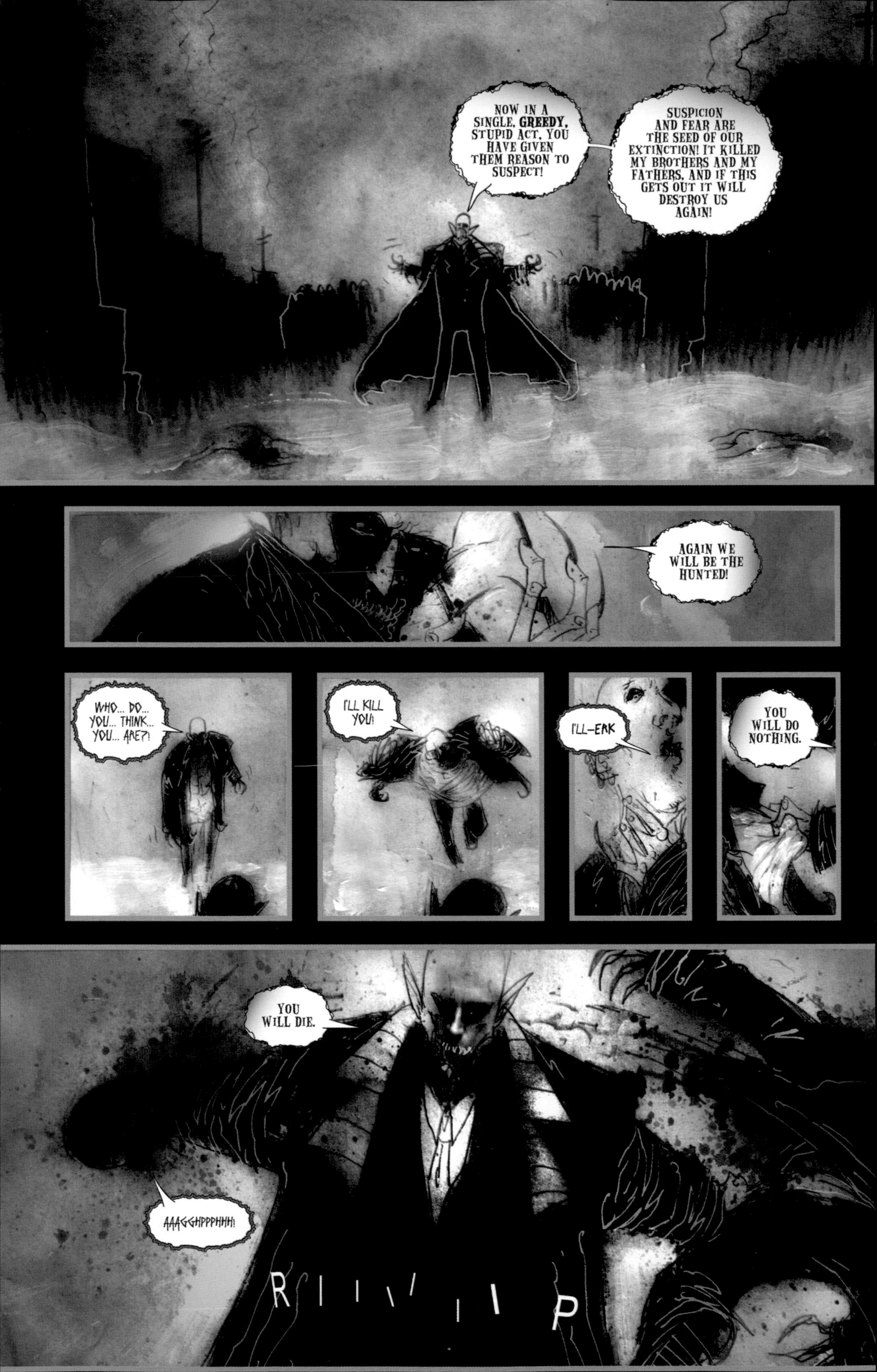
NOW IN A SINGLE, GREEDY, STUPID ACT, YOU HAVE GIVEN THEM REASON TO SUSPECT!
SUSPICION AND FEAR ARE THE SEED OF OUR EXTINCTION! IT KILLED MY BROTHERS AND MY FATHERS, AND IF THIS GETS OUT IT WILL DESTROY US AGAIN!
AGAIN WE WILL BE THE HUNTED!
WHO... DO... YOU... THINK... YOU... ARE?!
I'LL KILL YOU!
I'LL-EAK
YOU WILL DO NOTHING.
YOU WILL DIE.
AAAGGHPPPHHH!
RIIIIP

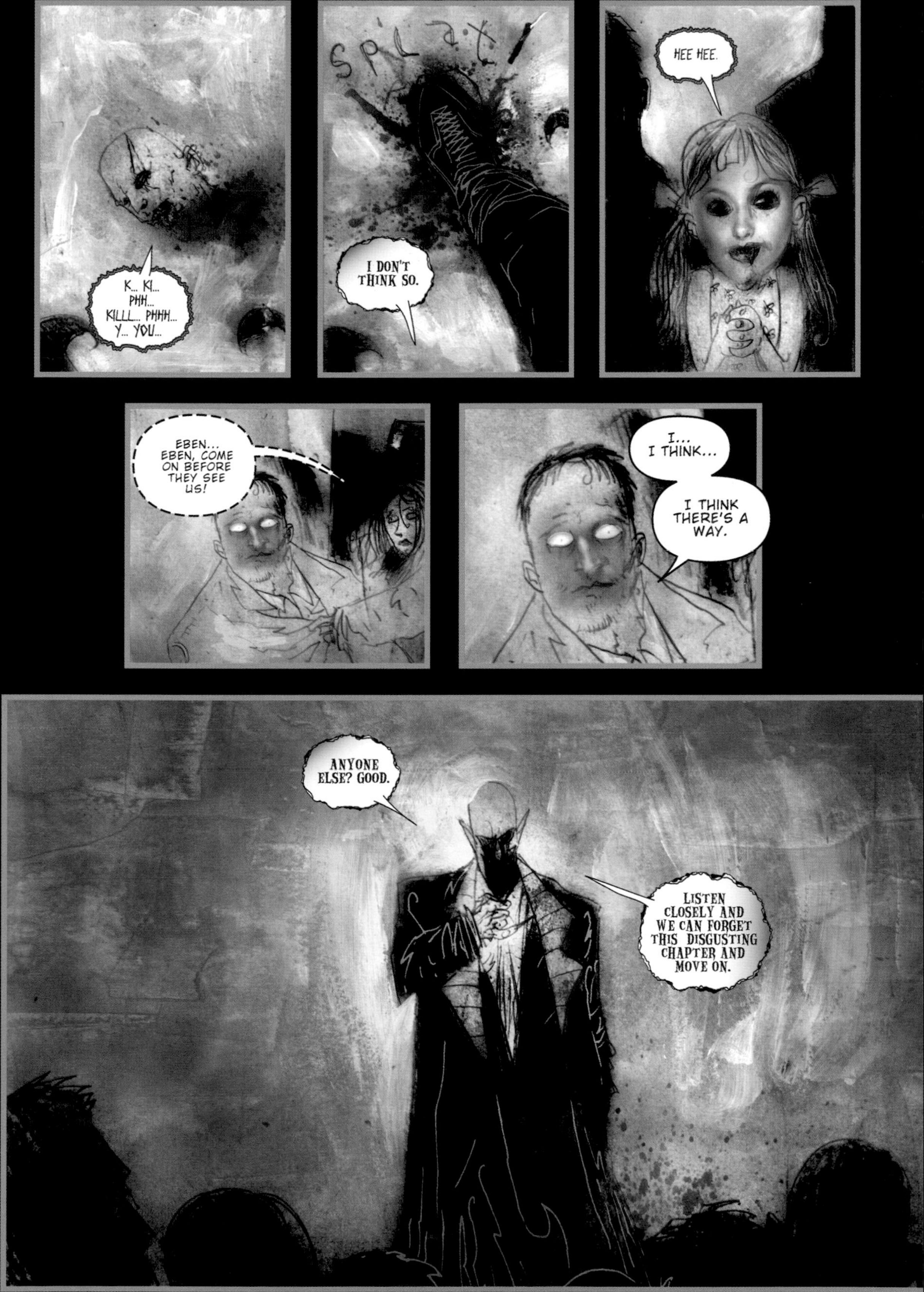
K... KI... PHH... KILLL... PHHH... Y... YOU...
SPLAT!
I DON'T THINK SO.
HEE HEE.
EBEN... EBEN, COME ON BEFORE THEY SEE US!
I... I THINK...
I THINK THERE'S A WAY.
ANYONE ELSE? GOOD.
LISTEN CLOSELY AND WE CAN FORGET THIS DISGUSTING CHAPTER AND MOVE ON.

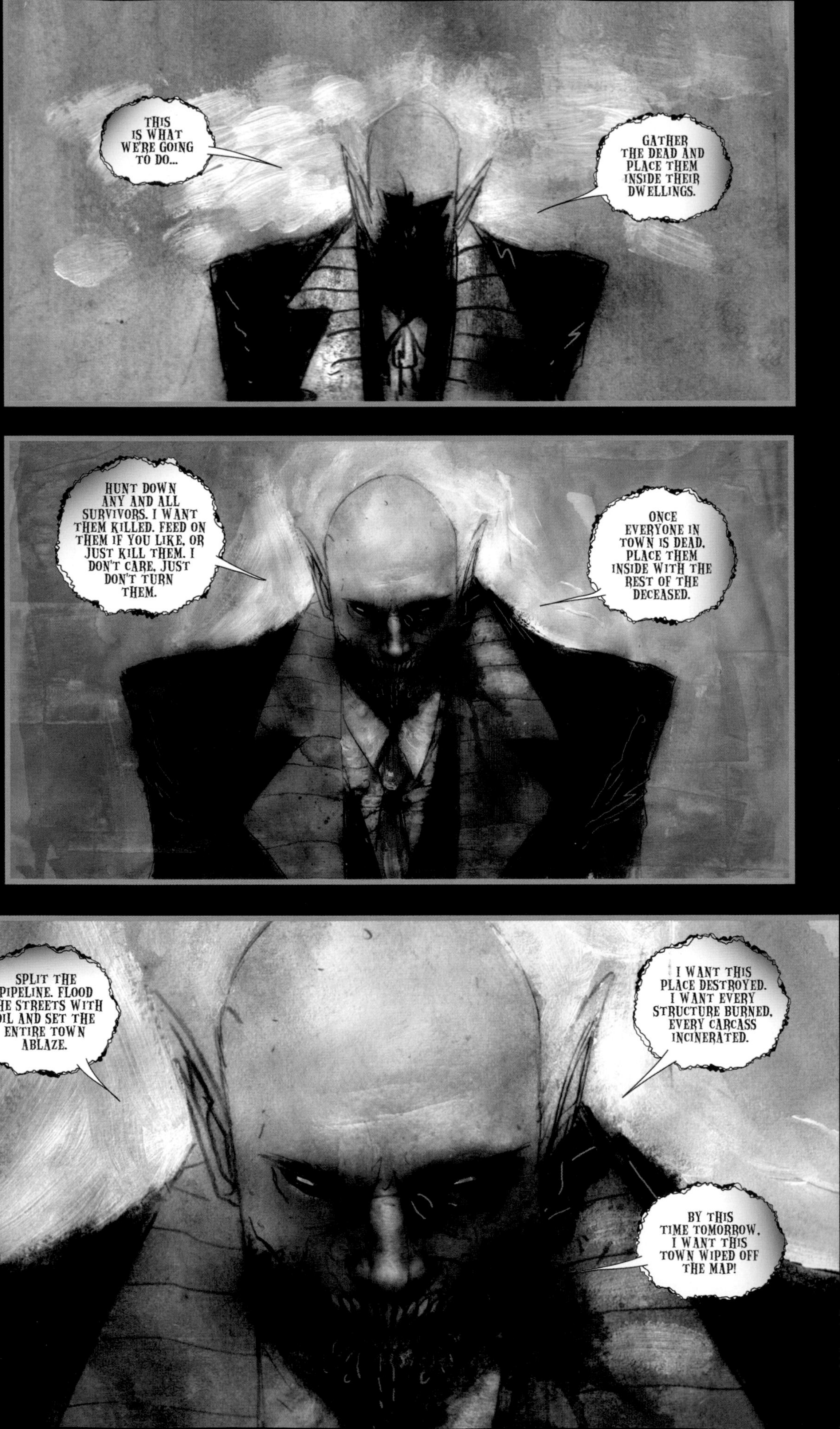
THIS IS WHAT WE'RE GOING TO DO...
GATHER THE DEAD AND PLACE THEM INSIDE THEIR DWELLINGS.
HUNT DOWN ANY AND ALL SURVIVORS. I WANT THEM KILLED. FEED ON THEM IF YOU LIKE, OR JUST KILL THEM. I DON'T CARE, JUST DON'T TURN THEM.
ONCE EVERYONE IN TOWN IS DEAD, PLACE THEM INSIDE WITH THE REST OF THE DECEASED.
SPLIT THE PIPELINE. FLOOD THE STREETS WITH OIL AND SET THE ENTIRE TOWN ABLAZE.
I WANT THIS PLACE DESTROYED. I WANT EVERY STRUCTURE BURNED, EVERY CARCASS INCINERATED.
BY THIS TIME TOMORROW, I WANT THIS TOWN WIPED OFF THE MAP!

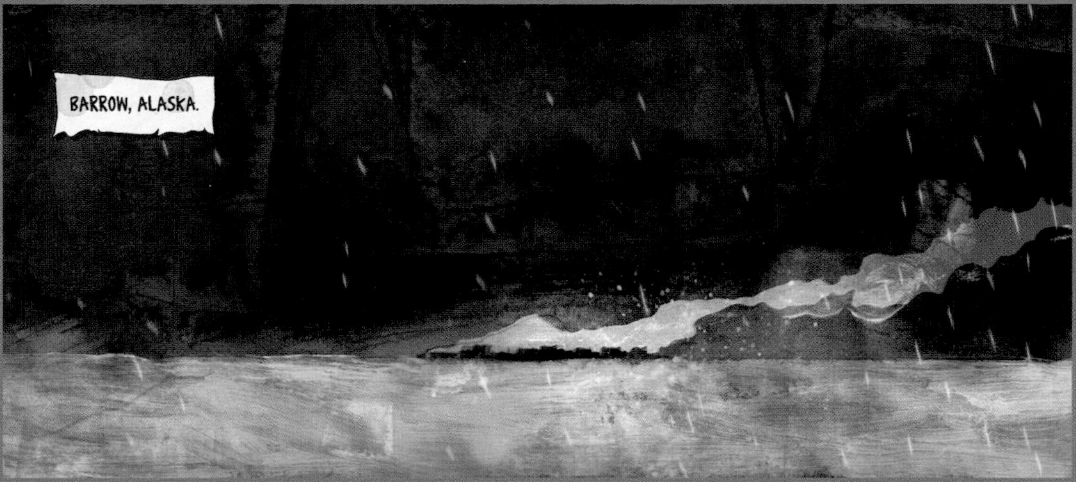
BARROW, ALASKA.

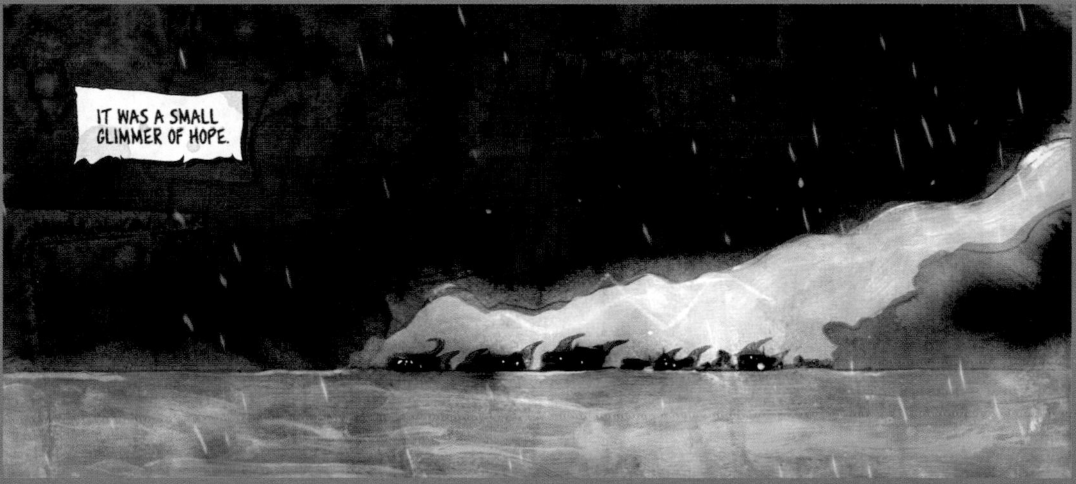
IT WAS A SMALL GLIMMER OF HOPE.

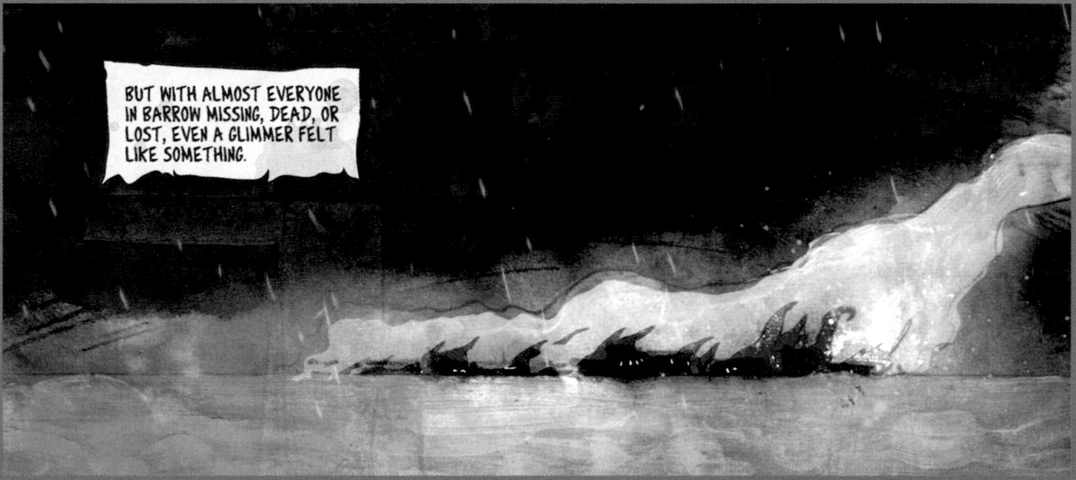
BUT WITH ALMOST EVERYONE IN BARROW MISSING, DEAD, OR LOST, EVEN A GLIMMER FELT LIKE SOMETHING.

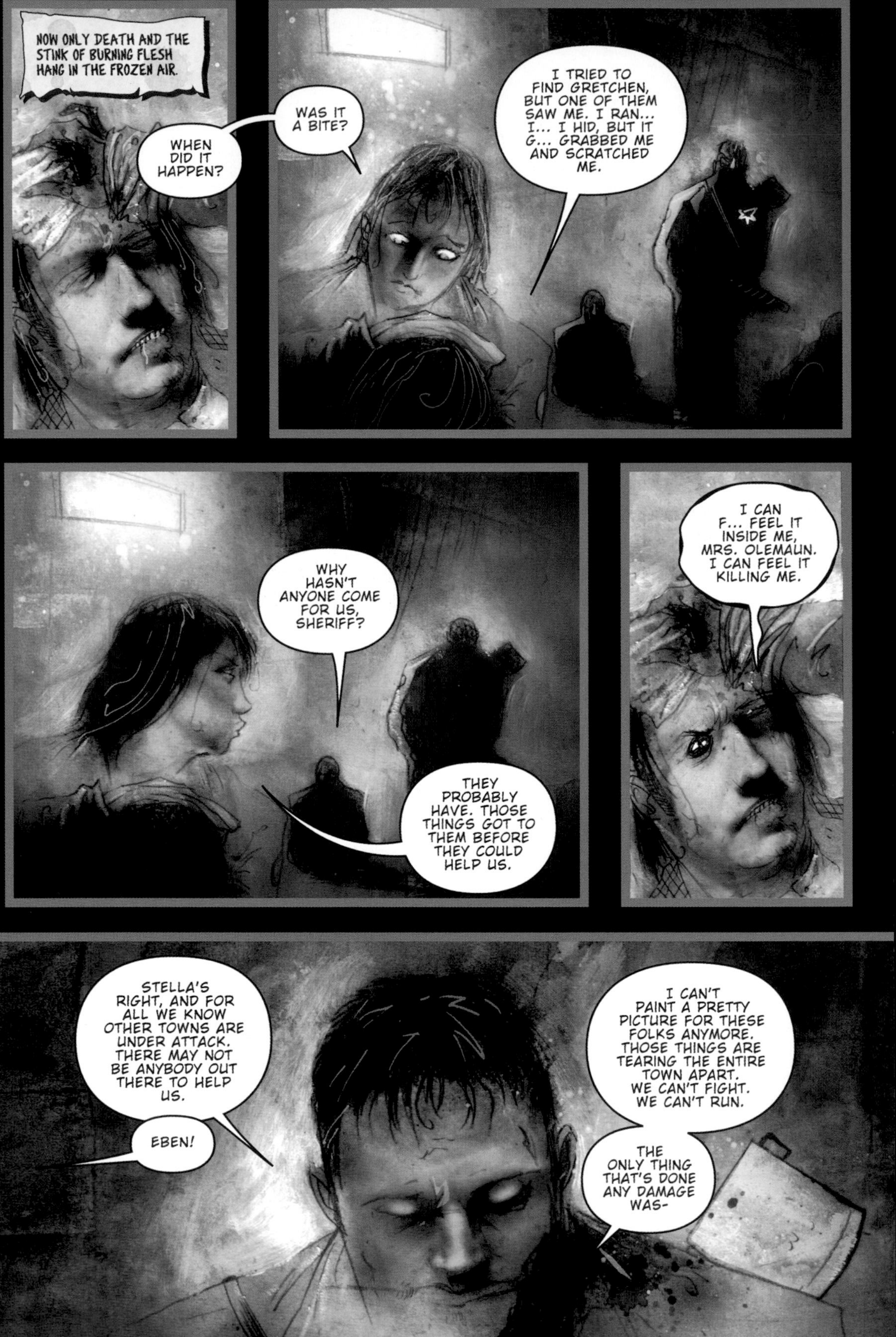
NOW ONLY DEATH AND THE STINK OF BURNING FLESH HANG IN THE FROZEN AIR.
WHEN DID IT HAPPEN?
WAS IT A BITE?
I TRIED TO FIND GRETCHEN, BUT ONE OF THEM SAW ME. I RAN... I... I HID, BUT IT G... GRABBED ME AND SCRATCHED ME.
WHY HASN'T ANYONE COME FOR US, SHERIFF?
THEY PROBABLY HAVE. THOSE THINGS GOT TO THEM BEFORE THEY COULD HELP US.
I CAN F... FEEL IT INSIDE ME, MRS. OLEMAUN. I CAN FEEL IT KILLING ME.
STELLA'S RIGHT, AND FOR ALL WE KNOW OTHER TOWNS ARE UNDER ATTACK. THERE MAY NOT BE ANYBODY OUT THERE TO HELP US.
EBEN!
I CAN'T PAINT A PRETTY PICTURE FOR THESE FOLKS ANYMORE. THOSE THINGS ARE TEARING THE ENTIRE TOWN APART. WE CAN'T FIGHT. WE CAN'T RUN.
THE ONLY THING THAT'S DONE ANY DAMAGE WAS-

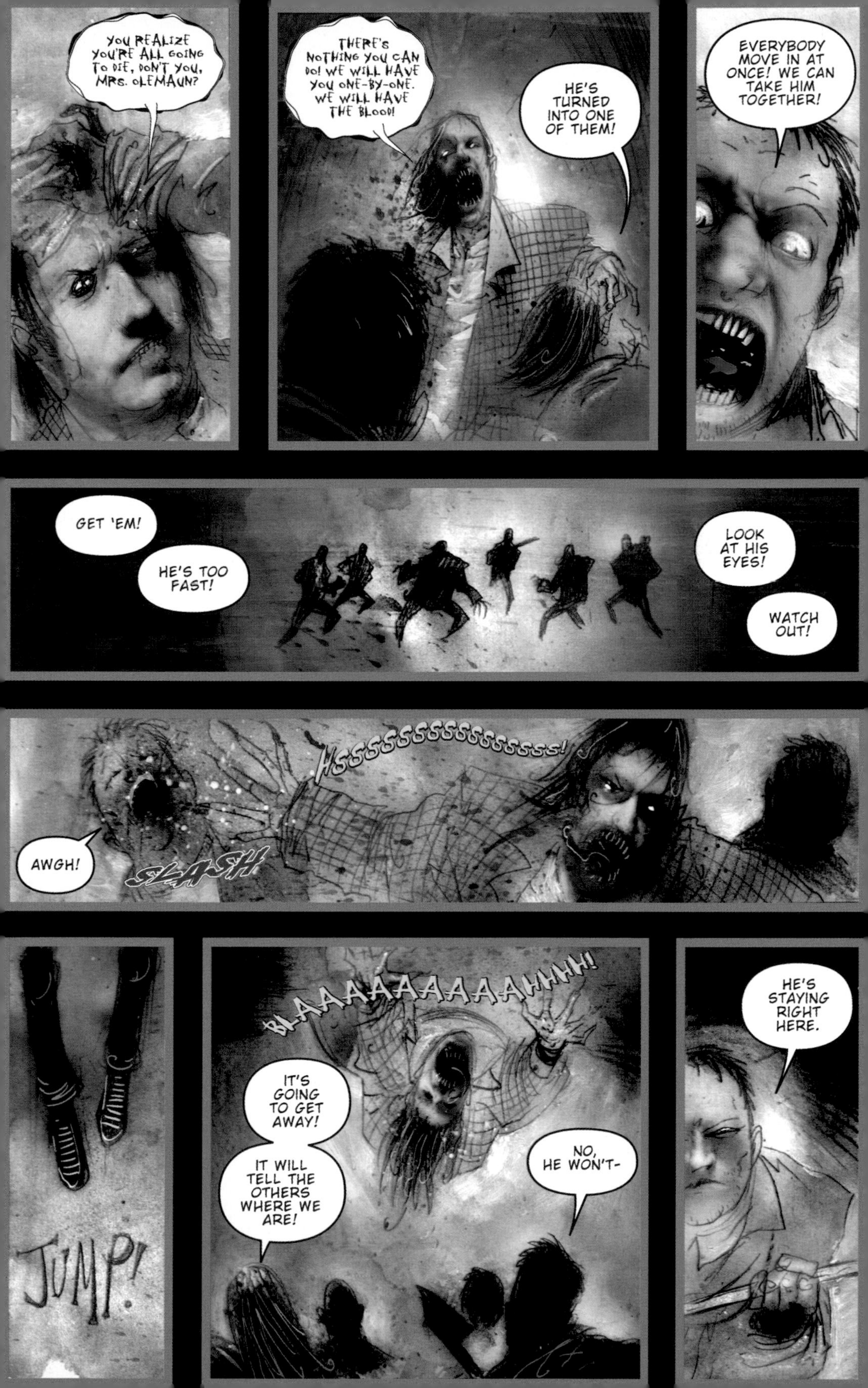
YOU REALIZE YOU'RE ALL GOING TO DIE, DON'T YOU, MRS. OLEMAUN?
THERE'S NOTHING YOU CAN DO! WE WILL HAVE YOU ONE-BY-ONE. WE WILL HAVE THE BLOOD!
HE'S TURNED INTO ONE OF THEM!
EVERYBODY MOVE IN AT ONCE! WE CAN TAKE HIM TOGETHER!
GET 'EM!
HE'S TOO FAST!
LOOK AT HIS EYES!
WATCH OUT!
HSSSSSSSSSSSSSSSSS!
AWGH!
SLASH
JUMP!
BLAAAAAAAAAAHHHH!
IT'S GOING TO GET AWAY!
IT WILL TELL THE OTHERS WHERE WE ARE!
NO, HE WON'T-
HE'S STAYING RIGHT HERE.

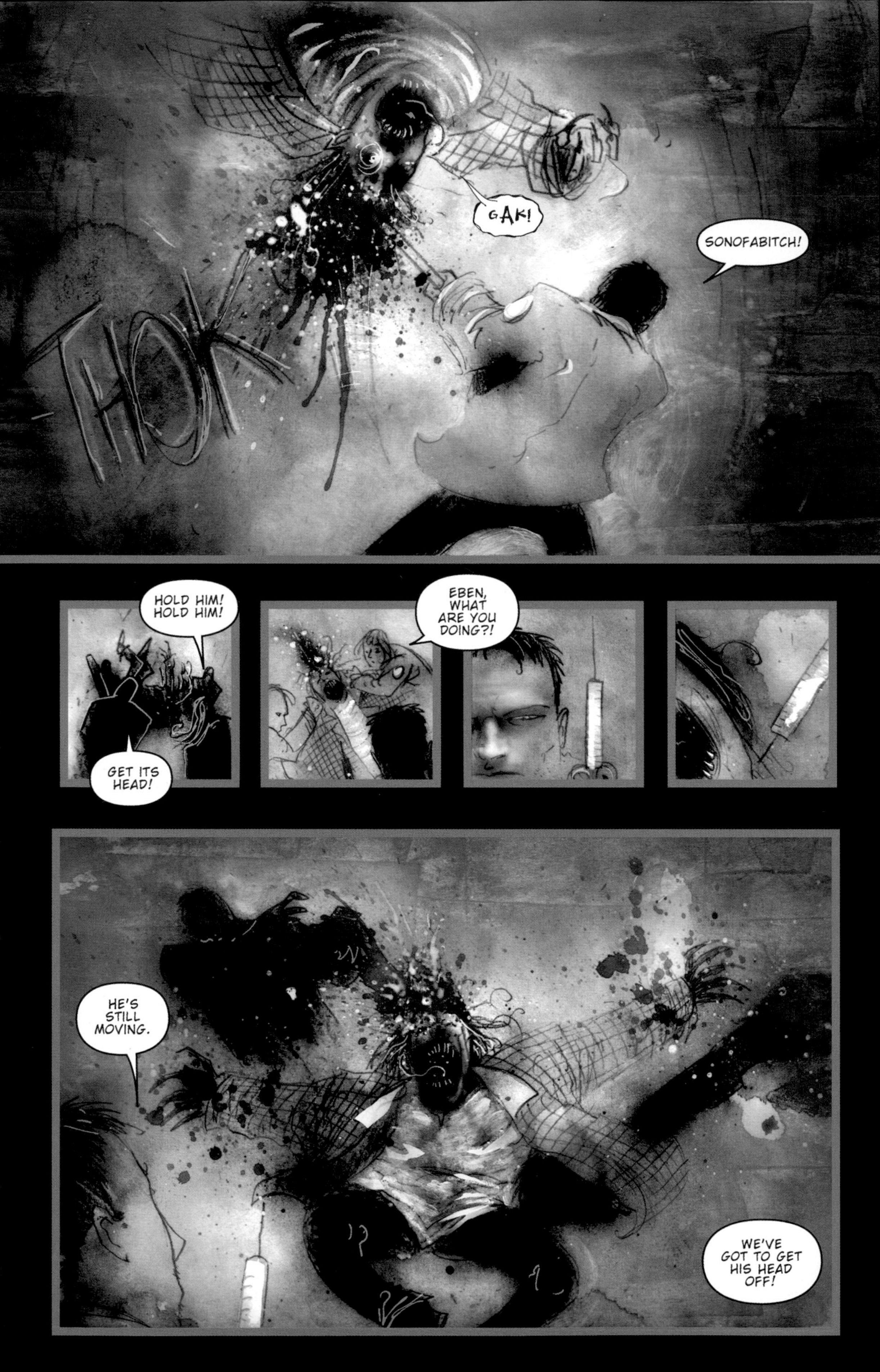
GAK!
SONOFABITCH!
THOK
HOLD HIM! HOLD HIM!
GET ITS HEAD!
EBEN, WHAT ARE YOU DOING?!
HE'S STILL MOVING.
WE'VE GOT TO GET HIS HEAD OFF!

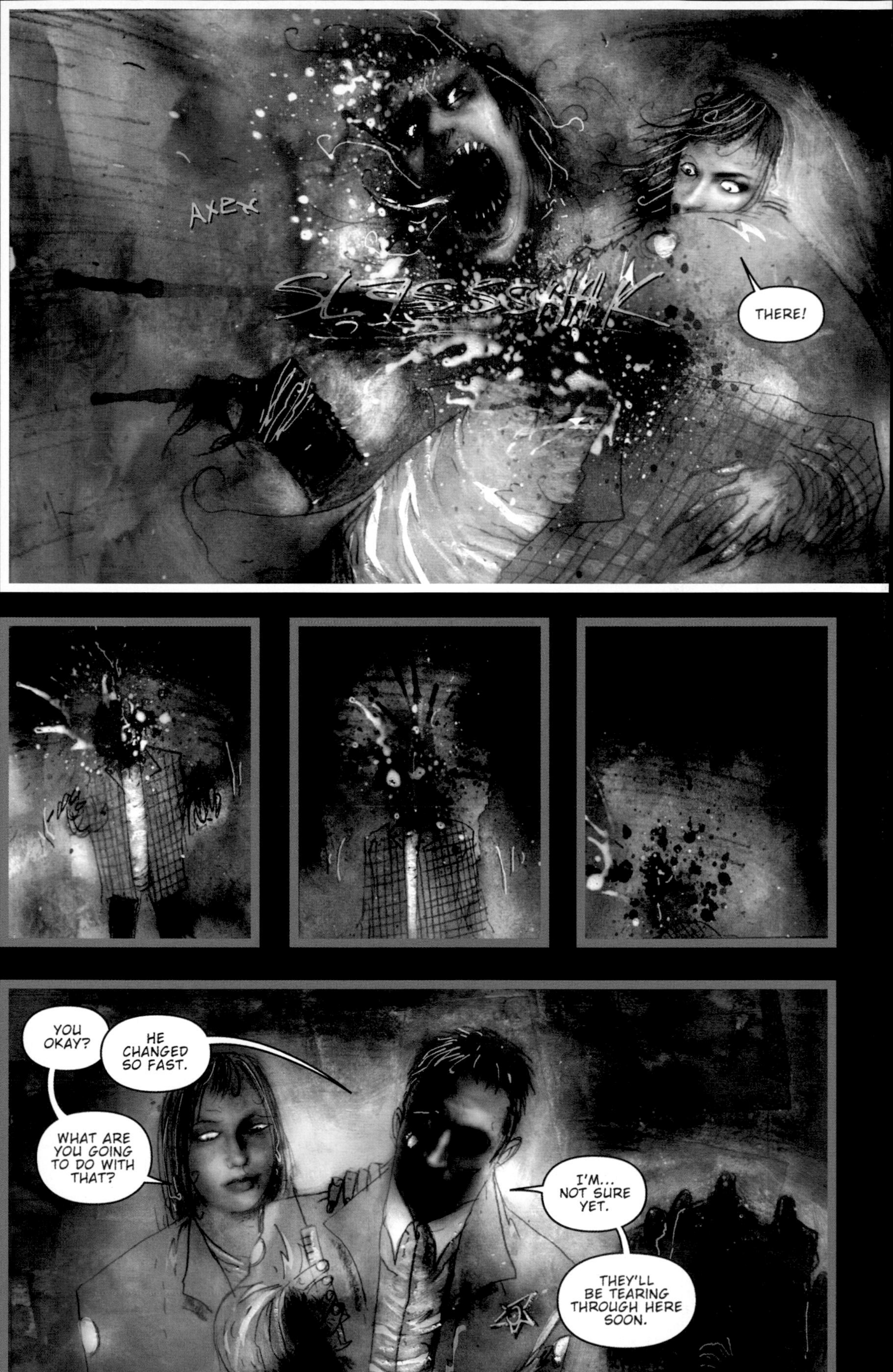
AXE
SLASSSHHK
THERE!
YOU OKAY?
HE CHANGED SO FAST.
WHAT ARE YOU GOING TO DO WITH THAT?
I'M... NOT SURE YET.
THEY'LL BE TEARING THROUGH HERE SOON.

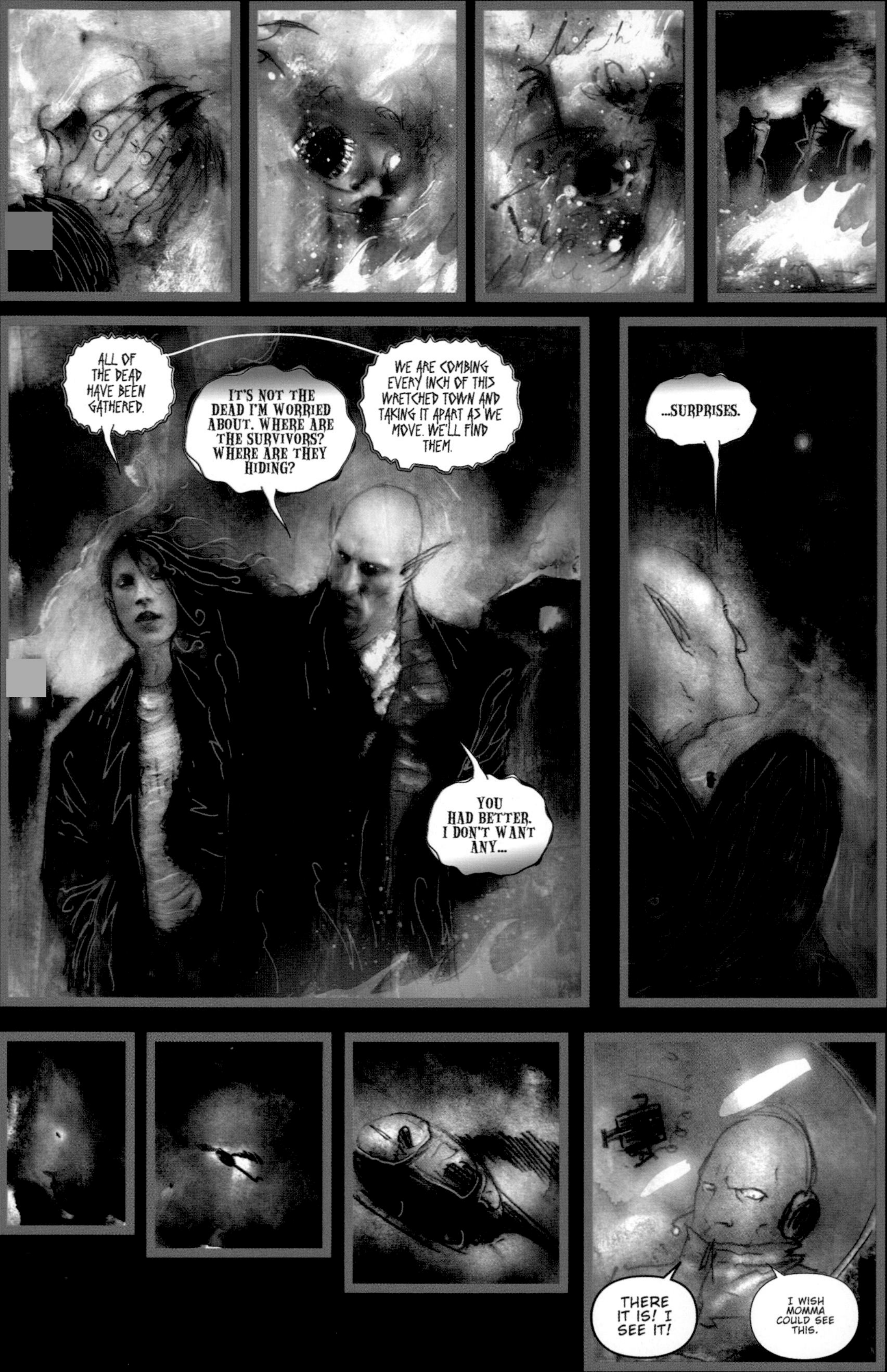
ALL OF THE DEAD HAVE BEEN GATHERED.
IT'S NOT THE DEAD I'M WORRIED ABOUT. WHERE ARE THE SURVIVORS? WHERE ARE THEY HIDING?
WE ARE COMBING EVERY INCH OF THIS WRETCHED TOWN AND TAKING IT APART AS WE MOVE. WE'LL FIND THEM.
YOU HAD BETTER. I DON'T WANT ANY...
...SURPRISES.
THERE IT IS! I SEE IT!
I WISH MOMMA COULD SEE THIS.

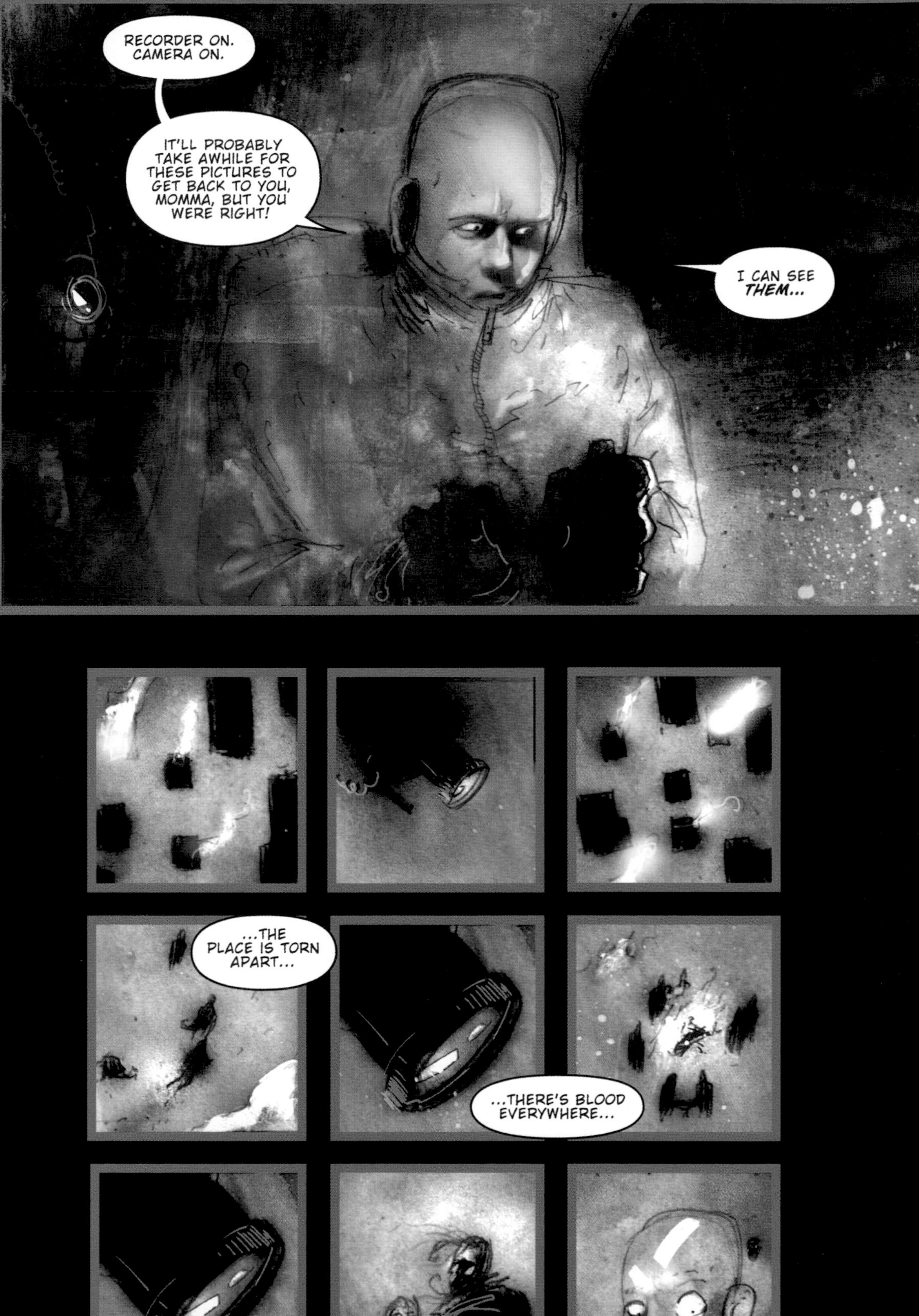
RECORDER ON. CAMERA ON.
IT'LL PROBABLY TAKE AWHILE FOR THESE PICTURES TO GET BACK TO YOU, MOMMA, BUT YOU WERE RIGHT!
I CAN SEE *THEM*...
...THE PLACE IS TORN APART...
...THERE'S BLOOD EVERYWHERE...
...OH NO...

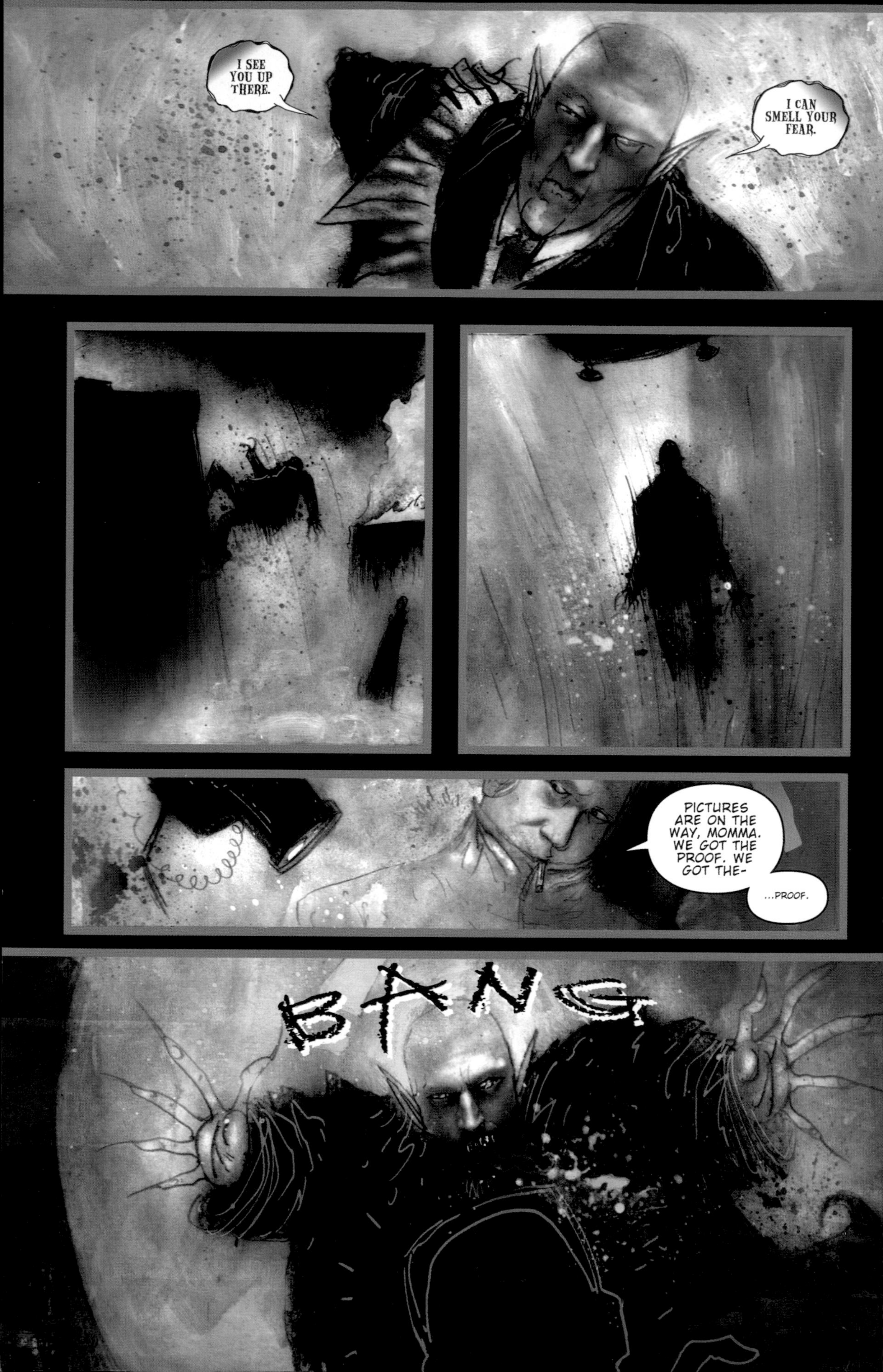
I SEE YOU UP THERE.
I CAN SMELL YOUR FEAR.
PICTURES ARE ON THE WAY, MOMMA. WE GOT THE PROOF. WE GOT THE-
...PROOF.
BANG

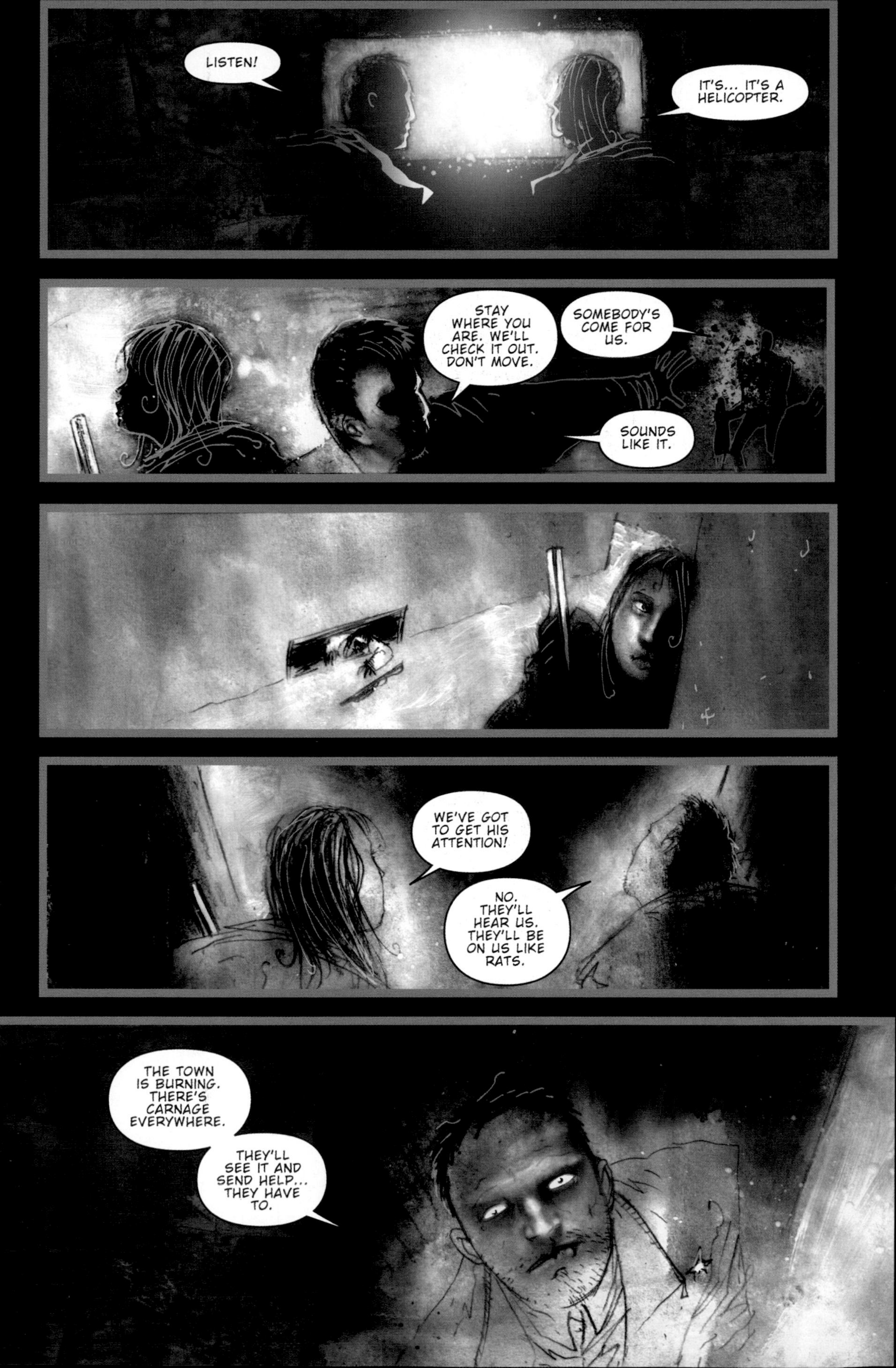
LISTEN!
IT'S... IT'S A HELICOPTER.
STAY WHERE YOU ARE. WE'LL CHECK IT OUT. DON'T MOVE.
SOMEBODY'S COME FOR US.
SOUNDS LIKE IT.
WE'VE GOT TO GET HIS ATTENTION!
NO. THEY'LL HEAR US. THEY'LL BE ON US LIKE RATS.
THE TOWN IS BURNING. THERE'S CARNAGE EVERYWHERE.
THEY'LL SEE IT AND SEND HELP... THEY HAVE TO.

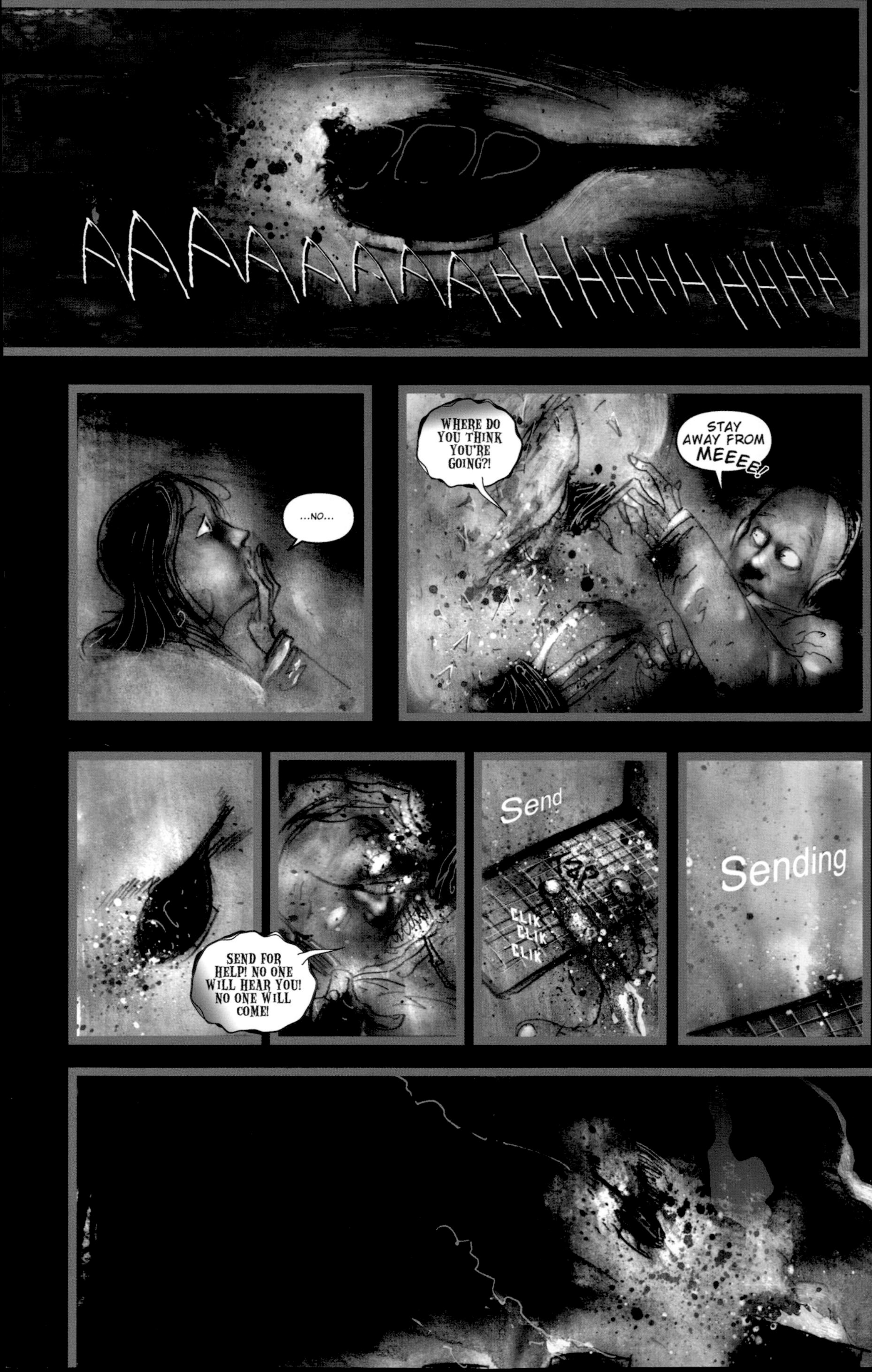
AAAAAAAAHHHHHHHHHHHH
...NO...
WHERE DO YOU THINK YOU'RE GOING?!
STAY AWAY FROM MEEEE!
SEND FOR HELP! NO ONE WILL HEAR YOU! NO ONE WILL COME!
Send
TAP
CLIK
CLIK
CLIK
Sending

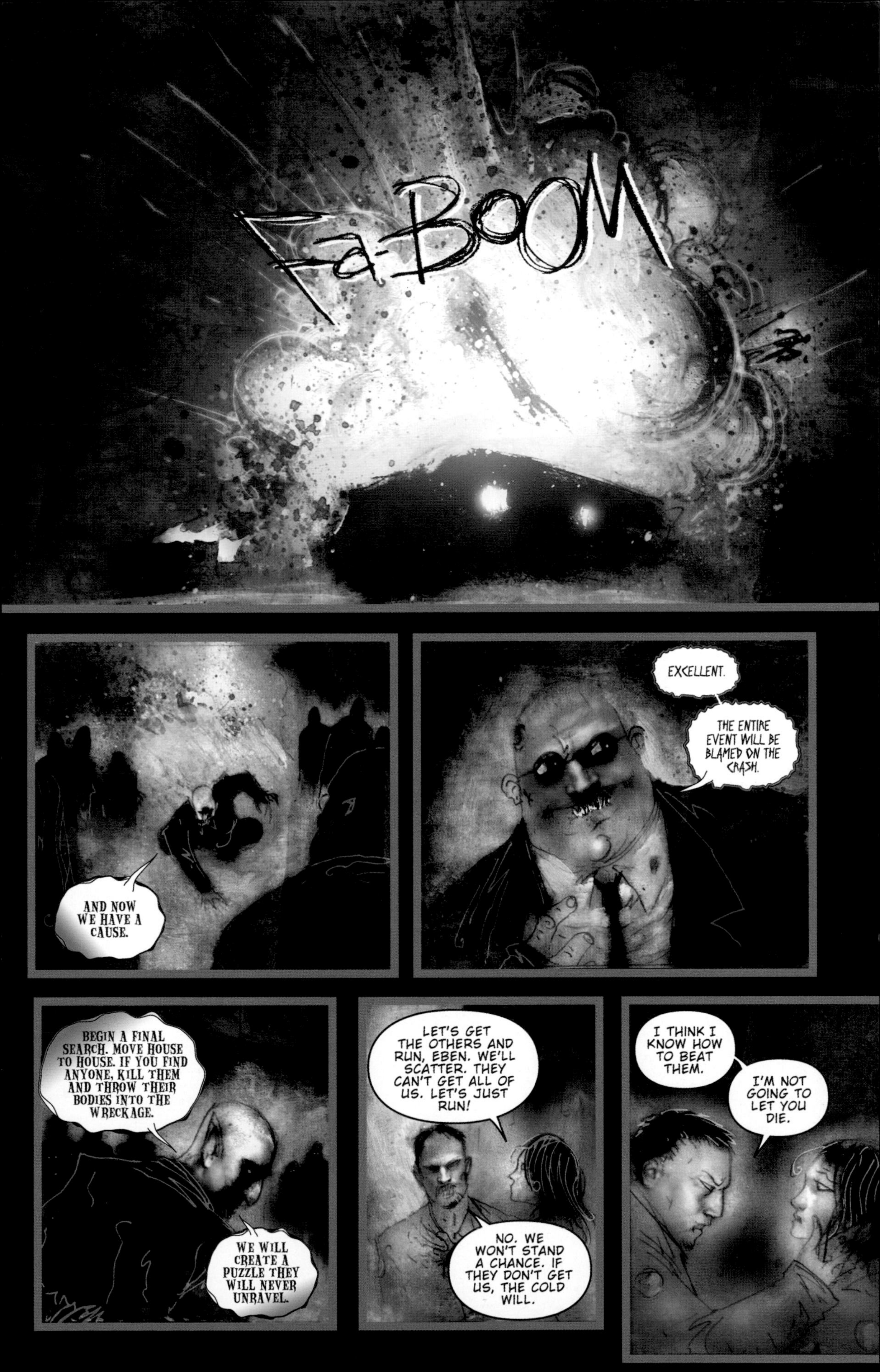

Ka-BOOM
AND NOW WE HAVE A CAUSE.
EXCELLENT.
THE ENTIRE EVENT WILL BE BLAMED ON THE CRASH.
BEGIN A FINAL SEARCH. MOVE HOUSE TO HOUSE. IF YOU FIND ANYONE, KILL THEM AND THROW THEIR BODIES INTO THE WRECKAGE.
WE WILL CREATE A PUZZLE THEY WILL NEVER UNRAVEL.
LET'S GET THE OTHERS AND RUN, EBEN. WE'LL SCATTER. THEY CAN'T GET ALL OF US. LET'S JUST RUN!
NO. WE WON'T STAND A CHANCE. IF THEY DON'T GET US, THE COLD WILL.
I THINK I KNOW HOW TO BEAT THEM.
I'M NOT GOING TO LET YOU DIE.

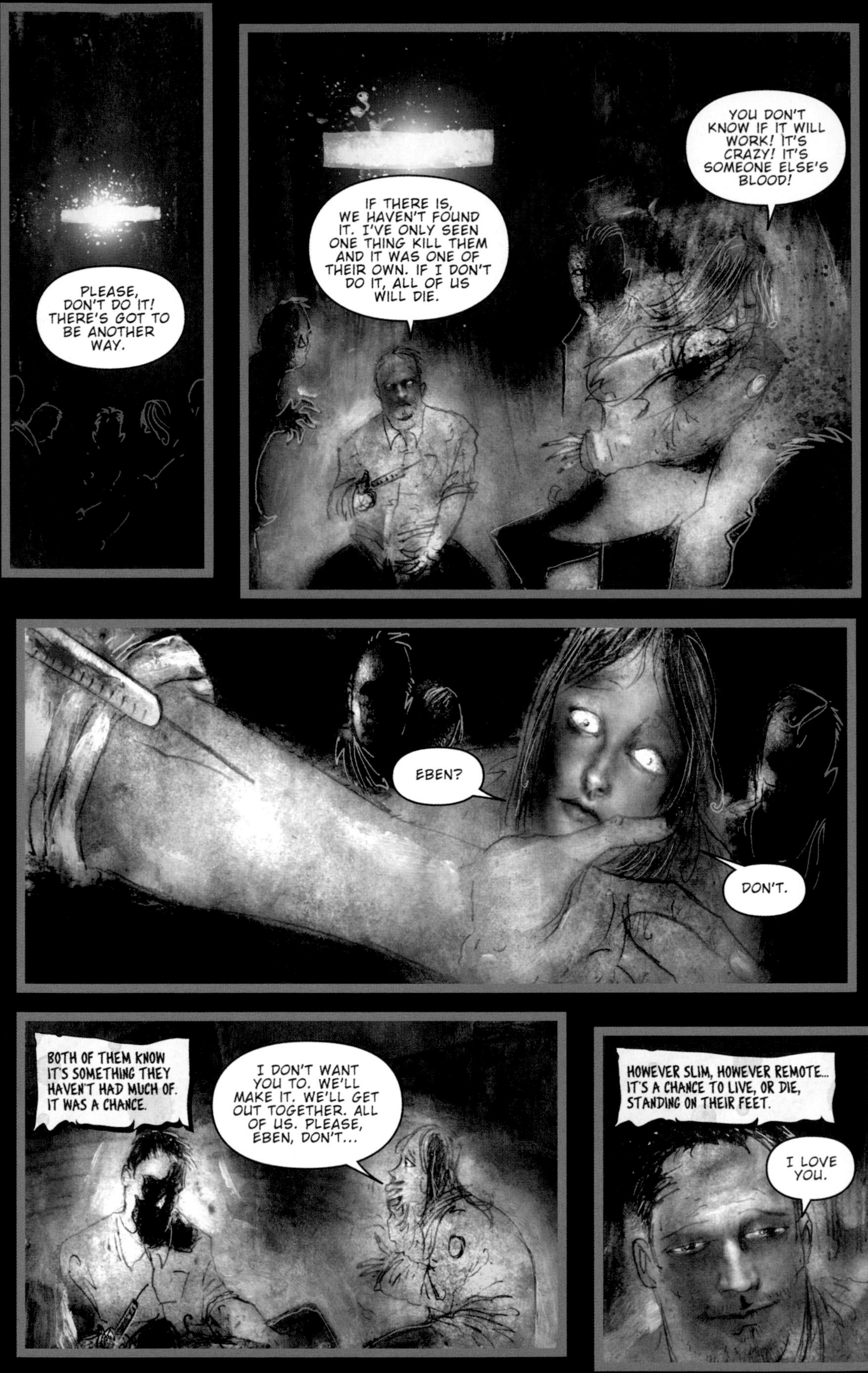

PLEASE, DON'T DO IT! THERE'S GOT TO BE ANOTHER WAY.
IF THERE IS, WE HAVEN'T FOUND IT. I'VE ONLY SEEN ONE THING KILL THEM AND IT WAS ONE OF THEIR OWN. IF I DON'T DO IT, ALL OF US WILL DIE.
YOU DON'T KNOW IF IT WILL WORK! IT'S CRAZY! IT'S SOMEONE ELSE'S BLOOD!
EBEN?
DON'T.
BOTH OF THEM KNOW IT'S SOMETHING THEY HAVEN'T HAD MUCH OF. IT WAS A CHANCE.
I DON'T WANT YOU TO. WE'LL MAKE IT. WE'LL GET OUT TOGETHER. ALL OF US. PLEASE, EBEN, DON'T...
HOWEVER SLIM, HOWEVER REMOTE... IT'S A CHANCE TO LIVE, OR DIE, STANDING ON THEIR FEET.
I LOVE YOU.

IT FEELS LIKE FIRE.

A FIRE THAT SPREADS MERCILESSLY THROUGH HIS VEINS IN SECONDS.

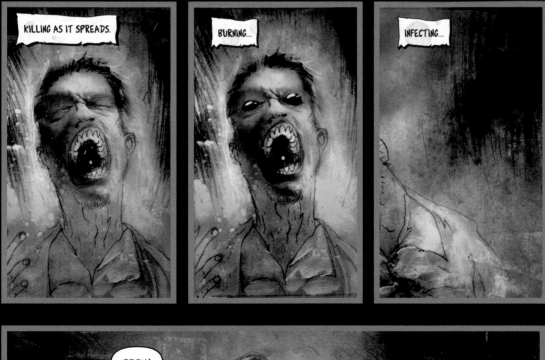

KILLING AS IT SPREADS.

BURNING...

INFECTING...

EBEN!

TRANSFORMING.

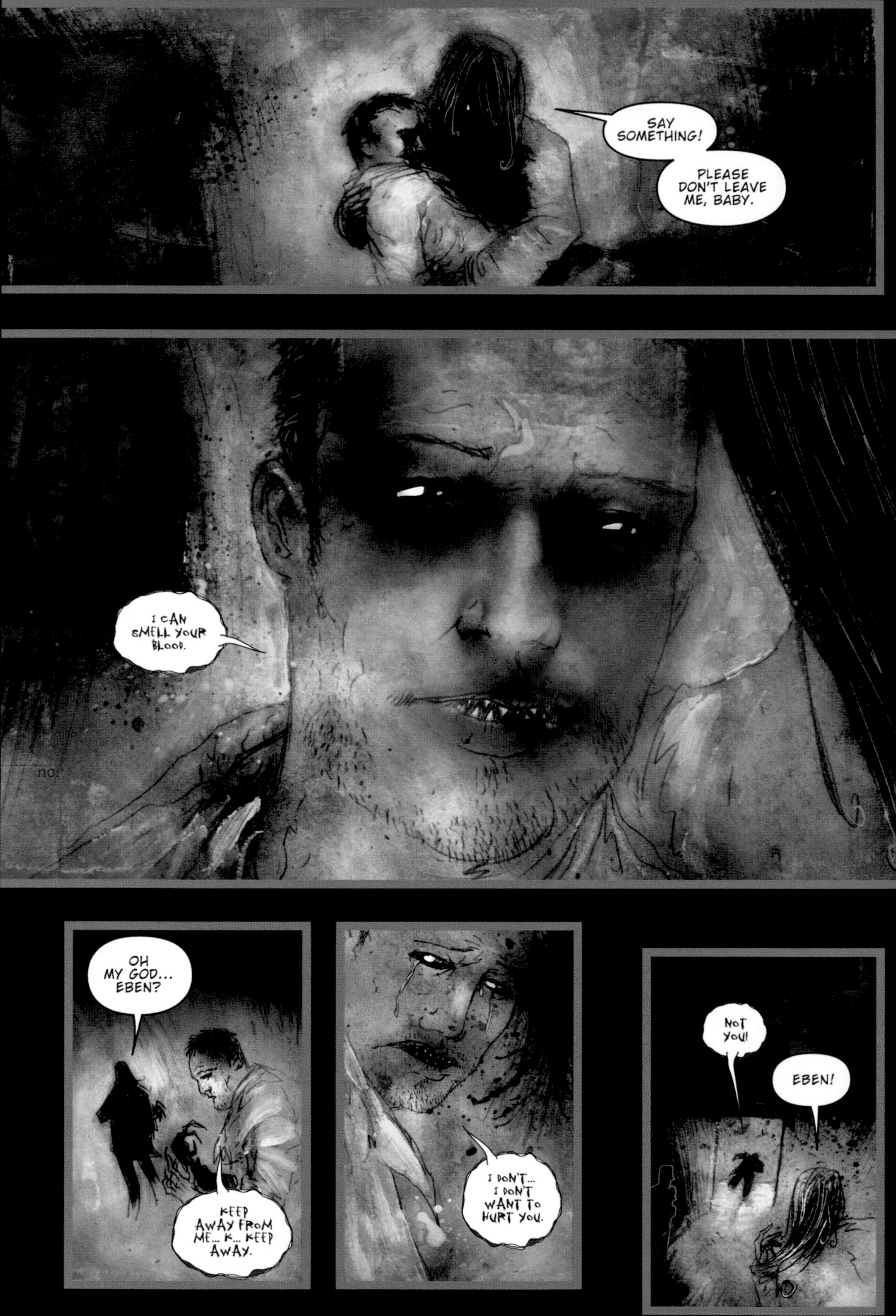
SAY SOMETHING!
PLEASE DON'T LEAVE ME, BABY.
I CAN SMELL YOUR BLOOD.
OH MY GOD... EBEN?
KEEP AWAY FROM ME... K... KEEP AWAY.
I DON'T... I DON'T WANT TO HURT YOU.
NOT YOU!
EBEN!

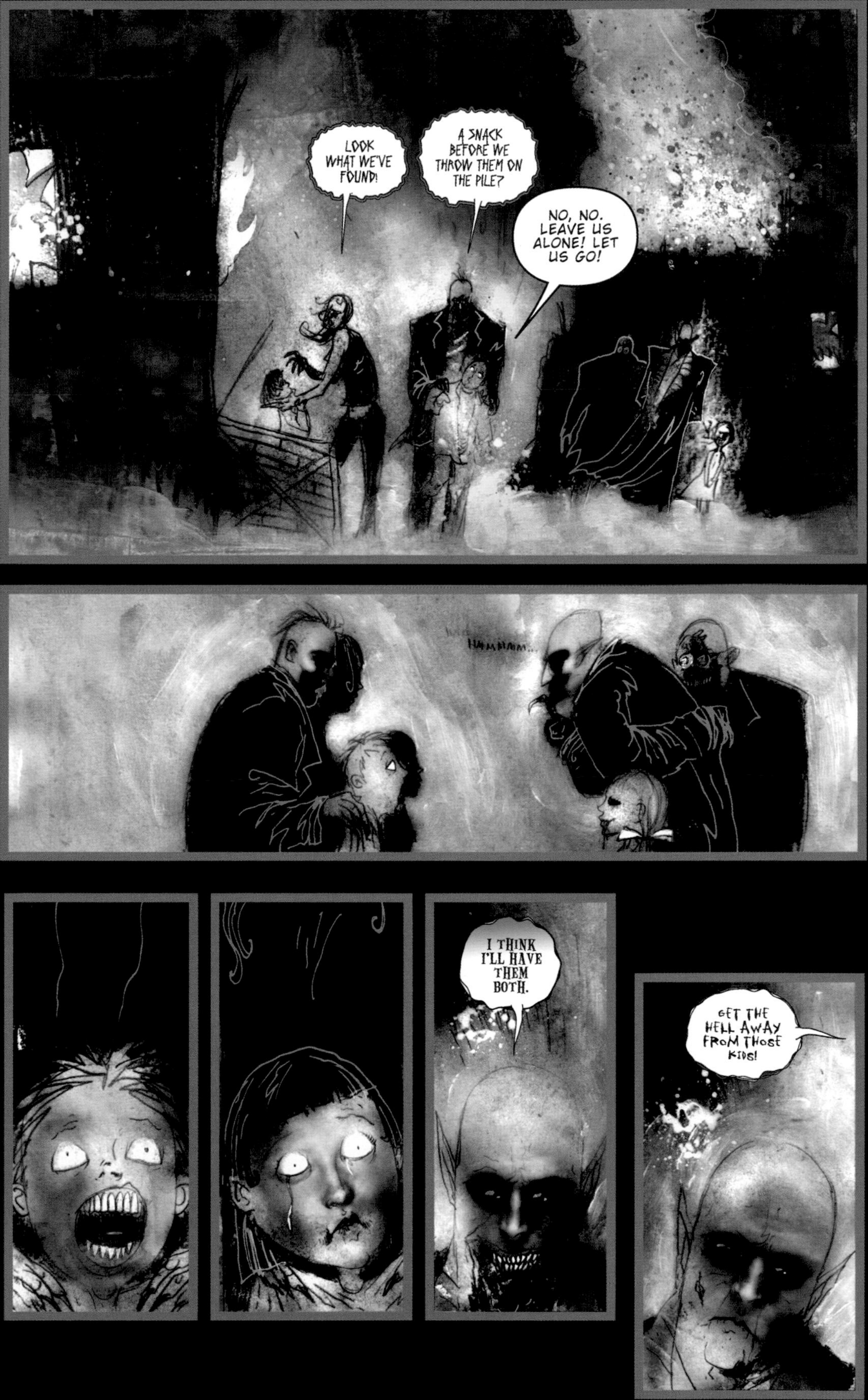
LOOK WHAT WE'VE FOUND!
A SNACK BEFORE WE THROW THEM ON THE PILE?
NO, NO. LEAVE US ALONE! LET US GO!
I THINK I'LL HAVE THEM BOTH.
GET THE HELL AWAY FROM THOSE KIDS!

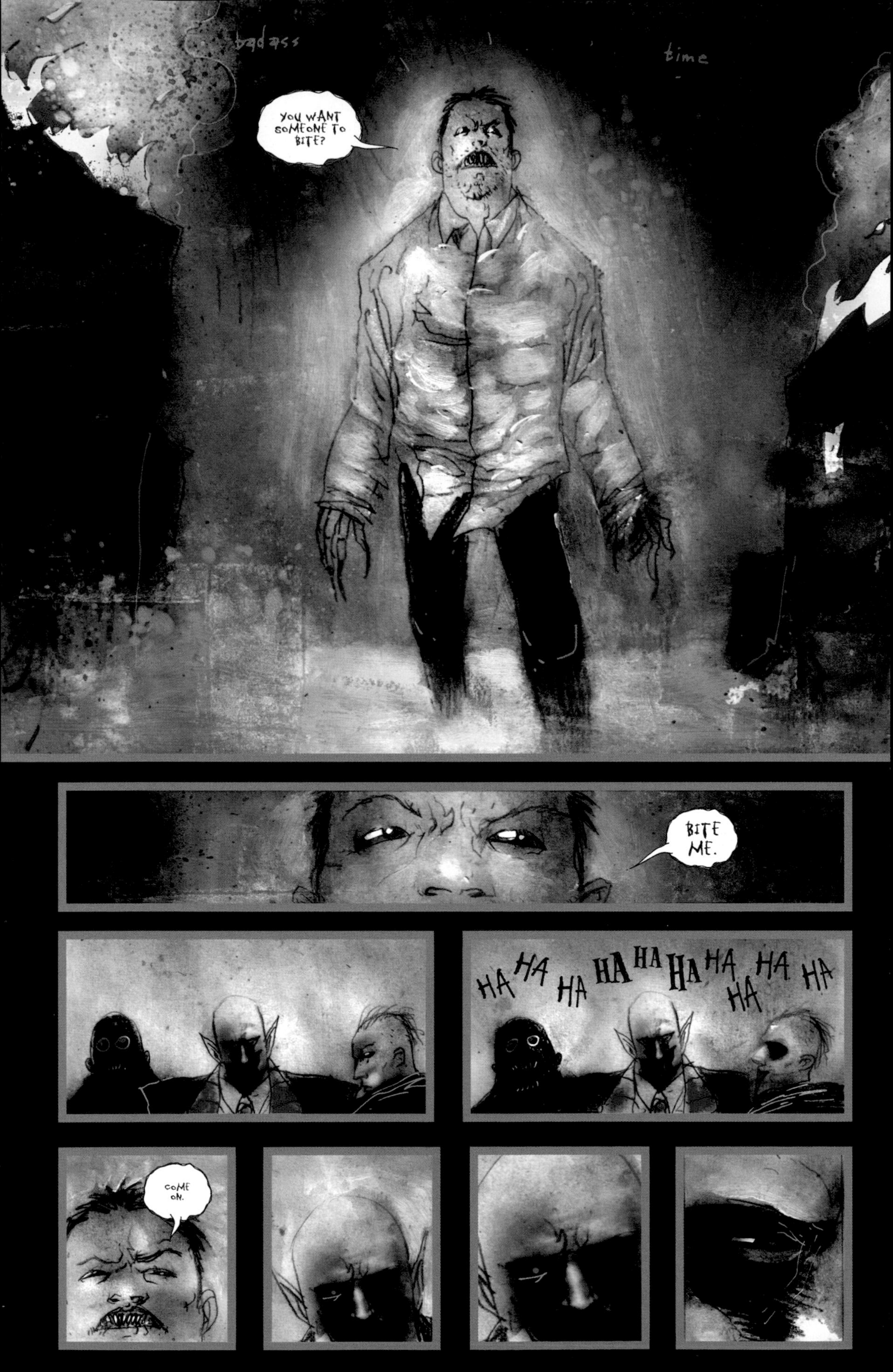
badass
time
YOU WANT SOMEONE TO BITE?
BITE ME.
HA HA HA HA HA HA HA HA HA HA HA
COME ON.

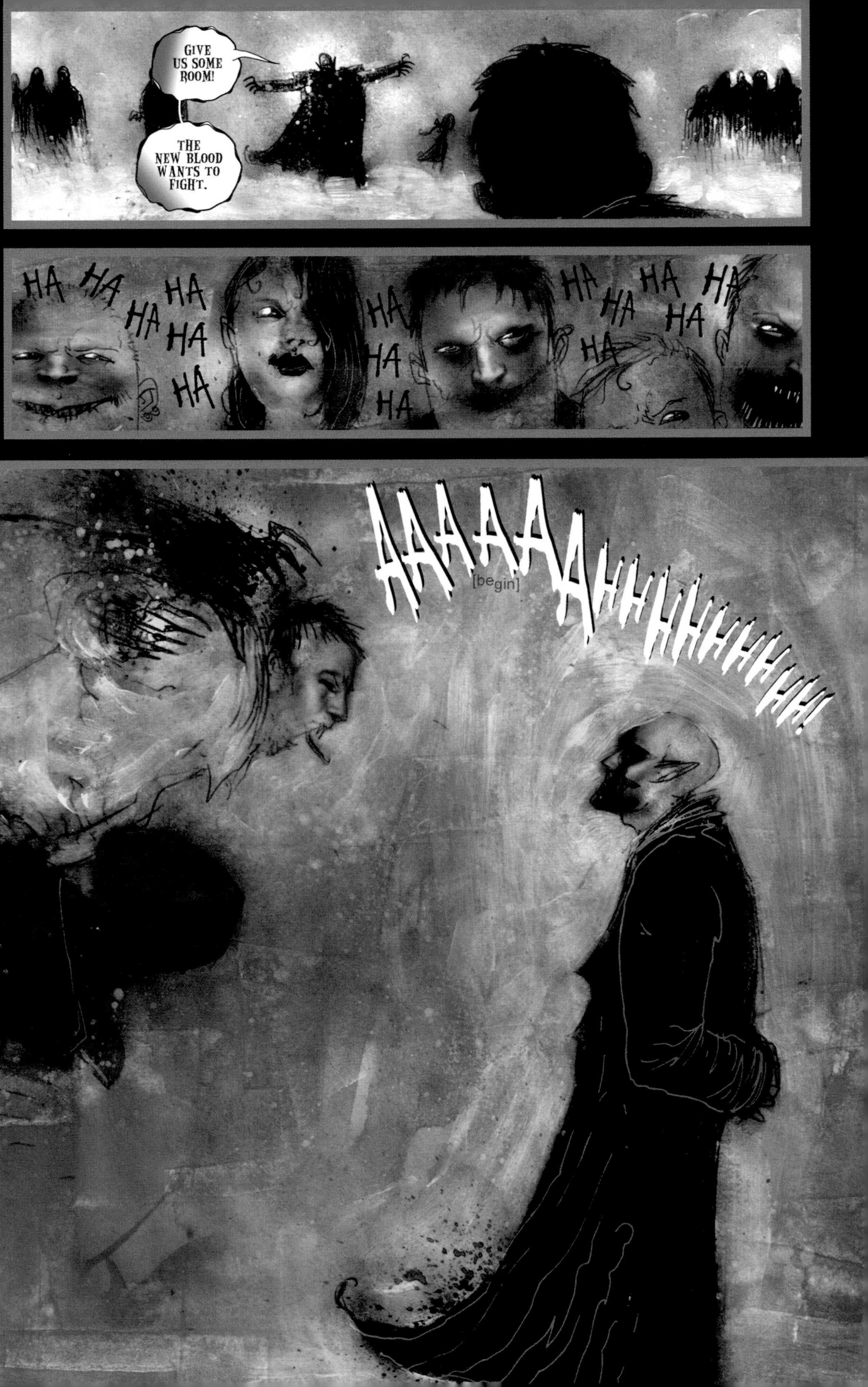
GIVE US SOME ROOM!
THE NEW BLOOD WANTS TO FIGHT.
HA HA HA HA HA HA
HA HA HA
HA HA HA HA HA HA
AAAAAAHHHHHHHHHHH!
[begin]

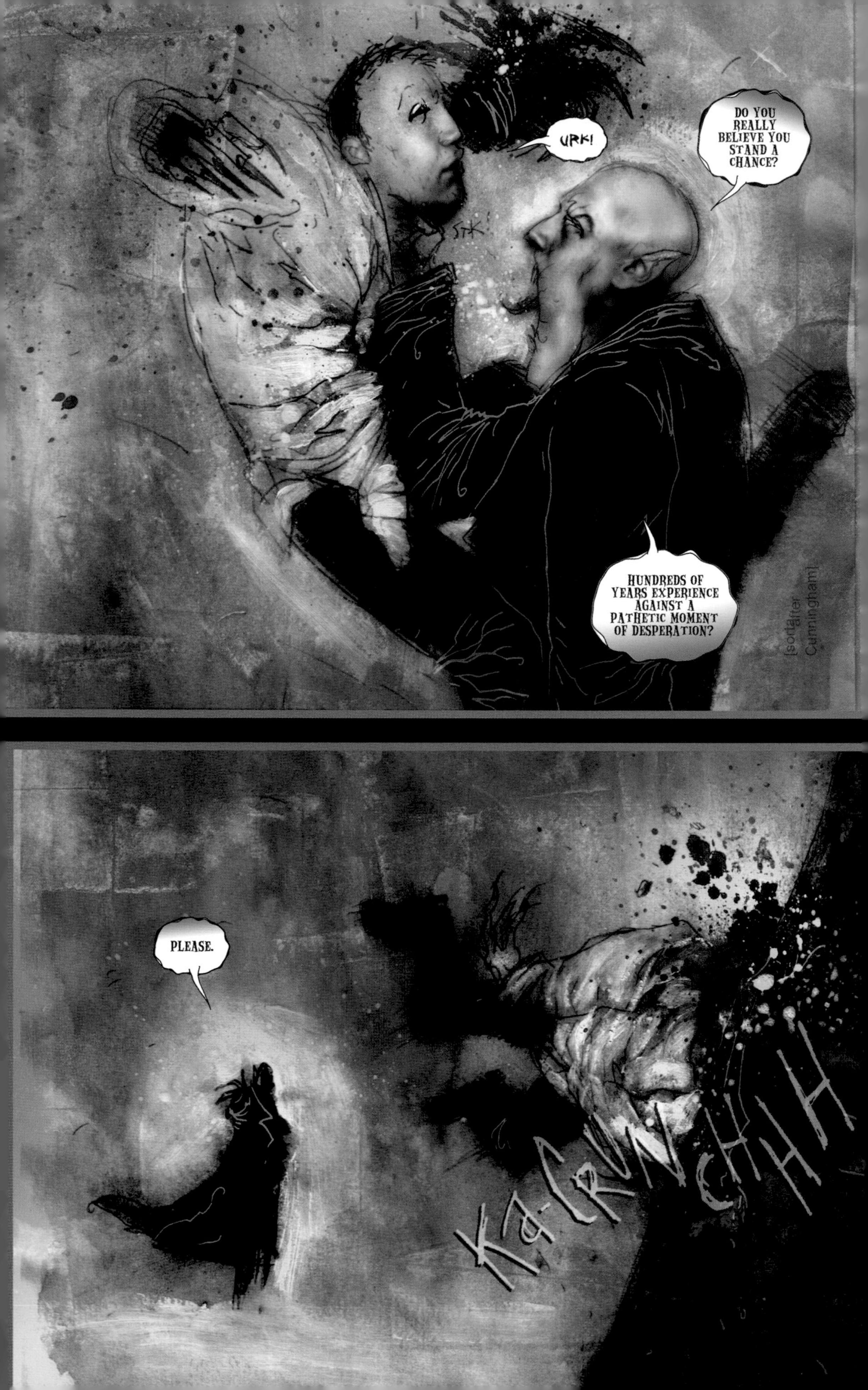
URK!
STK!
DO YOU REALLY BELIEVE YOU STAND A CHANCE?
HUNDREDS OF YEARS EXPERIENCE AGAINST A PATHETIC MOMENT OF DESPERATION?
[sort after Cunningham]
PLEASE.
Ka-CRUNCHHH

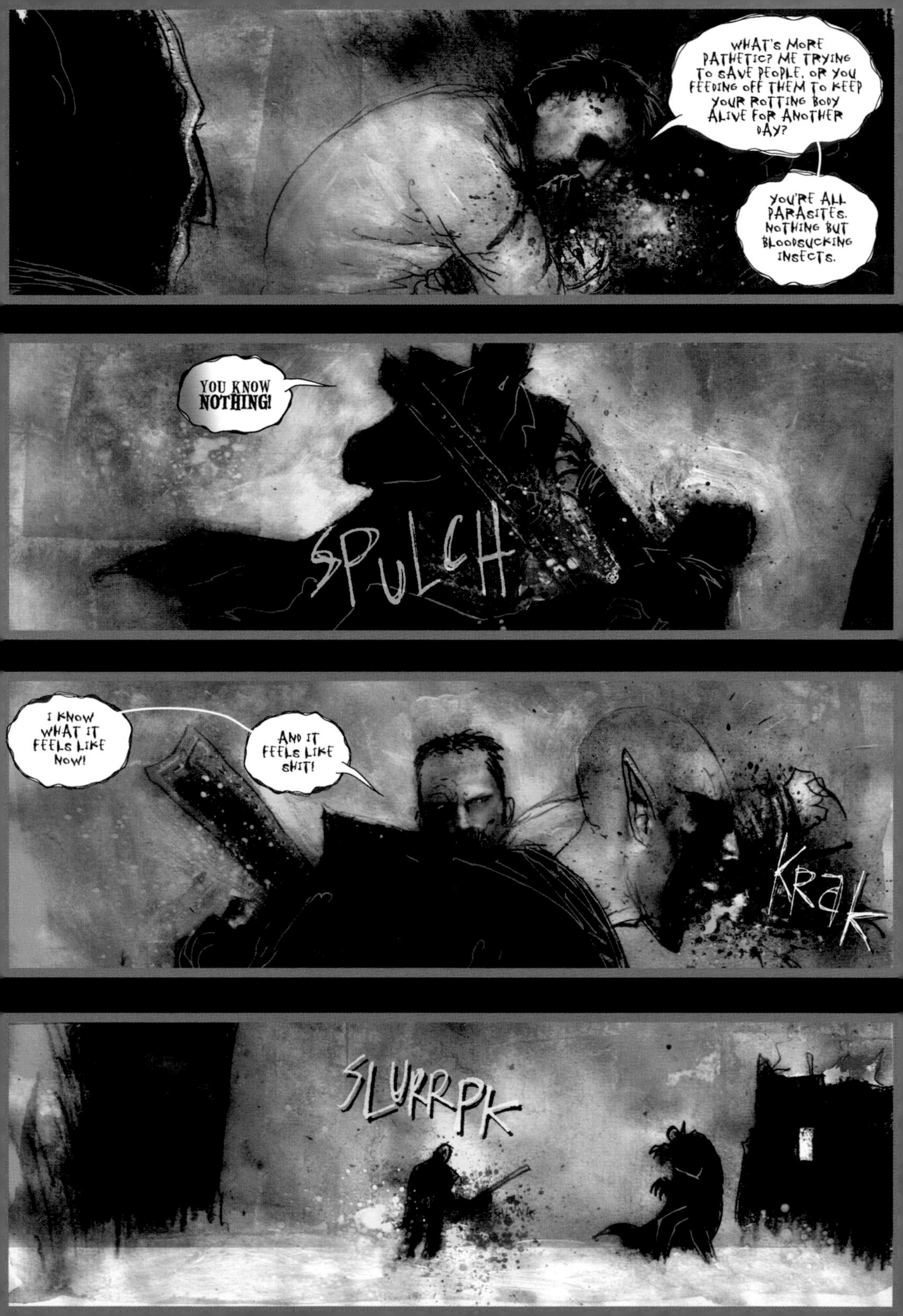
WHAT'S MORE PATHETIC? ME TRYING TO SAVE PEOPLE, OR YOU FEEDING OFF THEM TO KEEP YOUR ROTTING BODY ALIVE FOR ANOTHER DAY?
YOU'RE ALL PARASITES. NOTHING BUT BLOODSUCKING INSECTS.
YOU KNOW NOTHING!
SPULCH
I KNOW WHAT IT FEELS LIKE NOW!
AND IT FEELS LIKE SHIT!
KRAK
SLURRPK

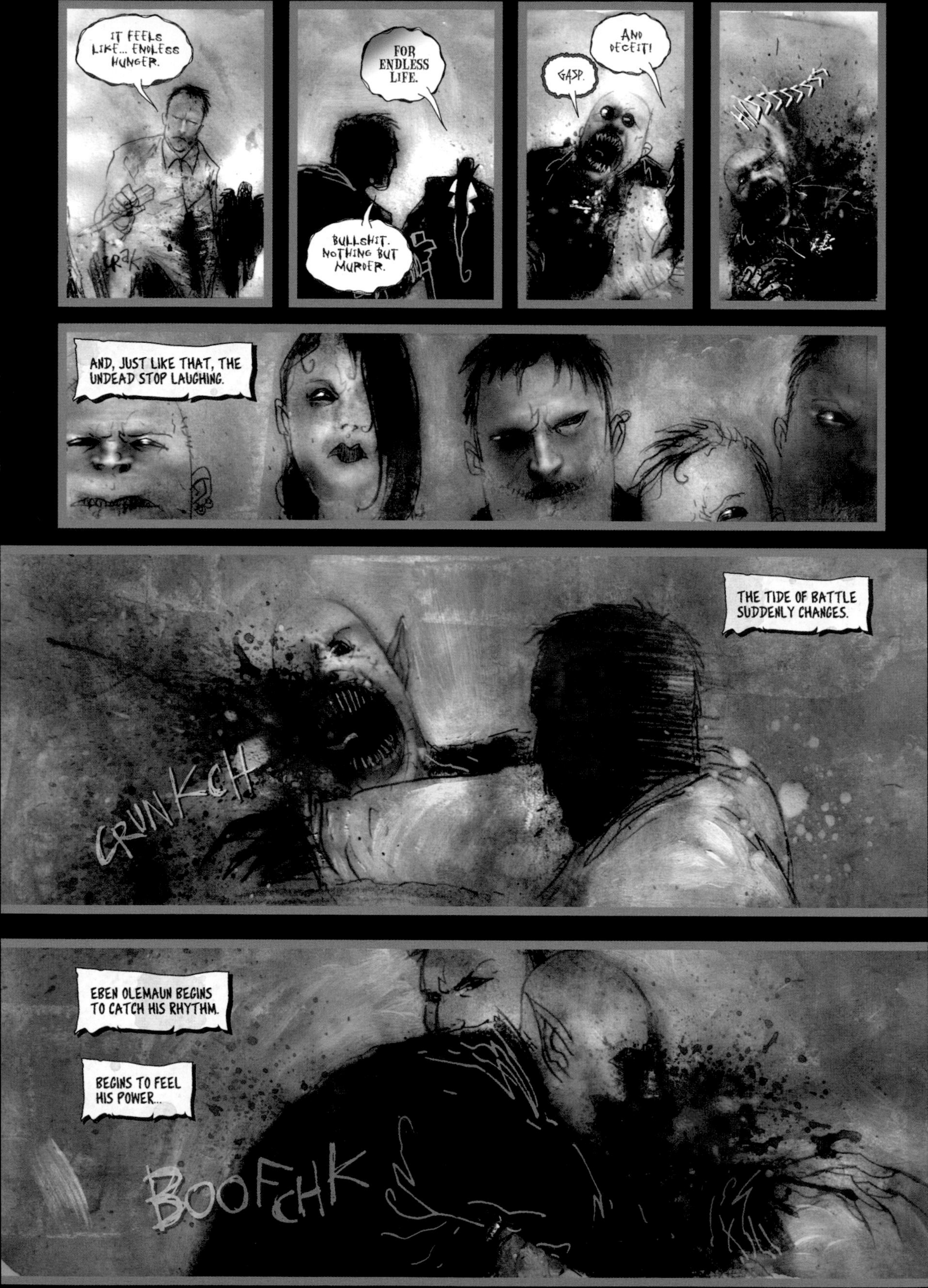
IT FEELS LIKE... ENDLESS HUNGER.
KRAK
FOR ENDLESS LIFE.
BULLSHIT. NOTHING BUT MURDER.
GASP.
AND DECEIT!
HISSSSSSSS
AND, JUST LIKE THAT, THE UNDEAD STOP LAUGHING.
THE TIDE OF BATTLE SUDDENLY CHANGES.
CRUNKCH
EBEN OLEMAUN BEGINS TO CATCH HIS RHYTHM.
BEGINS TO FEEL HIS POWER...
BOOFCHK

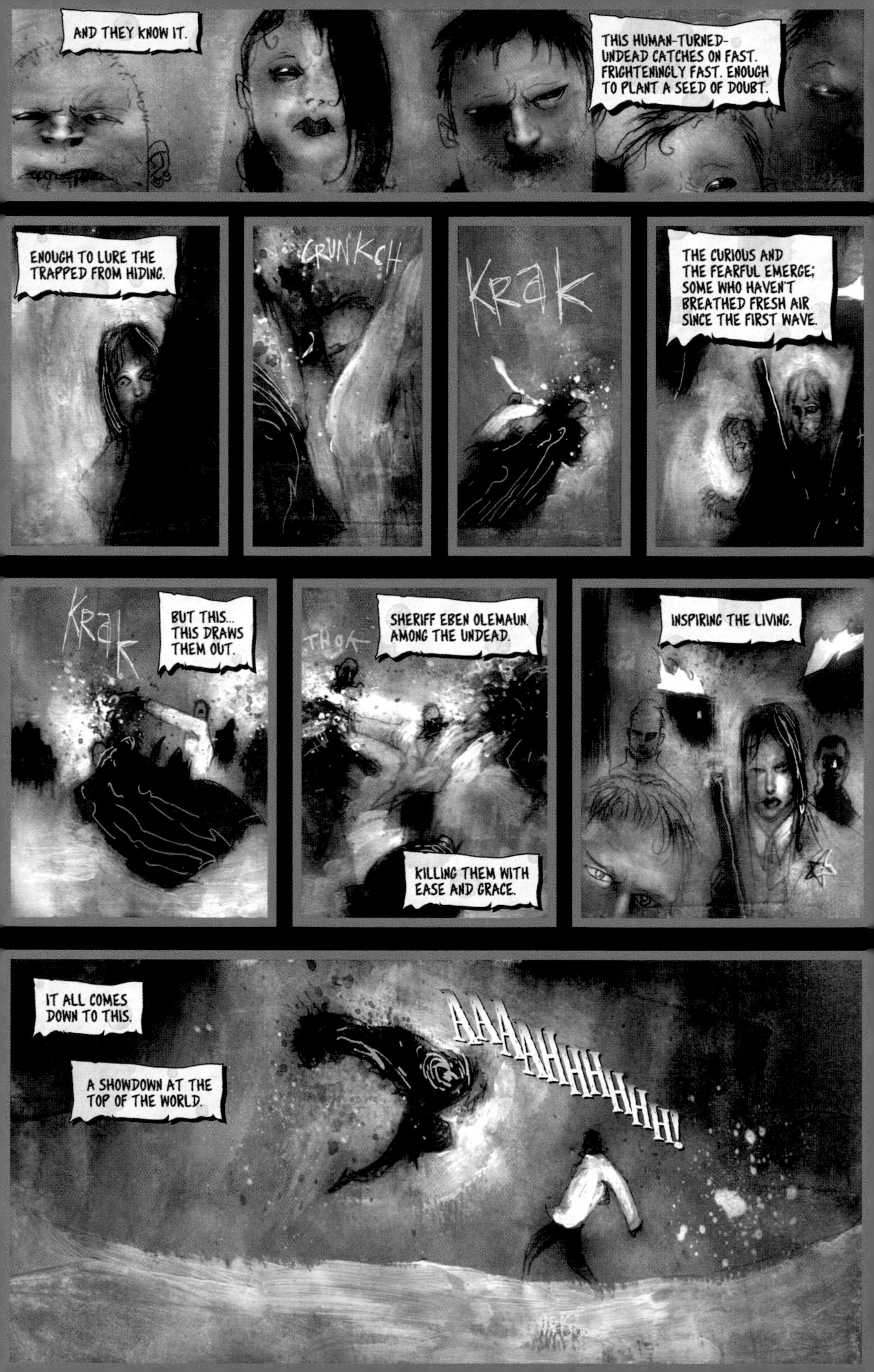
AND THEY KNOW IT.
THIS HUMAN-TURNED-UNDEAD CATCHES ON FAST. FRIGHTENINGLY FAST. ENOUGH TO PLANT A SEED OF DOUBT.
ENOUGH TO LURE THE TRAPPED FROM HIDING.
CRUNKCH
KRAK
THE CURIOUS AND THE FEARFUL EMERGE; SOME WHO HAVEN'T BREATHED FRESH AIR SINCE THE FIRST WAVE.
KRAK
BUT THIS... THIS DRAWS THEM OUT.
THOK
SHERIFF EBEN OLEMAUN. AMONG THE UNDEAD.
KILLING THEM WITH EASE AND GRACE.
INSPIRING THE LIVING.
IT ALL COMES DOWN TO THIS.
A SHOWDOWN AT THE TOP OF THE WORLD.
AAAAAHHHHHHHHH!

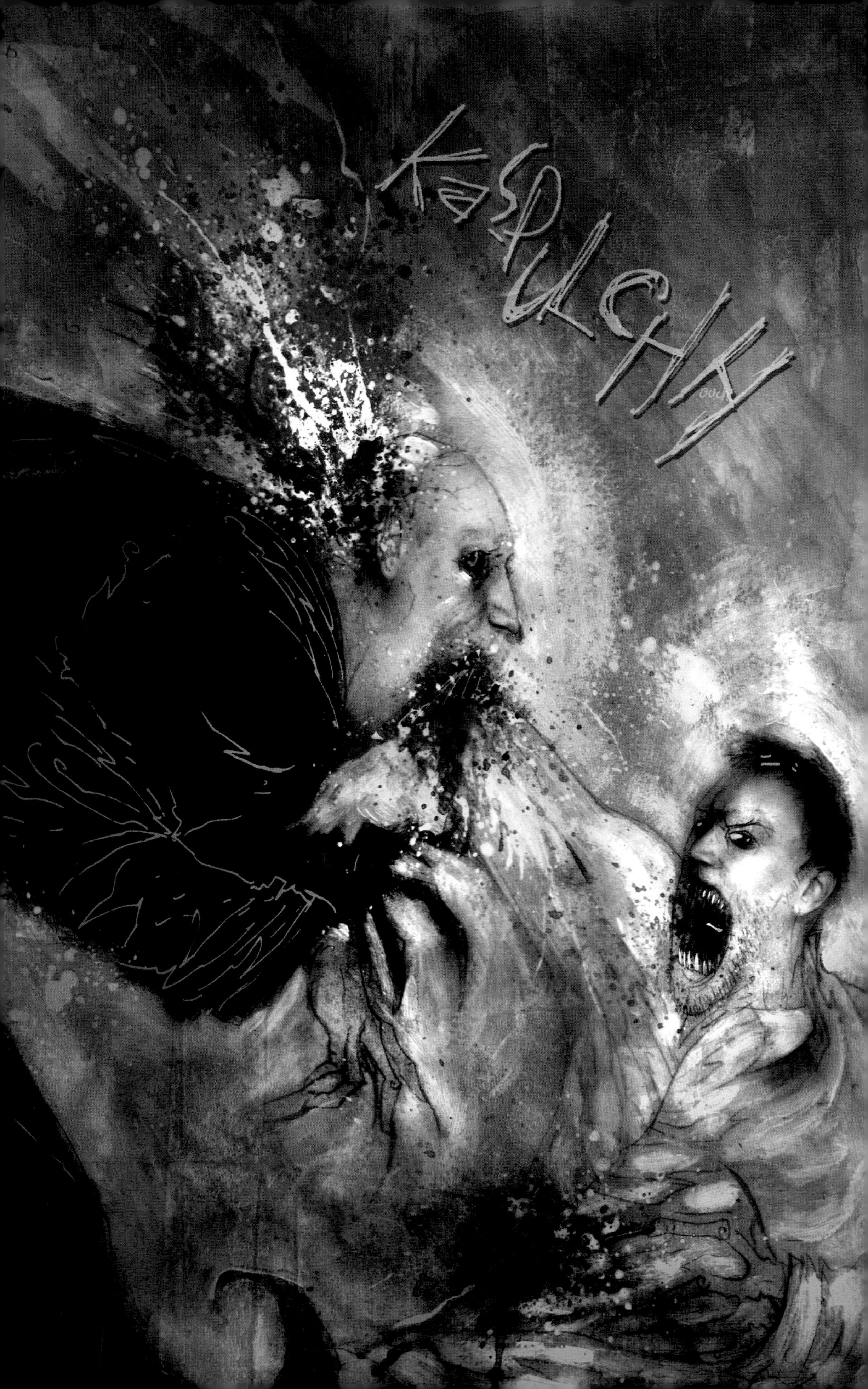
KaSPLUCHHH
ouch

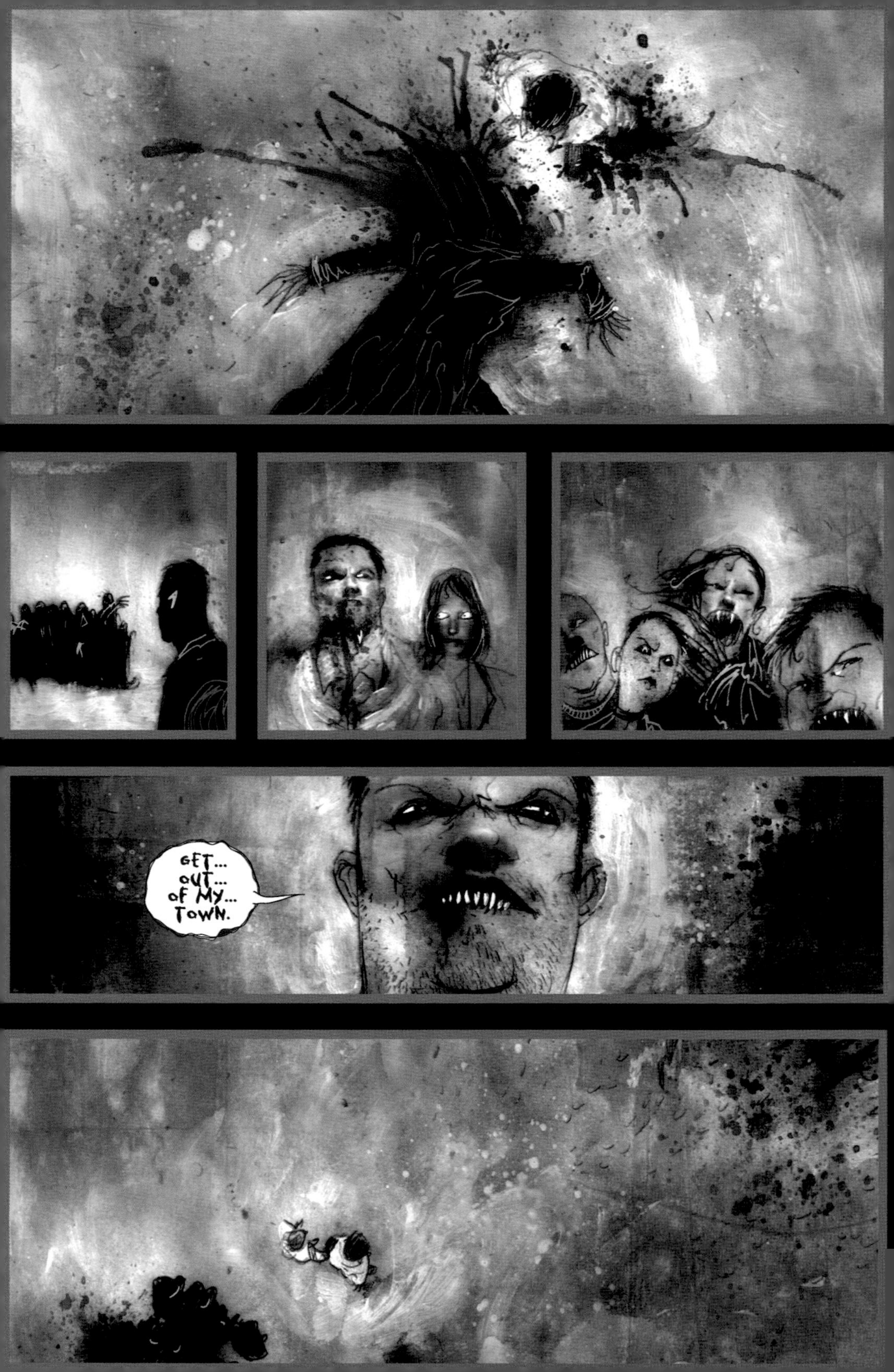
GET... OUT... OF MY... TOWN.

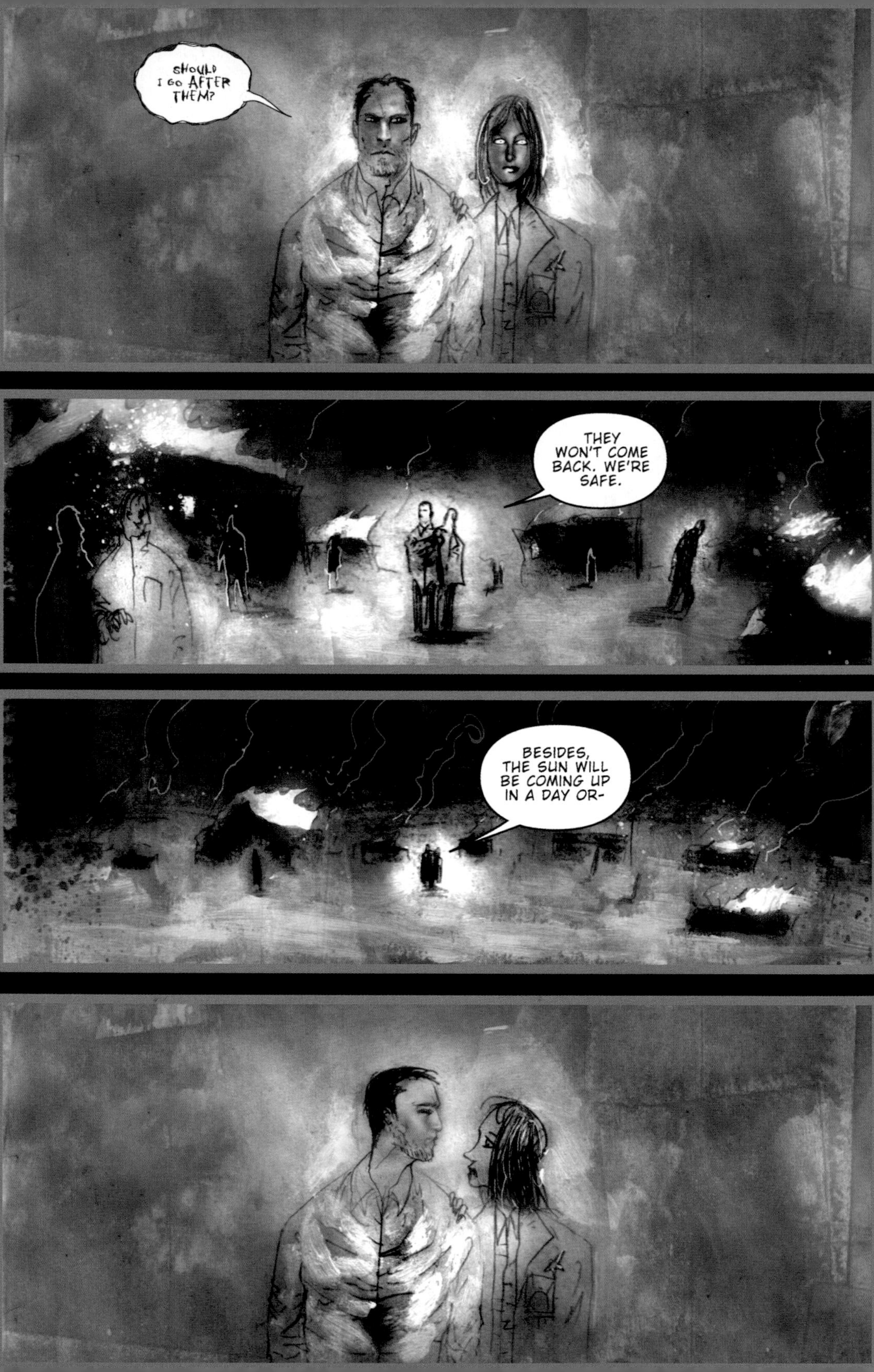
SHOULD I GO AFTER THEM?
THEY WON'T COME BACK. WE'RE SAFE.
BESIDES, THE SUN WILL BE COMING UP IN A DAY OR-

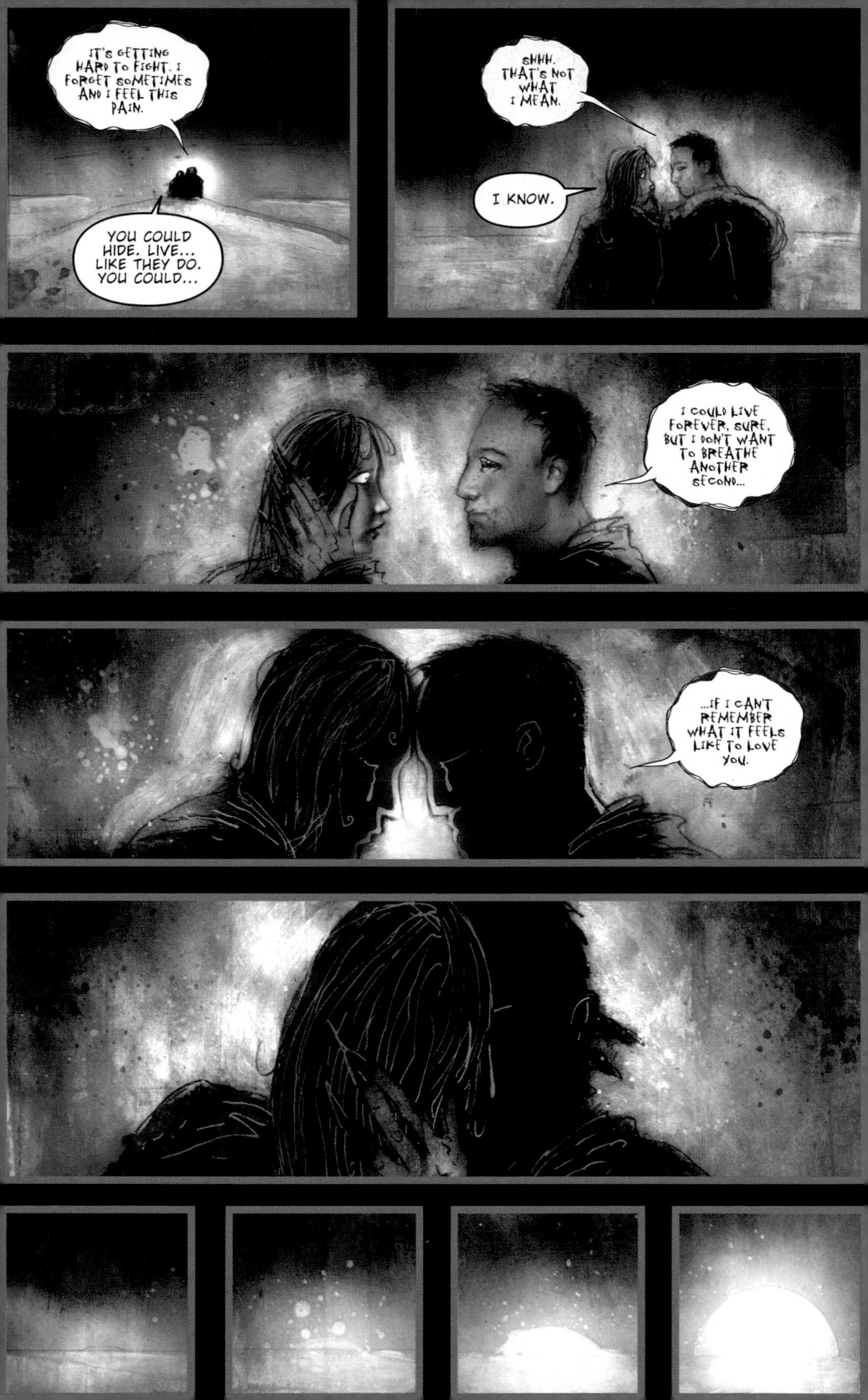
IT'S GETTING HARD TO FIGHT. I FORGET SOMETIMES AND I FEEL THIS PAIN.
YOU COULD HIDE. LIVE... LIKE THEY DO. YOU COULD...
SHHH. THAT'S NOT WHAT I MEAN.
I KNOW.
I COULD LIVE FOREVER, SURE, BUT I DON'T WANT TO BREATHE ANOTHER SECOND...
...IF I CAN'T REMEMBER WHAT IT FEELS LIKE TO LOVE YOU.

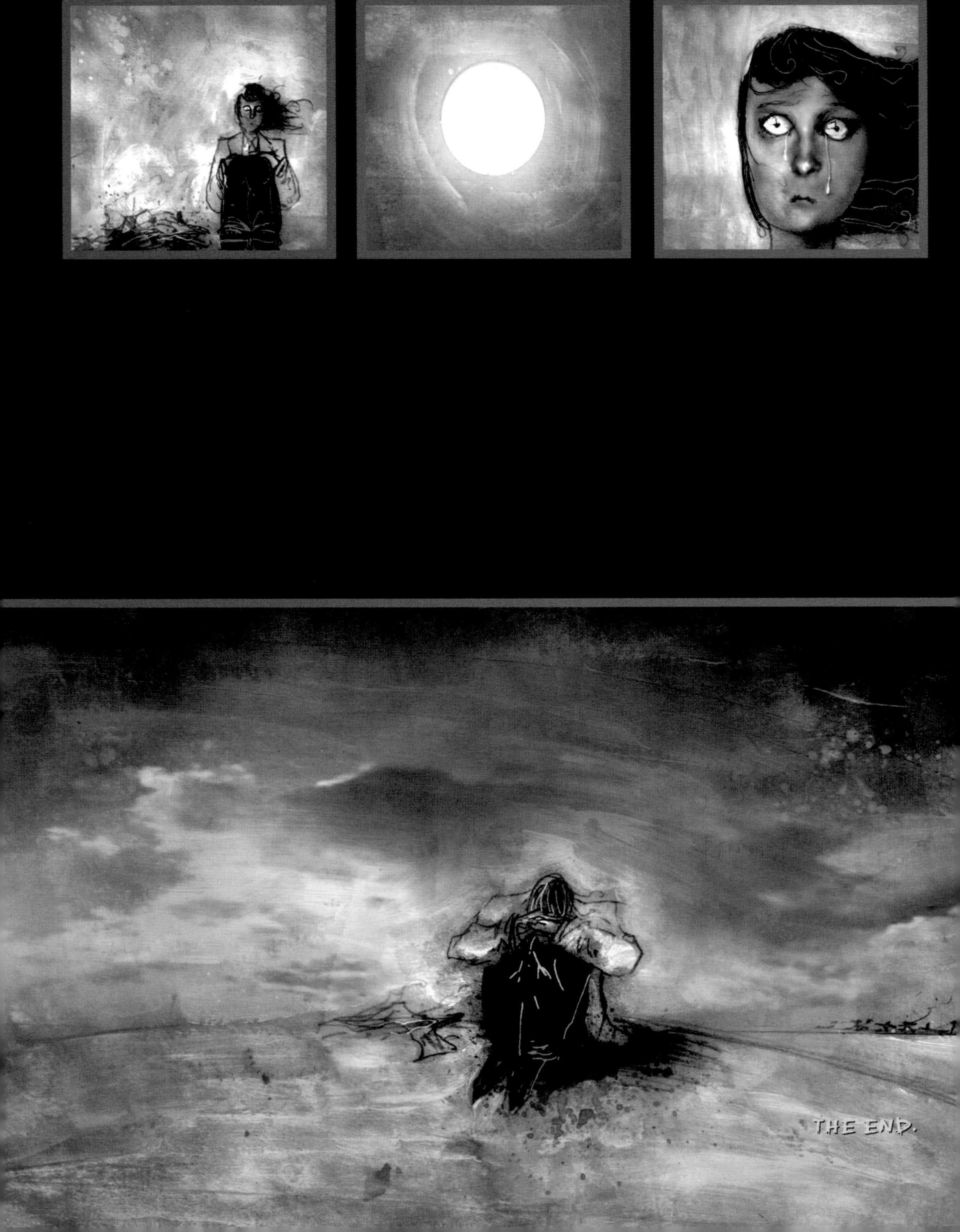
THE END.

Steve Niles

would like to thank:

Ted Adams and everyone at IDW.
Ben Templesmith, Jon Levin, Gretchen Rush
Sam Raimi, Michael Kirk, Mike Richardson,
Senator Films, Rob Tapert, Ashley Wood,
John Lawrence, and, as always,
my wife Nikki.

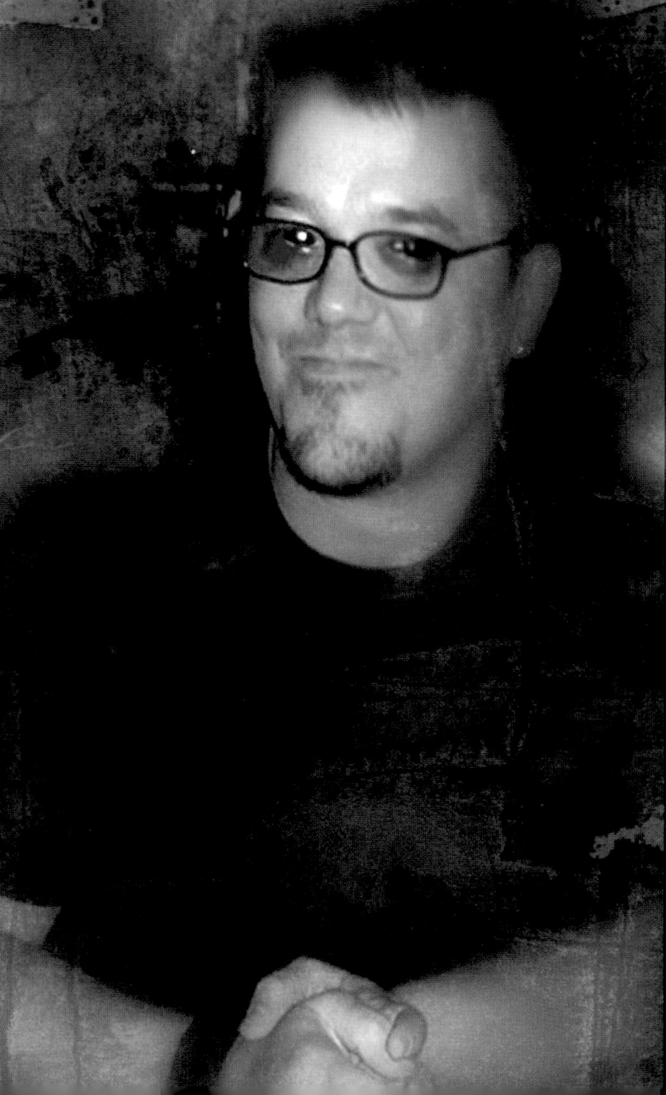

STEVE NILES IS CURRENTLY WORKING ON THE SCREENPLAY FOR THE MOTION PICTURE BASED ON THIS BOOK, AS WELL AS THE COMIC BOOK SEQUEL, **DARK DAYS**.

STEVE BEGAN HIS CAREER BY FOUNDING HIS OWN PUBLISHING COMPANY, ARCANE COMIX, WHERE HE PUBLISHED, EDITED AND ADAPTED COMICS AND ANTHOLOGIES FOR ECLIPSE COMICS. HIS ADAPTATIONS INCLUDE WORKS BY CLIVE BARKER, RICHARD MATHESON AND HARLAN ELLISON. HE HAS ALSO WRITTEN FOR DARK HORSE COMICS, CONTRIBUTING TO TITLES SUCH AS DARK HORSE PRESENTS AND 9-11: ARTISTS RESPOND.

ORIGINALLY FROM WASHINGTON DC, STEVE NOW RESIDES IN LOS ANGELES WITH HIS WIFE NIKKI AND THEIR THREE BLACK CATS.

Ben Templesmith
Would like to thank:

Ted Adams and all at IDW, Steve Niles,
Ashley Wood, Jon Levin, Mike Richardson,
Sam Raimi, Senator Films,
Lorelei Bunjes, John Lawrence,
Mark Hurst, Arni Gunnarsson,
Gareth Selby, Andrew Dabb,
Dave McKean, John Carpenter
nd the girl down at the local chinese take away.

BEN TEMPLESMITH WAS BORN IN THE ARSE END OF THE WORLD—PERTH, AUSTRALIA—IN 1978.

HE'S GOT A BA IN DESIGN FROM CURTIN UNIVERSITY AND A DIPLOMA OF CARTOON AND GRAPHIC ART FROM THE AUSTRALIAN COLLEGE OF JOURNALISM. HE'S DONE EDITORIAL CARTOONS, MAGAZINE WORK, SEQUENTIAL ART AND STICKER DESIGNS AMONG OTHER THINGS. HE ALSO DOESN'T REALLY UNDERSTAND WHY PEOPLE DO THESE THINGS IN THE THIRD PERSON SO MUCH.

HE ALSO HOPES TO GO TO EASTER ISLAND ONE DAY AND SHAKE HIS ODD LITTLE HABIT OF USING EMOTICONS IN NEARLY EVERY MESSAGE BOARD POST HE WRITES.

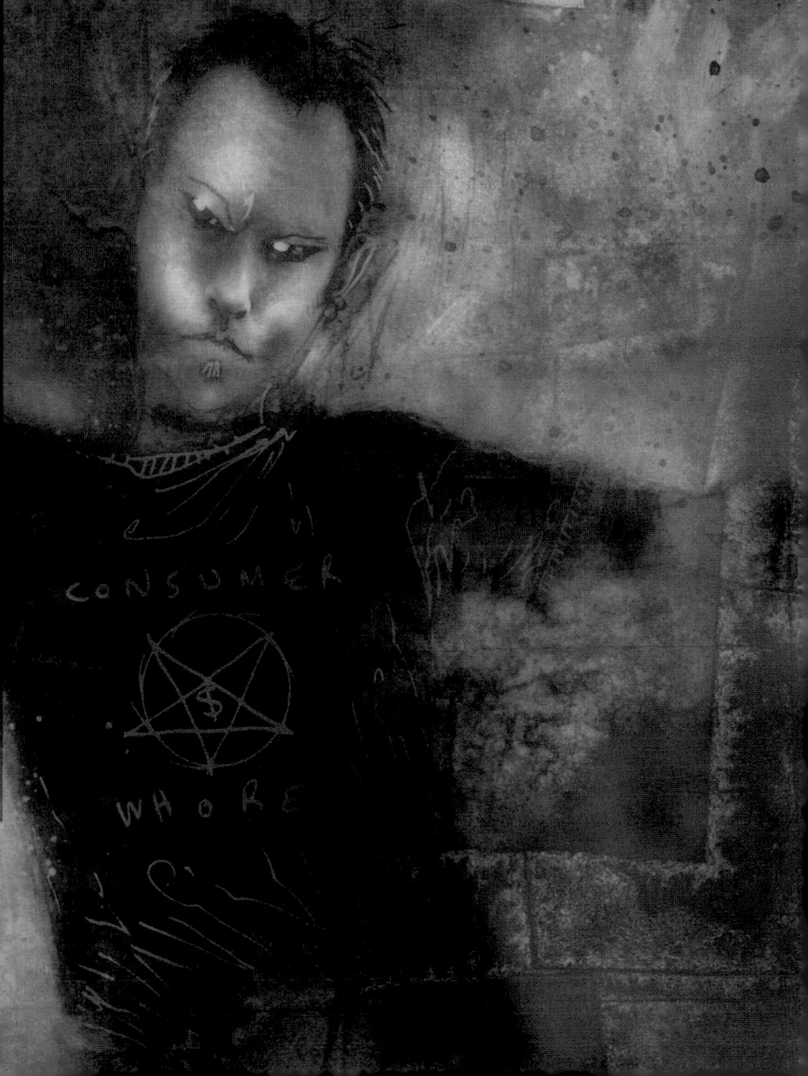
CONSUMER
$
WHORE

PAGE ONE

Panel 1: Three stacked rectangle panels. Each one slowly moving through the haze at ground level, until the town of Barrow is revealed. In this first panel, we are staring at a wasteland in the near distance. It's daylight but all we are looking at is a frozen tundra. Anything beyond the first few feet is covered by a thin sheet of blowing snow and ice.

Panel 2: Now we are moving closer and through the sheet of blowing snow. Ahead we can just begin to make out the sight of a remote town. We can see buildings up on props, trailers, and something flashing red.

CAPTION
Barrow, Alaska.

Panel 3: And this last panel is the town of BARROW, ALASKA in the near distance. We can just make out that a police vehicle of some kind is just heading away from the town proper.

CAPTION
November 17, 2001.

PAGE TWO & THREE

Panel 1: Big spread! Gray, snowy, winter day. We are looking at the frozen wasteland that is Barrow, Alaska. It looks like a modern old west town or as close as we get these days. The buildings are colorless and featureless, looking more like a mobile military camp than a town. Snow blankets everything and all over the town we can see strings of plain lights everywhere, like a constant, low-budget Christmas decoration. Tearing through this panoramic shot of the town is the POLICE JEEP with its lights flashing. We see several people on the streets, other vehicles.

CAPTION
The northernmost community in North America,
it lies 10 miles south of Point Barrow, from
which it takes its name.

CAPTION
It is a town used to two thing: temperatures
averaging below zero and darkness.

CAPTION
The climate of Barrow is arctic. Temperatures
range from cold as shit to fucking freezing.

CAPTION
The sun doesn't set between May 10th and
August 2nd, and doesn't rise between
November 18th and December 17th.

CAPTION
This is the last day the sun will shine for 30 days.

PAGE FOUR

Panel 1: We are looking through the windshield of the Police Jeep at SHERIFF EBEN OLEMAUN. He is Eskimo. Rugged, good-looking in a hard sort of way, and at the moment aggravated as all hell with the rough roads and his deputy on the radio. As he negotiates the rough ride, he yells into the CB microphone in his hand.

> CAPTION
> And today, of all days, a rare crime wave has broken out in the remote, frozen town.

> EBEN
> Goddammit, Stella! Just hold your horses! I'm on my way!

Panel 2: The Jeep plows over a wall of snow and leaps through the air. We see in the background a huge oil tanker propped on girders with a pipeline running from it.

> EBEN
> I gotta hang up!

Panel 3: We are looking at another police jeep parked in an open area as Sheriff Olemaun gets out of his jeep with the lights still flashing. In the clearing we see a Deputy (Stella) standing alone and staring down at a blackened hole in the snow.

> EBEN
> This better be good. Today's the last day of sunlight and we're having generator problems and theft reports springing up all over the place. Plus a storm's rolling in and...

> STELLA
> I think I've got something right here on the thefts.

> EBEN
> ...I got Richardson riding me, Union guys whining about the pipeline and—

Panel 4: Close on Deputy Stella. We see that she is a very beautiful young woman, and is shooting a flirtatious smile from beneath her ear-flapped deputy hat.

> STELLA
> Quit flapping your lips and kiss me before I become another one of your problems.

Panel 5: Eben and Stella kiss. Side view. Typical romantic shot.

PAGE FIVE

Panel 1: Eben is smiling at her while she looks toward the hole.

> EBEN
> That helped. Sorry I yelled at you.

> STELLA
> You'll pay for that later. You should look at this.

Panel 2: The Sheriff and his deputy/wife are looking down at the hole in the ground. The hole is filled with what looks like hundreds of burned and smashed CELL PHONES. Eben looks confused and disturbed.

> EBEN
> What the hell?!

> STELLA
> Saw smoke so I drove out here. I think we
> solved the mystery of the stolen cell phones.

> EBEN
> We've been getting calls since last night.
> Everybody in town is reporting theirs missing.

Panel 3: Eben is kneeling down and has picked up one of the melted phones. Stella is rubbing her hands together.

> STELLA
> Kids prank?

> EBEN
> Seems pretty elaborate for kids to pull off.
> I don't get it.

> STELLA
> The storm's almost here. If it's a prank,
> it's a bad one.

Panel 4: Eben is standing again and looking at his wife.

> EBEN
> Let's shake down the usuals. Call Sam at
> the Shepherd Inn and see if anybody new's
> checked in. Maybe we have a kleptomaniac
> in town.

> STELLA
> What do we tell everybody?

> EBEN
> The truth—we found everyone's cells burned in
> a hole and they'll just have to wait for new
> ones. Maybe if the town starts talking we'll
> smoke the thief out.

Panel 5: Stella is on her radio (pulling it out through her jeep window) as Eben heads back to his, his head turned as she calls out to him.

> EBEN
> Call it in. I'll see you back home.

> STELLA
> EXCUSE ME!

> EBEN
> Honey, seriously! I have so much
> to deal with. The power station
> wants me to—

PAGE SIX

Panel 1: Close on a pouting, semi-flirtatious Stella.

> STELLA
> The sun is setting for the last time until
> December. You're telling me you can't sit
> with your wife and watch? You promised.

Panel 2: Eben stares at her with a blank, helpless expression.

Panel 3: Eben smiles and puts out his hands and Stella runs at him with her arms open.

> EBEN
> Fine, but as soon as it's dark we get back to—

> STELLA
> Yaaaaaay!

> EBEN
> Okay, okay.

Panel 4: As Eben embraces his wife he looks up at the fading sun in the sky.

> STELLA
> Eben, you're the best!

> EBEN
> Like I had a choice.

PAGE SEVEN

Panel 1: Night. A frightened MAN has his back to an alley wall as he leans to peer around the corner to see if anybody is there. He is dirty looking, wearing tattered clothes and a knit hat. You can see the fear in his dark circled, wide eyes. You can see it in the sweat that mats his hair to his forehead. The sidewalk looks clear.

CAPTION
New Orleans, Louisiana.

Panel 2: The man darts down the sidewalk. He is gripping a shoulder bag and looking to his side with wide, frightened eyes as he shambles close to the wall.

Panel 3: The Man clutching the bag stops in front of a Voodoo Shop. There is no sign in the window or on the plain wooden door, but we can see dolls and other tell-tale signs in the window display. The Man is looking to the side while pulling a small chain that rings a bell on the inside.

SOUNDFX
bing! bing!

MAN
Come on, come on, come on!

Panel 4: Far shot, from down the sidewalk where the Man came as we watch the Man enter the store being ushered in by a large, muscular man whose features we can not make out.

MAN
Is she here?

LARGE MAN
She's here. What you got?

MAN
I watched what she told me to and I got what s...she said to look for right here! I got it, T-man! You'll see!

Panel 5: Same shot. The door is closed hard.

LARGE MAN (FROM DOOR)
Get on in before someone sees you, speed freak. And don't call me T-man.

SOUNDFX
Slam!

PAGE EIGHT

Panel 1: Now we are inside watching the Large Man lead. He's black, bald and muscular. He is wearing camouflage pants and a black T-shirt. The desperate Man clutches his bag and follows him. They are coming at us down a narrow corridor.

TAYLOR
When was the last time you slept, George?

GEORGE

Sleep? Who needs s...sleep? I hate sleep. I got
too much to do. The world's a cracklin'!

Panel 2: Taylor pushes through a wide door covered with beads and George is
right behind him. We can see the room is a cross between a VOODOO DEN and
a fortune telling room, with a pharmacy thrown in. There are bottles and bones
all over the place. There is a chair that both men are looking towards as they
come in, but all we see is the back of the chair and a woman's arm, resting.

TAYLOR

Momma, George here says he got something
for you.

GEORGE

Yeah, that's right. J...just what you asked for.
R...right where you asked—

VOICE

—George. Please, come in and sit down. Taylor
honey, would you mind mixing up a soothing
detox tea for our guest?

Panel 3: Now a big, full reveal of a beautiful but rugged looking black woman
who looks young enough to be Taylor's sister. Her name is MISS JUDITH. She
has dark skin and light brown eyes. Her face is very pleasant. As she looks,
jittery George digs through his shoulder bag like a maniac.

MISS JUDITH

What have you got there, George?

GEORGE

I've b...been monitoring the mail networks
based on the names and locations you speci-
fied. For months there was nothing, and then
BAM!—a s...sudden burst of activity. They tried
encrypting and all this other hacker crap, but
I chopped right through.

GEORGE 2

Most of them were pretty general... but late
last night they loosened up a bit...

Panel 4: George holds up a few pages of crumpled printouts with
e-mails on them. He looks like he just discovered the cure for cancer.

GEORGE

...and here they are!

Panel 5: Close on Miss Judith's multi-ringed hand taking the papers from
George as Taylor's big hand sticks a steaming skull mug in front of his face.

GEORGE (tiny whisper)

Thought I lost 'em there for a sec.

PAGE NINE

Panel 1: Miss Judith is sitting back in her ornate, dark wood and red velvet chair as she looks at the printouts. Taylor is standing behind her. The note that she reads will appear as a caption in text boxes that look like e-mail.

> CAPTION
> From: Sender blocked
> Sent: Friday, November 16, 2001 4:04 AM
> To: MARLOW Roderick
> Subject: none
>
> MARLOW —
>
> Received your last several correspondences,
> but I've been away and unable to access
> my e-mail. I do not approve of this electronic
> trail, but your idea has piqued my curiosity.
>
> In all my years I have never heard of Barrow.
> If what you say is true it could be worth
> gathering for an event.
>
> Sincerely,
>
> —V

Panel 2: Now we go over her shoulder as she puts aside the e-mail we just saw and reveals the next.

> CAPTION
> From: MARLOW Roderick
> Sent: Friday, November 16, 2001 5:44 AM
> To: Unknown
> Subject: none
>
> V—
>
> Everything I have told you is true. I have
> already sent a delegate to make all of the
> necessary arrangements for our arrival.
>
> I hope to see you there. The presence of
> one such as yourself will make the event
> truly one for the ages.
>
> I have sent all pertinent information to you
> by personal courier. We will meet in British
> Columbia and fly to a rendezvous point. The
> location is in the package. Thus far we have
> nineteen attendees.
>
> Sincerely,
>
> — MARLOW

Panel 3: And finally the last e-mail print out. The look on Miss Judith's face is no longer pleasant.

> CAPTION
> From: Sender Blocked
> Sent: Saturday, November 17, 2001 1:23 AM
> To: MARLOW Roderick
> Subject: none
>
> MARLOW —
>
> Make that an even twenty.
>
> —V

Panel 4: Miss Judith looks straight at us. She looks worried as Taylor reads one of the printout that he just picked up. He is still standing behind her.

> MISS JUDITH
> I don't like the looks of this.

> GEORGE
> Who's V?

> TAYLOR
> And what the hell is Barrow?

PAGE TEN

Panel 1: Back in Barrow, the Sheriff and his wife are sitting on a snowy hill (on a blanket) watching as the sun disappears over the flat, frozen horizon. This is a romantic shot from semi-behind them. He has his arm around her. She has her head resting on his shoulder and waving.

> EBEN
> There it goes.

> STELLA
> Bye-bye sun.

Panel 2: Close on the faces of the young couple with the romantic fading orange glow of the sun splashing across them.

Panel 3: Same.

> EBEN
> Can I go now?

> STELLA
> You ever want to have sex again?

> EBEN
> sigh.

Panel 4: And the sun is gone. In the lower portion of the panel we can see the two jeeps parked.

> RADIO (from Sheriff's jeep)
> ...KRRRSSHH...Sheriff?...KRRRSSHH—Sheriff
> Olemaun, do you read?...KRRRSSHH...

Panel 5: Eben looks over at Stella with a wide grin. She can't help but smile.

> STELLA
> Just go.

> STELLA
> I'll be right behind you.

PAGE ELEVEN

Panel 1: We are back in downtown Barrow. It's night, and will be for the duration of the story. IKOS DINER is little more than a gray house on blocks with a sign. There are snowmobiles and other vehicles parked outside, sort of scattered around. Eben is already out of his jeep and heading in as Stella drives up.

> EBEN
> Hey Sam.

Panel 2: Big reveal panel inside the diner. Eben has just entered the room. There are tables and a short counter. One OMINOUS MAN (this guy is our Renfield, a bug-eater scout: he is dressed in all black with ratty hair, sunken eyes and snot running from his nose) sits at the counter with some locals looking on but standing away. SAM, the owner stands on the other side of the counter and looks freaked out. The man is hunkered at the bar so we really don't get a very good look at his face, but what we can see tells us he isn't like anybody else in town.

> EBEN
> What's the problem?

> SAM
> I asked this gentleman to leave
> the premises and he refuses to go.

> MAN
> I'm just looking for a little hospitality.

Panel 3: Now Eben has moved to the counter and is standing next to the hunkered man who's face we can't see yet. Eben is looking at the side of the man but talking to Sam who is standing on the other side of the counter.

> SAM
> He wants stuff we don't serve, Sheriff, and
> when I told him that, he started in with the
> threats!

> EBEN
>
> That right? What kind of stuff you want, stranger?

> MAN
>
> A drink. I just wanted a drink and something to eat.

> SAM
>
> He asked for whiskey and a bowl of RAW hamburger meat!

Panel 4: Close on Eben.

> EBEN
>
> Well, alcohol possession and consumption are illegal here. With the dark winters, folks have a hard enough time without booze adding to the mess. As for the meat, it only comes two ways around here: frozen and burnt.

PAGE TWELVE

Panel 1: We reveal the face of the ominous man as he finally shoots a look up. By his crazed, unnaturally pale look, and his deep sunken dark eyes we can see he's unstable and most likely dangerous.

> MAN
>
> I like it raw! What's so hard to understand about a man wanting a little blood with his meat?!

Panel 2: The man is now standing. He's lanky and tall, taller than Eben. The man and the Sheriff are standing close. Eben has his hand on his holster as the man looms over him. The locals and Sam are all backing away.

> EBEN
>
> I'm going to have to ask you to leave, sir. If you refuse, I'll escort you out of here myself— and right out of town.

> MAN
>
> Oh yeah?!

Panel 3: Close on the man's head as a gun is pressed against his head from a low angle and behind. The Man looks startled, a little frightened even.

> SOUNDFX
>
> click click!

> VOICE (off panel)
>
> YEAH.

Panel 4: Pull back shot and we see Stella with her gun drawn and jammed into the back of the strange Man's head. The strange man has his hands raised. Eben is smiling. He loves how tough and aggressive his wife is.

                    STELLA
          Now you get to spend the night in a jail cell.

                    EBEN
          Hands behind your back!

Panel 5: They have the man handcuffed and are heading out of the diner. We are looking from the front so that we can see the menacing, evil expression/smirk on the man's face as he is being led away by Eben and Stella.

                    MAN
          Yeah, whatever.

PAGE THIRTEEN

Panel 1: The Barrow Satellite Communication Center. We are looking at a compact fenced in compound that looks like a power station with satellite dishes. In the darkness and the swirl we can see a portly man in a parka checking the fence alarm several feet from a closed door to the interior.

                    CAPTION
          When Gus Lambert left Chicago in 1983 he
          was running away from bad debt and a bad
          marriage.

Panel 2: Close in on as he tries to get the box to the security system open.

                    CAPTION
          It was a cowardly move, but if he hadn't done
          it, he'd have suffocated and died. He was sure
          of it.

                    GUS
          Ah, come OOOON! Don't putter out on me now!

                    CAPTION
          Now, almost eighteen years later, Gus KNOWS
          running was the smartest thing he ever did.

Panel 3: Gus stands and stares at the inside of the control box and sees that it has been torn to shreds. The wires are slashed, torn and ripped. The panel looks like a wolverine has been at it.

                    GUS
          What the hell?

                    CAPTION
          Coming to Barrow was a close second.

CAPTION
The cold didn't bother him a bit. And the 30
days of night, well, that kept him working.

GUS
Completely destroyed! Now that's just plain strange.

Panel 4: Suddenly Gus is looking up and seeing that there are tracks
everywhere in the snow around him, footprints.

CAPTION
But it was the people here who captured his
heart. They embraced him regardless of where
he came from or why he left.

Panel 5: Pull back shot and we see FIVE DARK STRANGERS standing some
distance away from Gus. We can't see them clearly. They seem strange and
out of place standing in the frozen landscape with their black clothing, stringy
bodies and their glistening eyes.

GUS
H...hello? Who's that?

Panel 6: Tight shot as Gus tries to look up and behind him, over his shoulder.

VOICE
Nobody you know.

CAPTION
Gus Lambert was damn lucky to come to Barrow.

GUS
What're you doing here? This place is
off limits.

PAGE FOURTEEN

Panel 1: Large panel. Gus is surrounded. He is frightened. The five who were
yards away only seconds ago are now all around him. The seeming leader,
MARLOW, is sitting on the ledge of the bunker lighting a smoke as he looks
down at poor Gus. Marlow is bald and one of his eyes is long gone. In its
place is a puncture-like scar. The others are all shapes and sizes, men and
women, kids and adults. They are all thin. They all have wild, stressed eyes
and hungry teeth.

CAPTION
Unfortunately, today is the day that his luck
runs dry.

MARLOW
Two questions... then we'll be on our way.

GUS
W...what?

> MARLOW
> This is the communication center for this
> blubber-smelling shit-hole, right?

> GUS
> Y...yes.

Panel 2: Close on Marlow.

> MARLOW
> All calls and television signals come through
> here, correct?

Panel 3: Back up shot and Marlow is standing in front of Gus as the rest
close in forming a tight circle around the portly man.

> GUS
> Y...yeah...mostly.

> MARLOW
> Mostly?

> GUS
> Except for short-wave and... Look—you need
> to identify yourselves and what the hell you're
> doing out here.

> MARLOW
> Questions, questions. I suppose you deserve
> some answers. Let's start with, "none of your
> business" and...

Panel 4: With a single violent, upward swipe, Marlow rips Gus open from belly
to throat, sending a shower-spray of crimson swirling into the frozen air. The
others cheer and bathe in the fountain.

> MARLOW
> ...THIS!

Panel 5: Marlow walks away, licking blood and meat from his hands as the
others converge on the building.

> MARLOW
> Tear the place apart.

PAGE FIFTEEN

Panel 1: The Sheriff, Eben, in his office. He's sitting, staring at a pile of
broken cell phones on his desk as his computer goes dead. The Sheriff's
office is basically one big room with two desks and a lock-up cell. Inside
the cell, the Crazy Man from the diner (we'll call him Freak) is standing,
holding onto the bars and giggling. Stella is at her desk looking at Eben.
She is just putting down the phone receiver.

EBEN

Oh, Christ. Not now!

STELLA

What?

EBEN

Computer's down.

STELLA

Phone's not working. Gus probably fell asleep
again. Give it a couple minutes.

FREAK

Hee, hee, hee.

Panel 2: Close on Freak with his face shoved up against the bars. He's
grinning, his rotten teeth chipped and brown.

FREAK

You can wait all you want. All you have left
is time. Hee, hee.

Panel 3: Eben and Stella are looking pretty calm as they swivel their chairs
and face the crazy man in the cell.

STELLA

What are you going on about?

FREAK

Believe me, Mr. & Mrs. Sheriff, there's nuthin'
you can do to stop what's coming.

EBEN

All I'm hearing from you is a whole lot of
nothing. Sit down and zip it before Stella loses
her temper.

Panel 3: Close on the Freak rubbing his face on the bars.

FREAK

Mmmm, I'd like that. Your little lady could
have some fun with a guy like me. I like to
take a beating now and again. Maybe she'd
like to come in here and—

EBEN(off panel)

SHUT UP!

Panel 4: Eben is standing, glaring at the freak in the cage. He is clearly
rattled. Stella is still sitting, but is reaching out for her husband. The Freak
is laughing in the cell.

STELLA

Eben, don't. He's just trying to get your blood up.

> EBEN
>
> It's working.

> FREAK
>
> Hee, hee, hee.

Panel 5: Close on Stella, her face worried, yet gentle.

> STELLA
>
> Don't let it. We have enough to worry about.
> I think we should check on Gus.

Panel 6: Tight close-up of the freak, spitting and wide-eyed.

> FREAK
>
> Now you're catching on. Check on Gus! Board
> the windows! Sandbag the doors! You'll try it
> ALL! But one by one they'll pick you off and
> strip THE MEAT from your bones!

> FREAK
>
> It's gonna be beautiful! And then I get to be
> with them!

PAGE SIXTEEN

Panel 1: Eben and Stella are reaching for their guns as the freak inside
the cell begins to PULL the bars apart with his bare hands.

> EBEN
>
> What the hell?! Stop!

> STELLA
>
> OH MY GOD! Impossible!

Panel 2: The freak has pulled the bars open enough for him to step through
and he is glaring at Eben and Stella with a hungry, crazy stare.

> FREAK
>
> You are so FUCKED.

Panel 3: Frozen action shot. Eben has his pistol raised and has fired. We
see the path of the bullet from the end of the barrel all the way INTO and
THROUGH the Freak's head, where the bullet is exiting in an explosion of
blood. The Freak is sprawling in the air as his head blows out the back.

> SOUNDFX (big)
>
> BLAMM!

Panel 4: Stella and Eben look at the Freak laying sprawled on the
floor next to the broken cell as a pool of blood grows around his
still-intact head.

> EBEN
>
> Is he dead?

PAGE SEVENTEEN

Panel 1: With the body out of the shot, and Eben surprised, Stella angrily unloads a clip down into where the head would be.

SOUNDFX
BLAMM! BLAMM! BLAMM! BLAMM! BLAMM!
BLAMM! BLAMM! BLAMM! BLAMM! BLAMM!

Panel 2: Up shot. The Freak's head is now a comical smear of black, red and bone-white splattered all over the floor. Eben stares at his wife in shock as she jams in another clip.

STELLA
He's dead now.

Panel 3: Eben is holding his head. Stella is shaky but trying to stay calm.

EBEN
I need a minute.

STELLA
We might not have a minute, honey.
Something's going on. First, we've gotta
figure out why all our communications
are down.

Panel 4: A shot of Stella and Eben driving over the frozen tundra.

Panel 5: Close on Eben looking as scared as a little boy lost in the dark. We are seeing him through the jeeps windshield.

EBEN
Gus?

STELLA
Gus!

PAGE EIGHTEEN

Panel 1: We are outside. Stella is throwing up. Eben is down on his knees, catching his breath. They are outside in the snow at the Communication Center, but we don't see it yet. We can see blood soaked into the snow and a sheet of steel shredded like paper.

STELLA
Blarrrrwlp...oh God... Blarrrrwlp...Eben...

Panel 2: Now reveal the entire scene and we see Eben and Stella standing before the Communication Center. It is COMPLETELY destroyed, almost unrecognizable as a building. There's blood everywhere. Atop one lone pole we can see Gus' head. His arm is here, his torso there. It's an unbelievable nightmare. The satellite dishes are destroyed--twisted like aluminum beer cans. Eben is close to Stella in this shot, holding her up, comforting her as he looks around, now really scared.

Panel 3: Small panel. Tight. Paranoid. Close on Eben, his frightened eyes searching.

> EBEN
> H...here's what we do. We stay calm. We drive back to the station, then to the diner to check on everybody.

Panel 4: Small panel. Tight. Paranoid. Pull back and show Stella holding her husband as he looks around. He has his gun out.

> EBEN
> We'll round everyone up.

Panel 3: Small panel. Tight. Paranoid. Close on Eben again.

> EBEN
> Get 'em all together while I make a RUN for HELP.

PAGE NINETEEN

Panel 1: They are back in the the jeep. Eben is driving, looking ahead, squinting. Stella is looking over at him. She looks worried.

> STELLA
> I think it's my turn to freak out.

> EBEN
> You hang in there, sweetie. I've got an idea. We're dealing with numbers here, right? Maybe some kind of gang. Maybe escaped prisoners—

> STELLA
> But why would anyone escape from prison and come here?

Panel 2: Stella has gone from worried to panic. Eben is trying to maintain, but he can't see, and he's frightened.

> EBEN
> Maybe it's terrorists trying to get at the pipeline again.

> STELLA
> He bent the bars, Eben! He said they were coming! What was that?!

> EBEN
> I don't know. I don't know. Everything is happening too fast! Let me think!

Panel 3: Neither talk for a beat as they drive and consider what is happening.

Panel 4: Stella sees something through the window on Eben's side. She is leaning forward trying to get a better look.

>   STELLA
>   What's that?

>   EBEN
>   What?

>   STELLA
>   Out there... Look... a light!

PAGE TWENTY

Panel 1: Outside, the jeep comes to a side-sliding halt. In the background we can see the town of Barrow.

Panel 2: Eben is standing outside the jeep as Stella comes running up to his side with high-tech binoculars and hands them to him.

Panel 3: Eben looking through the binoculars.

>   EBEN
>   Something's moving out there. It might be the
>   locals, or...wait.

Panel 4: Now we are seeing what Eben is seeing through the binoculars. In the distance we see a starless black sky and a horizon of white snow. There is something, a mass moving towards us, but we can't make it out. Something seems to glimmer.

PAGE TWENTY-ONE

Panel 1: Binocular point of view. The mass in the distance is closer now and we can see that it might not be an object at all, but possibly a group of people.

Panel 2: Closer still. Now we can see that it IS a group of people, more than 20, walking in the middle of the frozen tundra. We can't make out anything more specific.

Panel 3: Back on Eben with Stella standing next to him, waiting for him to say something—but he doesn't. He just lowers the binoculars slightly. The look on his face tells us that he doesn't believe what he is seeing through the lenses.

>   STELLA
>   Eben? What is it? What do you see?

Panel 4: Stay on Eben and Stella. Eben looks back through the lenses without saying a word to his wife. Stella looks horrified as she squints, trying to see into the distance.

PAGE TWENTY-TWO

Panel 1: The whole top half of the page is the image Eben is seeing through the zoomed binocular lenses. It is a CROWD. They are a rough looking group and completely varied from one to the other, except for their fierce eyes. Some have traditional fangs. Some have fangs at the bottom and top of their teeth. Some have rows of razor teeth like a wild dog. They wear mostly black, but some are in leather and others are in suits with a white shirt and tie. There are woman and children among them. These are the nastiest looking pack of people we have ever seen. Within each face we see pure evil. They are the UNDEAD and they are moving in a pack directly towards us!

Panel 2: Back on Eben. He has the binoculars lowered. Stella looks near tears. She has never seen her husband like this. He is staring off, his eyes wide. He is in shock.

> STELLA
> Eben?

Panel 3: Repeat, except Stella is staring off, worried, trying to see what he saw.

> EBEN
> G...get in the car. We have to warn the others while there's still time...

> CAPTION
> To be continued...